To Papa—
Hope y...

Jenny

Chosen Quarry

By

Jenny Kanevsky

PublishAmerica
Baltimore

First printing

ISBN: 1-4137-2759-X
PUBLISHED BY PUBLISHAMERICA, LLLP
www.publishamerica.com
Baltimore

Printed in the United States of America

For Tim and Theo

1

July 5th, 6:12 a.m.

Sophia heard the shrill ring of the phone as she grabbed the newspaper and stumbled backwards into the vestibule. She balanced her bike on one shoulder, shoved the door closed with the other and made her way up the single flight of stairs to her apartment. *Who the hell is calling me at six o'clock in the morning? It can't be a client. The ring sounds like the home line,* she thought. *Phone lines should be silent before six a.m. Maybe it's an emergency.* She struggled with the bike, the newspaper, her keys and fell inside. The bike clattered to the floor. The ringing stopped. She cursed herself for dropping a thousand dollars worth of steel and hung the bicycle on a hook she'd installed just inside her apartment door. She proceeded to disrobe, shoes first, setting them toe-clip side up so as not to mar the hardwoods.

Sophia worked out of her apartment, her bathroom doubling as a darkroom, her living room, an office. She had a second phone line for business calls and her listing in the yellow pages gave a PO Box, Internet address, phone number and fax. Client meetings, whether for photography or private investigative services, were conducted either at The Commissary or Pete's Diner, depending on the client.

The ringing started again—it was definitely her home line. She grabbed it on the first ring.

"Oh good, you're there, I've been calling for an hour."

"I was out on my bike," she skipped a beat. "Martin? Martin Duncan? What is it? Why the hell are you calling me at six in the morning?"

"Easy Sophie, don't bite my head off."

"Sorry, it's just early."

"Sophia Bella Gold, did I wake you from your beauty sleep?"

"No. I said I was on my bike. But, it's still early. Look, if you called to spar, I only do that by appointment these days, have your girl call my gi—"

He cut her off. "This is big Sophia, I can't tell you over the phone. Plus, I'm missing every other word," Martin said, sounding far away. "Can you come to my office today at nine?"

"What's going on?" Sophia asked. "Gone are the days when I drop everything for you, you know. Where are you by the way? This connection is terrible."

"I'm in the car, on my way back from the shore. I came down for the Fourth." The phone line fizzed and popped, reminding them of its cellular path. "This is not a secure line. I can't tell you more. A possible missing person—that's right up your alley, isn't it? Can you come?" He was more serious now, talking in clipped sentences, his voice raised an octave.

So he was tossing some work her way. She wasn't busy, having planned to take the weekend off, shoot some film, ride, relax. Would have been nice to have some warning, but oh well, she was flexible. She better be—she was freelance.

"Doesn't the firm have an in-house PI?" she asked.

"We do but not for this. It's too sensitive. Well?"

"Okay, I'll be there at nine."

"Oh and Sophie?" He stopped her from hanging up. "No jeans, okay?"

You know, fuck you. For that I will wear jeans, she thought. "Jesus Martin, what am I eight? You don't have to tell me how to dress—sorry listen, you sound freaked out. Stop at Starbucks, get yourself some decaf. I'll be there. It can't be that bad, can it?"

"It's bad. I'll see you soon." He hung up.

Sophia gazed around her apartment. Her heart still raced from the ride, and now there was a pit in her stomach, adrenaline mixed with anxiety—or is that redundant? Sunlight streamed in the windows and it was already hot. Luigi stretched as he walked and rubbed against her leg.

"Hey buddy, you hungry?" He pushed his head further into her leg and went to sit by his bowl. Sophia fed him, started the coffee pot and got in the shower still thinking about Martin's urgent voice.

She hadn't talked to Martin Duncan in months, maybe a year. She'd heard he was making a name for himself in all the right Philadelphia circles. He had married Regan Whitehouse—just blonde enough to not be an airhead, perfect blue eyes and an ever so slightly upturned nose. With the marriage, Martin immediately jettisoned himself from blue-collar boy-makes-good to socialite and big-time lawyer. They were both beautiful—Martin and Regan— and considered one of Philadelphia's hottest couples. Was she jealous? She didn't want to be but maybe she was. She didn't want that life. *Hmm, that's a crock*, she thought, dropping the soap and dripping shampoo into her eyes. *There is something about that life I want*, she thought, *although maybe it's just the idea of it*. She shook off the self-pity, rubbing her corneas raw.

She turned off the hot water and examined her profile in the foggy mirror. Even through the condensation she saw familiar aquiline features. A Michelangelo nose dominated the image. She wiped the mirror with a towel. Dark eyes peered back at her; the skin around them still tight and creamy olive smooth. *Nothing like Regan Whitehouse*, she thought. This face makes a statement. She ran fingers through wet hair releasing curl after curl after curl. A Mediterranean heritage pulsed through her body—fiery personality, dominant face, lithe figure. What was that expression? Long, tall drink of water? Sophia grinned. I'm a drink of something—but I pack more of a punch than water—might as well embrace it. She finished her post-shower routine, leaving her hair loose and make-up understated.

Now, back to business. Someone is missing and I have to find them. She dressed in a classic suit with a searing hot pink silk blouse and chose her favorite Manolo Blahnik's—edging her up to the six foot mark—grabbed her bag and went into the day.

2

Sophia arrived at Centre Square just before nine o'clock, pushing past the throngs at The Clothespin, a modern sculpture that when first erected caused a flurry of controversy— Philadelphia being a conservative city, artistically and otherwise. Progress had prevailed and the enormous statue sat defiant, rusting aesthetically near City Hall and the illustrious William Penn who was covered in scaffolding, again. Centre Square sat across from the city's political hub housing lawyers, bankers, and lots of other people in blue suits. Sophia remembered walking past the building as a child, marveling at the busy corner on which it stood, traffic converging from multiple directions at the intersection of Market Street with City Hall. The pulse of the city.

How many times had she cut across the City Hall courtyard to get to Wanamaker's, a Philadelphia department store long since gone but not forgotten? She used to lunch there with her grandmother. They would take the escalator to The Crystal Tea Room, so named for a majestic crystal chandelier glimmering above the restaurant. They would eat tiny finger sandwiches and listen to the delicate tinkling of spoons against teacups. Sophia always felt out of place among proper ladies with linen napkins carefully folded on their laps. Her grandmother had reveled in it, having matured into hard-earned wealth and stature. The elegant room was tall windows, sunlight, lucent water glasses and well-mannered wait staff. The Cossacks storming her grandmother's childhood home were worlds away—a distant but painful memory.

Sophia fell into a revolving door at Centre Square, spilled into the air-conditioned lobby and ducked into an open elevator cramped with blank-faced suits. In the past, she'd have envied them their snappy clothes and seemingly important jobs. Today she knew she would have suffocated, day after day going to the same place, sitting at the same desk, doing the same thing. She reached around a portly, sweaty three-piece suited gentleman, pressed "30" and steeled herself against the quick ascent.

******

Charlotte Keats sat back in the Town Car, oblivious to the steamy air and Friday morning traffic. She leaned into the plush leather and touched a well-manicured hand to her triple-strand pearls. Charlotte smoothed the cool white orbs against her skin and settled every pearl on every strand.

Despite the long holiday weekend, traffic swarmed around Logan Circle. The streets were busy, borderline hysterical, in a way that comes only with East Coast moxie, oppressive humidity and the knowledge that Sunday night would come soon, bringing an end to a long holiday weekend. Charlotte, perfumed and coiffed, sat in her own world buffeted by tinted glass and thick cool air. Her life was of privilege with the inexplicable but unmistakable quality of unwilling pretension.

She tolerated the traffic and workers clamoring for a weekend getaway at the shore. She had other things on her mind. The Town Car pulled up behind a SEPTA bus billowing smoke and spitting passengers onto the sidewalk. The driver appeared at Charlotte's door and opened it for her with a gentle click. She plucked her handbag from the seat and slid into the steamy morning.

In the building lobby an elevator sat open, empty. Charlotte rode alone to the thirtieth floor where the door opened to the reception area at Whitehouse Robbins. Design scheme: Elegant Lawyer. A striking, ethnic-looking woman waited by the office door. Her eyes were a deep brown, almost black, and her eyebrows were thick— too full. Charlotte smiled to herself. *Unruly hair, but she is quite beautiful in a loud, decisive way. Although, she won't age well. Her dark curls will soon take on shades of gray. She must be Greek or Italian,* Charlotte thought, pondering sharp features and pouty lips. Charlotte was again thankful for her classic good looks and blue blood. The woman crossed and uncrossed her bare legs with a childlike energy. She wore spindly shoes that looked expensive, Italian and uncomfortable. Charlotte was intrigued.

Just then, Martin Duncan came into the reception area and moved directly to her.

"My dear, I am so sorry. How are you holding up?" he asked.

"Thank you Martin, yes, it is difficult," Charlotte said. "We must contain this story and find out what has happened. Poor Zoë is beside herself."

******

Sophia's ears perked up. Here was her new client. No wonder Martin had been cagey on the phone. Sophia had recognized Charlotte Keats when she'd entered the lobby—a woman famous for her local philanthropic activities. And, based on the publicity those activities generated, her energy, time and charitable dollars were endless.

In person, Charlotte Keats' presence was more commanding than any newspaper article or television sound byte could describe. Sophia wondered about that kind of altruism. Were people really that good, or did giving serve some other purpose? Martin interrupted her thoughts.

"Charlotte Keats, I'd like you to meet Sophia Gold," he said. Sophia stood and put out her hand, taking the edge off her usual handshake. Charlotte Keats shook with a delicate, skeletal grip; her hands were frigid.

"Yes, Martin tells me you can be discreet," said Charlotte, skipping the pleasantries.

"Yes, ma'am, absolutely." Ma'am? Was that too formal?

"Ladies, why don't we go back to my office?" Martin asked. "I'll have some coffee sent in and we can talk." He led them to a spacious room with an impressive view of City Hall. William Penn's likeness, the statue atop the city's epicenter, peeked out from behind green netting. Charlotte strode into the office as if it were her own and stood behind a side chair. Clearly, she did not plan to sit down. Yet. She gave Sophia a tight smile that said, "I don't quite trust you, nor do I like you." Sophia perched on the chair beside her and waited.

"Charlotte, why don't you tell us what happened," Martin began.

"Yes." The woman remained standing and held a hand to her neck. "First, I must emphasize how sensitive this is. Obviously I want to find my son, but we must be very careful about publicity. Despite what the press seems to think, we are a private family," she said, "and involving the police is out of the question."

Sophia stepped in. "Mrs. Keats, I want to assure you, it is my job to be discreet. If you decide to hire me, my only allegiance is to you, my client.

Our relationship is confidential." *Meaning, if you don't hire me*, Sophia thought, *I could poke around as much as I want. So, it's your choice, Mrs. Talbots catalog.*

"Fine. Well, that's settled. What are your fees?" Charlotte opened her purse and immediately plucked out a leather-bound checkbook as if there was a little hand in there waiting at the ready. Sure enough, out came a fountain pen.

Whenever a client went right to the money—before even telling her story—Sophia's red flags waved. Paying is good, but when it comes first, it says something about the client. *In this case*, Sophia thought, *the woman is either in denial, has to be in control, or both.* If Charlotte had waited for Sophia to mention her fees, she would be *compensating* Sophia for valuable services. By raising the issue herself, she was *hiring* Sophia. It was a subtle difference, but it was there.

"Five hundred dollars a day plus expenses." Sophia raised her rates in that split second, never having had such a high profile client. It was time. *In the first place*, she thought, *I never put a high enough value on my work. And in the second place this woman can not only afford it, she expects it.* Martin grinned like a proud parent and sat quietly at his desk.

"A retainer of two thousand dollars is standard," she continued, "with a refund of any unused portion, if necessary." The words were still the air when the woman handed her a check. Sophia took it gingerly, noticing the ink glistening.

She resisted the urge to blow on the writing; it was still wet.

"This should cover us for awhile. I am hoping Campbell will be found immediately, but you may need this for expenses," Charlotte said, the pen and checkbook going back into her purse as stealthily as they had appeared.

Four thousand dollars in expenses? Was she paying Sophia in advance to keep quiet about something she might find or was she just a wealthy woman to whom money had a different relative value? Since this was always the awkward part of any client interaction, and Sophia was still a little surprised at herself having raised her rates on the spot, she simply said, "Thank you, Mrs. Keats."

The woman smiled and sat down.

Martin leaned back in his chair, relaxing his posture.

"Tell us what happened," Sophia said.

"Well, the family was at my home for July Fourth," she began, "we have a celebration every year. Often the children stay overnight, I don't like them driving back into Center City. People overdo it on holidays, drinking and driving, not watching the road. Campbell and his wife Zoë were staying at my home in Chestnut Hill," Charlotte paused.

"You said the children, Mrs. Keats, do you have others?" As soon as she asked, Sophia remembered the headlines from years ago. Campbell's younger brother Clayton had drowned while racing in a regatta. He had been an Olympic-caliber athlete, rowing his way through the University of Pennsylvania when he was killed in a horrible freak accident. Sophia knew that Charlotte's late husband Jackson Keats, also a renowned oarsman, had died of a heart attack last year. "I'm sorry," she said. "I didn't mean to bring that up."

"Yes, well, no. There are no other children. Campbell is my only son now, although the cousins were there as well, my sister, some other guests," Charlotte replied evenly.

Sophia nodded. "Please go on."

"Zoë, Campbell's wife…" Charlotte started.

Also your daughter-in-law, Sophia thought.

"…was exhausted. Poor dear is eight months pregnant with my first grandson," she continued.

Or Zoë's first child, whichever is more significant. Sophia pinched her own leg. *That's enough. Pay attention.*

"Zoë had gone to bed, although the fireworks had not yet started. Jane Howard was there as well. The D.C. Howards?" Rhetorical. Unless the D.C. Howards were in the White House, Sophia didn't know them. The woman smoothed her skirt.

"Her father and Jackson knew each other well," Charlotte said as way of explanation. "Jane went to bed also, if I recall. I don't remember. Everyone else was gathered in the garden. It was a lovely evening." The woman placed an age-spotted hand on her neck and continued. "Campbell pulled me aside and said he needed to go to the quarry. I wasn't happy about it and told him so. He said he wouldn't be long. As it was a holiday weekend, he said he wanted to make sure everything was battened down. He's so conscientious really, how could I fault him?" There was a glimmer of fear or sadness in her face. Sophia was relieved to see a chink in the armor.

Keats Quarry was the oldest and largest limestone quarry in the nation. Sophia assumed, hearing Charlotte speak, that Campbell had been running the business since his father had passed away last year. Rumor had it that the quarry was to be sold but Sophia would not bring that up now. The Keats family had a long history in Philadelphia, and an excellent reputation in the stone industry. She was sure the company was a source of great pride—the legacy of Charlotte's late husband, and now of her son. There was something raw in Charlotte Keats, something beneath the surface of pearls and starched linen. Tenderness or anger; Sophia couldn't be sure which.

Sophia said, "What time was this? When did he leave?"

"It was about nine o'clock, I think. At midnight, I called his cell phone but there was no answer. I assumed he had left it in his car and was in the office working. He probably didn't call because it was so late. I went to bed," she said.

"Did you call the office?" Sophia asked.

"Oh, no. No, I suppose I could have. No," she paused, "I think the phones roll to a service on weekends and holidays."

"That's alright, tell me more." That was odd. She was worried, assumed he was working but didn't call the office. Answering service or not, the line would ring, wouldn't it? Martin glanced at Sophia as if thinking the same thing. Charlotte was deep in thought and missed the exchange.

"I expected he would be home in the morning," Charlotte continued. "At about three o'clock in the morning, Zoë came into my room crying hysterically. He wasn't home yet. That's when I called Martin. He said to wait a few hours; that Campbell had probably fallen asleep at the office—there's a couch there—and he'd surely be calling any minute. But Zoë was frantic and in her state, she cannot afford to be. So, Martin offered to return to the city immediately. In the meantime, I drove over to the quarry. Campbell's Jeep was there, but there was no sign of him. I haven't slept a wink."

Sophia and Martin were silent.

Sophia remembered her own mother's face when she had run away at seventeen. They were fighting, about sex of course. What else did teenagers fight about with their parents? Sophia wanted to sleep over at her boyfriend's; Sylvia was putting her foot down. Sophia had called her a hippie hypocrite, thinking herself clever and alliterative. "How old were *you*, Ma?" she'd shrieked.

"That doesn't matter, young lady, I'm still your mother."

"Not for long!" Sophia had stormed out the door, returning after sundown. She'd found Sylvia going door-to-door in the neighborhood, panic etched in her face, sweating despite the October chill, searching for her daughter who had merely thrown a long temper tantrum. This woman's son had been gone overnight and she was complaining about missing a night's sleep.

******

"She's awfully cool for someone with a missing child," Sophia said. "I know, he's not a child," she held up her hands in protest, "but from what I understand, they're always your babies, no matter how old they get." Charlotte had disappeared in a cloud of Chanel N°5, leaving Sophia puzzled and up four grand.

Martin had been quiet while Charlotte was in the room. He spoke forcefully now. "Soph, first of all, you're right, he's not a child. Plus, she's the quintessential WASP. She doesn't show her hand, ever." He took a swig of cold coffee and made a face. *Even a grimace can't make Martin Duncan look bad*, she thought, taking him in. She'd put off looking at him earlier, focusing on her new client. Now she drank in the dimples, clear green eyes and Nantucket sun-kissed hair— *he could be a Kennedy*, she thought.

"Can you stay for a bit, talk this through?" he asked. "I need fresh coffee though." He held out his hand for her cup and she caught a subtle wave of aftershave. Her senses reeled—it was the same brand he'd worn when they were together. Something classic, she didn't remember what, only the smell. It was him. "You wait here. No snooping."

Sophia gave a mock salute and settled into a leather chair that could have paid her rent for a year. She peered over Martin's desk. Hmm, files. Wonder what those are? She stood, paced casually around the room, eyeing the manila tabs for clues as to their contents.

"Cream, no sugar, right?" Martin said as he opened the office door with care.

"Yes, thanks." She took the steaming mug from him as he came in the room.

"Find anything?"

"Why did you tell me not to snoop if you knew I would? Why didn't you just drag me with you like a little puppy dog?"

"Sophia, think back, we've known each other a long time. Do you think I would leave anything out that I didn't want you to see?" Martin asked.

"Humph." Was she more embarrassed at having been caught, or at having been so predictable? She shifted gears. "I notice you aren't wearing your wedding ring, what's the matter, trouble in white-bread paradise?"

"It's in the shop," he said and gave her a cold stare. "We're having some problems. Can we drop it for now?"

She softened. "Jesus Marty, I'm sorry, what happ—?"

"Look," he interrupted, "I have to be in court in an hour, can we do this Keats thing and talk about my marriage later?" He was simmering with emotion, anger on the surface.

"Sure." Sophia eyed him warily. She settled back into her chair and took out her notebook. She hadn't taken notes earlier, keeping her full attention on the subtle and reserved—almost choreographed—performance of Charlotte Keats. Now, it was time to get down to the business of dissecting the case.

3

July 5th, 12:30 p.m.

Sophia wove the Saab through Center City and onto Kelly Drive, enjoying the scenery as the road snaked by Greek Row, past the boathouses and Lemon Hill. The streets of Philadelphia were eerily quiet. Instead of focusing on other cars and traffic, she watched the flow of city into neighborhoods and suburbia. Sophia rarely took the expressway—it had no character, and no bike path. She passed a group of Penn rowers and their megaphone-bearing coxswain gliding across the Schuylkill. She turned right onto Midvale Avenue, taking the long route past East Falls and through Germantown, Mount Airy and into Chestnut Hill, a route that traced the gradual transformation of city landmark to blue collar row-house, gentrifying middle class home and finally to old money stone mansion steeped in history and genteel advantage.

Sophia planned to drive around the Keats' neighborhood and then to retrace Campbell's steps to the quarry.

She had asked Charlotte for keys to the quarry office and to Campbell's car. "I'll just stop by and pick them up," she'd promised. "I won't stay and I won't disturb your daughter-in-law." An envelope was waiting for Sophia at the entrance to the house in front of a closed gate.

Subtle. Inside the envelope were two sets of keys and a map highlighting Campbell's probable route.

She would return to the house after visiting the quarry. She wanted to meet Zoë, size up her mood, and ask the family some questions. Charlotte seemed to think Sophia would return with Campbell in tow and all would be resolved. Sophia had her doubts, saying she would take the investigation one step at a time, and not to expect too much too soon. The matron had visibly bristled.

At one o'clock, Sophia pulled into the quarry parking lot. And, although Sophia had never been to a quarry before, it seemed unusually still.

Campbell's Jeep, with KEATS QUARRY emblazoned on the side, sat haphazardly parked across the parking lot's white lines. Of course with no one else here, Campbell would have had no reason to park in a designated spot, but she'd have done so anyway. Was Campbell a rule-breaker? She looked around at the massive piles of rock. The air was heavy but oddly peaceful. There was no dust, she realized. When rock is being worked with, there must be dust and noise. The heaviness in the air then was humidity—not work, sweat, toil.

Any fantasies of scooping Campbell Keats into her arms and whisking him back to his grateful mother were dashed. The place was deserted. As much as Sophia loved a good investigation, she still harbored a Wonder Woman fantasy. She had the costume: the cuffs, red boots, special bulletproof belt, and skimpy red, white and blue bodysuit. As a child she had imagined herself running at lightning speed nabbing villains and returning lost dogs and children to their loving families.

She sighed, glancing down at her jeans and work boots, slid the Saab in a spot near the Jeep and got out of the car, cameras in tow.

She started shooting. Sophia liked to shoot the scene before looking with the naked eye, unless it was a known crime scene with evidence to protect.

She was always careful, wore gloves when touching things, and kept a look out for errant footprints and other clues. The camera, unencumbered by preconceptions, picked up what her eye missed. Often a seemingly insignificant detail would later reveal itself as the key to the case. Having photos was better than memory, notes, or even returning to the scene. A photo was a pure immediate impression. The first time Sophia had used her camera eye before her naked eye had been an epiphany. In her excitement, she'd ruined the roll with sloppy handling in her darkroom. She only had to do that once.

She shot the outside of the Jeep first, then got in the driver's seat searching the floor. Campbell kept his Jeep spotless. It still smelled like new car and new leather. It had fewer than ten thousand miles on the odometer. She opened the storage compartment, checked the visors. She got out her notebook and jotted down what she saw: a well-thumbed wire-bound atlas of the Five County Metro area, a flashlight, tin of Altoids, cell phone stand base with phone (turned off), a pair of sunglasses. In the back was a polar fleece vest with KEATS QUARRY embroidered on the right corner and a dog bed lined with a worn gray sweatshirt covered in long red hairs. Looked like Irish Setter.

Sophia examined the sweatshirt and found a logo, faded from years of washing. Chestnut Hill Academy. Ah yes, education for the understated elite.

She shot a few more pictures, locked up and moved toward the office entrance. She thought of something and stopped. Maybe Campbell had run out of gas or had a dead battery and had set off on foot. Not likely. He had any number of phones available to call for a tow, or Mommy. Sophia went back to the Jeep, hopped in, and turned the key. Dead. She flicked switches at random, as one is wont to do in a strange car, and found the headlights had been left on. *Overnight I suppose that could blow the battery*, she thought. But why had he left them on? There were no outside lights that Sophia could see and Campbell had arrived in the dark. He would know the area though. Did he leave the lights on out of fear? She turned them off, not that it mattered, as the car would need to be towed or jumped anyway, locked up again and went to the office. Two rolls of film later, she dusted herself off and started up the Saab.

******

The large gate was open when Sophia pulled into the Keats' driveway. She parked in the shade under a centuries-old weeping willow tree.

Charlotte greeted her at the door wearing a skirt and sweater ensemble that defined conservative chic. Her hair was Grace Kelly perfect. The signature pearls gleamed at her neckline; her bony ankles were graceful in sensible, untarnished pumps. She looked more put together than a person had a right to, especially with a missing child.

They both glanced down at Sophia's dusty work boots and jeans. "I'm sorry Mrs. Keats. I'm a mess from the quarry. I can take off my bo—" Sophia stammered.

She was, again, an overwhelming presence among the cool and understated. Grateful that she'd taken the time to remove her hat, brush her hair and smooth it into a ponytail, Sophia tried to appear just the right combination of apologetic and yet self-confident. It was trying, to say the least.

"Oh, I'm used to it." Charlotte said, surprising her. "Between Jackson and Campbell, there has always been quarry dust all over this house. I've had someone clean every day for the last thirty years," she explained. "Do come in."

Sophia looked around and wondered who the poor sap was who cleaned this place every day. She could have performed open-heart surgery on those antiseptic, gleaming marble floors.

"Please, have a seat in here." Charlotte pointed to an open door. "I'll get Zoë and have some lemonade brought in. Do you like lemonade? Of course you do, everyone does. Excuse me a moment." And she was gone.

"Why yes ma'am I do like lemonade, thank you," Sophia whispered to herself. *That's good, your client's son is missing and you have one of two reactions: intimidation or sarcasm. Something about Mrs. Keats bothers me,* she thought, *I just can't put my finger on it yet.*

Sophia looked around the room. The perfectly matched, perfectly furnished sitting room was perfectly devoid of dust, quarry or otherwise. She looked down at her jeans—oh well—and sat in a Queen Anne armchair by the fireplace. A woman entered with a silver tray.

Sophia stood back up and went to her. The woman looked startled but her hand stayed steady as she passed Sophia a glass of lemonade. Sophia put the glass down on a coaster and held out her hand.

"Hello, I'm Sophia Gold." She looked the woman in the eye. Clearly, most visitors did not introduce themselves.

"I'm the cook, the housekeeper. My name is Virginia. Ginny."

Aha, the poor sap herself. "Nice to meet you Ginny. Thank you for the lemonade."

"You're very welcome miss." Ginny smiled broadly and this time made solid eye contact. She thrust her shoulders back, and carried herself proudly out of the room.

As if on cue, Charlotte Keats entered with a very pregnant, puffy-eyed woman.

Aside from the swollen eyes, Zoë Keats looked fantastic in a clingy cotton knit dress the color of pink grapefruit.

Her Hollywood pregnant body would be back to normal, and by normal, that's a neat little size four, within days of giving birth. Her blond shag had a consciously tousled "I don't care" look; a look that requires a lot of caring, frequent trims and multiple gels and sprays to achieve. She was stunning—Twiggy and Tinkerbell wrapped into one compact package brimming with both sadness and new life. *But, her husband is missing, you superficial ass.*

The doorway then filled with a tall, athletic-looking woman with long thick red hair and an attractive, just-came-from-the-country-club look. She wore a kelly green and white sleeveless blouse revealing pencil-thin but ropy arms and navy golf shorts that skimmed her knees. Her tanned legs were muscular and long. She strode like a gazelle to the couch, sat next to Zoë and crossed her legs.

"Sophia Gold." She went to them and reached to shake Zoë's hand.

The woman burst into tears and fell into a heap on her friend's shoulder. Sophia sat next to her. "It's going to be okay, we'll find him," she said unconvinced.

The redhead smiled evenly and put out a strong but perfectly manicured hand, "I'm Jane Howard. A friend of the family from Washington. I came up for the holiday weekend."

"Yes," Charlotte added with a disdain incongruous to her words. "Jane's father went to school with my late husband, Jackson. The Howards are a prominent Washington family. She's been like this all day," Charlotte said gesturing to her daughter-in-law. "I have been trying to get her to calm down, for my future grandson, of course. Since she's expecting, she can't take anything."

Sophia wondered if that was the key to Charlotte's calm demeanor, a few well-timed tranquilizers. Sophia sat listening to Zoë sob, absorbing the situation's emotional gravity. Initially, she had been taken aback by Mrs. Keats' calm.

Zoë Keats was about to give birth to her first child. Her husband had disappeared. Sophia felt her chest constrict. What if I don't find him? What if he's dead? The questions flitted through her mind. She took a deep breath.

"Listen, Zoë, let's have some lemonade," Sophia said. *Like that's going to help.* "I'll make a deal with you." Zoë stopped crying and looked up at the stranger barking orders at her. "All you have to do is take care of yourself and answer my questions. If you are not healthy, you can't help me. You have to trust me."

Zoë nodded and whipped a kerchief from her sleeve, blew her nose. She snorted and laughed a little. She was not completely inconsolable.

Charlotte watched the exchange in silence but shifted her weight slightly, as if to get Sophia's attention. Sophia did not look up; Charlotte might be paying the bill, but Zoë was the man's wife.

"Okay, what do you need to know?" Zoë asked.

Jane sat motionless beside her friend. Sophia noticed the faintest sheen of freckles across the bridge of Jane's nose and along her arms. The woman was beautiful, equestrian, stately. She reeked of money.

"Well, let's start with why Campbell went to the quarry in the first place," Sophia said. "Was he meeting someone? Anything you can tell me about that would—"

Zoë was already shaking her head violently. "Nothing. I can't tell you anything. He didn't tell me anything about it. I didn't even know he'd gone until the middle of the night. We were here at the party and I was exhausted. I'm so big now," she caressed her belly, smiling, "I get so tired, and don't always sleep through the night. I toss and turn. Well, I try to toss and turn but my belly stops me. The baby wakes me up." Her smile faded and she started to cry again. "But, I slept last night. I mean, I fell asleep easily. I was so tired. I hoped I might even sleep through, you know," she looked up at Sophia and Charlotte, "if only I had woken up earlier, noticed he wasn't there, maybe—" she wept heavily.

Charlotte interrupted her tears, "There, there dear, you needed your rest, it's not your fault." Zoë slumped into the couch. "You need to stay calm for the baby, dear. Try not to excite yourself."

Sophia stood and paced as Zoë's sobs filled the room. Jane patted Zoë's knee.

The women sat lined up along the sofa like mismatched statues.

Sophia remembered how her own mother used to hold her when she cried. Sylvia would allow her to weep for a few minutes and then breathe dramatically through her nose, lifting her shoulders up to her ears. "C'mon Sophie, be a robot with me," she would say. And soon, they would be laughing and moving their arms and shoulders up and down in the air like mechanical dolls.

Sophia looked over at a now calmer Zoë. Charlotte sat stonily to her right, Jane to Zoë's left, her freckled fingers laced across her knee. Sophia thought she saw the subtle line of a scar along Jane's leg—orthoscopy, the surgery of the elite athlete. If the scar was there, it came from an expert hand because Sophia lost it in the light when Jane shifted positions and re-crossed her legs. They were perfect again.

Sophia said, "Listen, Zoë, I'm going to get to work. I need you to rest and to think about anything that's happened recently. Anything unusual, appointments, phone calls, meetings, that sort of thing. Mrs. Keats, you too, please. Think about it. I will be in touch. I may want to come back to ask more questions tomorrow. Zoë, will you be here?"

Zoë looked up at Charlotte, then to Jane. "I'll be home," she said. "In case Campbell calls, or comes home, you know. Plus, I'll have Max with me, our dog. And Jane is going to stay with me at the house for a few days." Jane nodded decisively at Sophia.

"Okay, that's good, great," Sophia said. "Where do you live Zoë?"

"Twentieth and Delancey Place."

"That's near me." *Although I'm not in the high rent district*, she thought. "I'm on Twenty-third and Pine. Across from Fitler Square. So, I'm close if you need me."

Downtown Philadelphia, affectionately known as Center City, had many flavors. Sophia rented a one-bedroom with hardwood floors just close enough to Rittenhouse Square to be considered almost classy. As you went south and west, it was still Center City, although seedier.

Over the South Street Bridge heading west were the University of Pennsylvania, Children's Hospital, and the Civic Center, all intellectual and financial draws contrasting with many of the neighborhood's inhabitants, students and lower income minorities.

Sophia turned to Charlotte. "Mrs. Keats," she began diplomatically, "It will be very important for you to be available here in case Campbell contacts you. I also may need to talk with you again and other family members. Is anyone still here from the Fourth?"

Charlotte shook her head. "They have gone home, but I can give you names and phone numbers if you must. Remember, dear, we must keep this in the family." She seemed eager to have something to do and to remind Sophia of who was paying the bills.

"I understand." *Give it a rest with the publicity already.* "A list would be good—everyone who was here, including your staff," Sophia added quickly. The woman could call her dear all day and all night, Sophia would still drive this investigation.

"Staff? I don't really see how that would be relevant to Camp—oh, I suppose there's no harm in talking to Cook and the others. They'll certainly be discreet."

Right, or they're fired, Sophia thought. "Zoë," Sophia asked, "Did Campbell have a briefcase or appointment book or anything I might take a look at?"

"His Palm Pilot—it's here in our room. I'll get it." She started to stand up, hefting herself from the couch. Jane gave her a gentle push and stood herself.

"May I join you?" Sophia asked. She wanted to see the room; maybe there would be something else, a clue.

Charlotte Keats interrupted. She stood and smoothed her clothes. "I will compile the list. Please excuse me." And she left without saying goodbye.

******

Charlotte Keats slipped into the library closing the door softly and locking it behind her. She could hear footsteps on the stairs as the women moved to the guest room. *They'll find nothing there*, she thought. *The room has been cleaned twice since the party.* Perhaps the Palm Pilot, Campbell's favorite new toy, would reveal something.

She wondered just how much her son documented on that silly little computer.

Charlotte thought of her late husband Jackson and his leather-bound appointment book. He'd used his father's antique quill pen to note meetings and appointments. He was meticulous and reliable—the ink a permanent notation of what had been and what was to come.

She went to the desk, took the quill pen and began to make a list of family, friends and staff who had attended what would likely be her last Fourth of July celebration. When she finished the list she unlocked the door and summoned the maid from the kitchen.

"Virginia, please seal this in an envelope and take it to the private detective." She handed the woman a sheet of Jackson's personal stationery still damp with ink.

"Yes, ma'am," Ginny replied, opening a desk drawer, her movements like a subtle breeze.

Charlotte held Jackson's pen in hand, the grip polished smooth from years of use. She stood and moved swiftly to the wall safe, hoping the physical movement would jar her out of the memory. The lock clicked and Charlotte removed a wood-paneled box, opening it slowly. She didn't need to re-read the notes. She'd read them a hundred times.

She just felt safer knowing where they were, folded in fours and locked away in a safe to which only she knew the combination.

4

Sophia parked in front of her apartment building. A great parking space: one of the perks of having nothing to do on a holiday weekend. Across the street Fitler Square was quiet. She could never shake the memories of that park. As a child, she'd played there almost daily—her home was just a block away.

She remembered learning to ride her bike. She'd started off so well, motoring along on two wheels. When she got to the park, her jeans got caught in the bike chain and she went down. Hard. The next day, she was at it again, defiant in success. In her own way, she'd never left home. Today, her apartment overlooked the small park now peppered unevenly with children playing and the homeless sleeping, drinking. Philadelphia was a tougher city now, and scarier in many ways, the contrasts more glaring.

She grabbed her gear and took the stairs two at a time, anxious to get inside. She turned the air conditioner to high. Luigi started, gave an annoyed you-woke-me-up look, vaulted from the couch, stretched and went to bathe in peace.

The darkroom/bathroom would be stifling today. She could usually get through the process of the changing bag, reels, and tanks in under a half hour. Locked in a tiny room with no ventilation, that time passed slowly. She took a cold shower, washed her hair and left it wet—anything to lower her body temperature. She put on a tank top and shorts and began to dismantle her bathroom.

Someday, I'll have a real darkroom—an entire studio, she thought wearily.

Instead, Sophia had rolling carts whereby makeup, toothpaste and hairbrushes quickly swapped with tongs, clips, changing bag, reels, tanks and bottles of chemicals. Her fantasy darkroom was state of the art, cavernous, climate controlled with a deep utility sink and the best equipment money could by.

Working with evidence photos was basic, but when she did her art, purity was critical. Developing film while sitting on a closed toilet seemed wrong. *I bet Diane Arbus never sat on a closed toilet seat*, she thought. Some women hung stockings in the shower; Sophia hung negative strips.

She locked herself in the darkroom and felt a familiar twinge of excitement. She loved the time before the unveiling. She held images she'd created but could not yet touch or see. Soon they would be ghosts and then they would come alive and tell a story. She worked quickly, her movements spare and efficient. Twenty minutes later, five rolls of film hung from clothespins attached to a thin dowel she'd installed parallel to her shower curtain.

Suspense built slowly as the negatives dried in the shower, their images shadows glimmering on the emulsion.

Once the negatives were dry, the real exposition began. Sophia fed the strips into her Nikon Cool Pics, automatically opening PhotoShop on her computer. Within seconds she was clicking through thumbnail previews of photographs of limestone, the interior of the Jeep, the grounds around the Keats Mansion and the quarry office.

Sophia had invested in good, professional equipment. Her scanner, the Nikon Cool Pics, was standard. Today, Polaroid was hitting the market hard with better models.

Still, Sophia tried to be satisfied with what she had. Upgrading was not an option. Although she had the money, she wouldn't spend it. *This machine is fine*, she thought. In fact, the computer, scanner and cameras were the most expensive things she owned—besides the Saab and a nice collection of Manolo Blahnik's. For a freelance artist doubling as a PI, she was doing just fine.

By dark, the case began taking shape before her eyes. Although she hadn't figured anything out, seeing the images and having the printouts scattered around her work area made her feel like she had accomplished something. Hunger and exhaustion hit her at once like a truck. She stretched and looked up at the clock. It was after eleven. She'd been working for five hours. *When did I eat last?* she wondered. As if on cue, Luigi came meandering into the room, back legs dragging in a lazy stretch behind him and gave a short deep meow that said, "Feed me, too."

"Worked up an appetite sleeping all day, huh Louie?" She reached out her hand and the cat fell into it, closing his eyes and raising his chin for a scratch. "Okay, let's have some kibble." She got up from her desk, did a few knee bends to loosen up her back and went to the kitchen. The cat trotted along behind her.

"What about me Louie? What am I going to eat?" Sophia opened the refrigerator, closed it again, opened the cupboards, went back to the refrigerator. She opened it again, hopeful, as if the contents would be different. Nothing new: milk, some fruit, juice, bread. She glanced at the clock again, not different there either. Still bedtime. She knew she'd never fall asleep hungry and settled on a peanut butter and banana sandwich and a glass of milk, inhaled them both and crawled into bed. Next thing she knew, Luigi snored next to her pillow and the sun snuck through the window shades.

The neighborhood was dead quiet, more than usual at seven a.m. on a Saturday. *Oh, yes*, she remembered, *it's still the holiday weekend.* Sophia had spent July Fourth at her mother's, leaving before the fireworks began. Sylvia had been displeased, but was quiet about it. Sylvia's friends envied her having a daughter so close by—their kids had all moved off to New York or Seattle or somewhere else equally hip.

After a quick visit with Mom, Mom's new man and an aging hippie entourage, Sophia ended up at the Benson's Annual Fourth of July Party. This year, the Benson's had something to show off. Rita was pregnant, and Sam had just been promoted to Director-of-something-or-other at Rohm & Haas, the local chemical giant. They had bought a townhouse in Society Hill, had a great view of Camden (if any view of Camden can be called great) and a balcony where yuppies congregated drinking microbrews and Cosmopolitans. Sophia wondered how she had grown so far from her friends. It had been a depressing night and as soon as the fireworks were over she went home to bed. Martin's call had been a welcome diversion from what was turning into a lonely weekend.

By dawn Saturday, Sophia felt invigorated. She skipped her bike ride that morning and got right to work on the photos. She'd gone to sleep with more questions than answers. She made a pot of strong coffee and sat down at her desk.

5

July 6th, 9:05 a.m.

"Martin, are you there? Pick up?"

"Wha—hello?" Martin's voice was thick with sleep. "Hello," he cleared his throat. "Sophie? God, what time—guess it's your turn to wake me up." He quickly shook off sleep and was now talking in a clear voice.

"Sorry, is it early?" she paused. "It's after nine o'clock, you lazy bum." She was amazed at how easily the banter came even after all this time. When she'd picked up the phone to call, it had dialed itself, and before Sophia could think his number might have changed, she heard his gruff sleepy voice. Mornings had always been especially nice; she would wake up first and then wake him up slowly, gently. She hadn't realized how much she missed him.

"What is it Sophie?"

"I think I found him. I mean, I think so anyway, but I think he's dead."

"What?!"

"Sorry. I could have broken it to you gently. Something showed up in one of my pictures. Can you come over?"

"Yeah, sure, I guess. Wait, let me get this straight, you found Campbell Keats' dead body?"

"I don't know. But, I found *something*. We need to go out to the quarry. I think you should come with me. I may need some help. If we suspect anything, we're going to need to talk to Charlotte." Sophia heard sheets rustling and movement from Martin's side of the phone. She wondered if he still slept in the nude. "Martin?"

"Yeah, I'm getting ready. Listen, I'll be right over, okay? Don't call Charlotte or anything yet, wait for me." He hung up.

Sophia did a cursory walk through the apartment, checking for foul odors and rousting dust bunnies. She straightened the place up a little, Luigi staring at her from his favorite chair with a disappointed look.

"I know, I know—I shouldn't care. Who are you to judge anyway?" she asked. He put his head back down, sighed and went back to sleep. Sophia brushed her teeth, washed her face, daubed on some lipstick—coincidentally, Martin's favorite shade—and put on a fresh pot of coffee.

******

Martin had showered. His hair was damp, glistening colors of goldenrod and honey and he smelled like apples and something else familiar and warm. They hugged, his lanky athletic frame enveloping her in comfort. He seemed different, softer. He was out of the office and those stuffy suits. *That was probably it,* Sophia thought.

"Well, hello," she said smiling.

"Sophie. It's good to see you again, you know?" She did. He brushed past her as he entered. "Anyway, I'm here. Luigi! Hello, sir." He went to the cat who immediately stuck out his chin to be rubbed. Luigi did not like many people, but he liked Martin Duncan. Sophia knew it was cliché, but she felt that meant something. Maybe not.

"He's bulked up."

"Hey, he's not fat, just—" she searched for the word. "Full." They both laughed. "Coffee?" she asked.

"Yeah, great. I showered and came right over. What is it, what did you find?"

"Go sit down, I'll be right in." Sophia gestured to her large desk strewn with photographs from the quarry. The computer glowed with an enlarged fun-house-like image on the screen. She had moved an extra chair next to her desk. Martin sat down and started shuffling through papers.

"Here you go, black, one sugar, right?" She handed him a mug.

"Good memory." Martin took a gulp of coffee. "Hey what's this?" He pointed to a form on her desk.

"Oh, sorry, that's my E-Trade account." Sophia blushed.

"Holy shit woman, you're rich." Martin stared at the balance.

"Jesus Martin, how rude. Can you give that to me please?" She grabbed the papers from him. "I thought I'd put that away," she mumbled.

"Sorry, Sophie, guess I picked up the wrong pile." He put down the stack of papers and she handed him the photographs. He said, "Don't be embarrassed. Having money is a good thing." Martin watched her until she made eye contact with him.

"I know. I just still can't get used to it. I mean it's been what, two years since my grandparents died?" She took a sip of coffee. "I'm so lucky living like this, but still I feel a little weird about it all. It's more money than I'll ever need. I'm set for life," she said apologetically.

Sophia Bella Gold had been conceived at Woodstock. Her mother Sylvia had caravanned to the festival in her Volkswagen bus and there met a sexy Italian who spoke no English. She and the mysterious stranger got stoned and, to the incomparable Janis Joplin, made love not war under a scratchy wool poncho. Neither Sophia nor her mother ever knew more about him than his first name: Piero.

Sophia's maternal, and thrifty, grandparents never forgave Sylvia her dalliance: a daughter conceived out of wedlock, at Woodstock, with a stranger—a non-Jew no less. When they died, they skipped a generation and left Sophia their large inheritance. So, as a young adult, Sophia was blessed with a fortune, an artist's eye and a financial wizard's brain. She'd invested wisely and lived comfortably on small PI jobs and the occasional sale of her photographs.

"Sophie? Hello? You've got to stop feeling guilty about this. You deserve it. It's great. Shit, I'm jealous, I wish I had money like this." Martin blew on his coffee.

"Oh for Christ sake, you do have money like this," she said.

"Well, I do now," he said referring to marrying well.

"Anyway. Can we get back to the subject?" she asked, eager to move on. "Check this out. Here are the pictures from the quarry." She clicked the mouse and paged through the printouts quickly setting up the panorama, showing a full 360-degrees of rock, a deep cavern, a row of fork lifts neatly parked along one side, and the quarry office. "Nothing special here, right? But look at this." Sophia moved to the computer keyboard and pointed to the screen. She double clicked on the image.

"I can't tell what that is Soph, it looks strange."

"Right, because it has been enlarged. Look." She boxed out a section of the screen and clicked on it, the image became clearer, it was a string of some kind.

"What the hell? Is that a shoelace?"

"Very good. That's what I think it is. It could also be a twig, but there are no other sticks or pieces of wood anywhere else in these shots. A twig there is just as out of place as a shoelace." She spoke quickly, excited by the discovery—or rather Martin's reaction to it. She had been looking at this image now for hours.

"I think we need to go out there, take another look around. We might need to climb down to where this shot is. It's down in the cavern of the quarry. Is that what it's called, a cavern?" she asked.

"How the hell should I know? I'm just a lawyer." Martin flashed a full smile. Ten thousand dollars of orthodontia, caps and whatever else the dentist could scare up had served him well. His teeth were straight, white and inviting.

Sophia remembered seeing school pictures of Martin smiling tin and looking embarrassed, but still genetically superior to his classmates.

"Will you come with me?" Sophia asked.

He nodded. "Let's go."

******

Sophia wove along Kelly Drive while Martin hunkered down in the passenger seat leafing through the photos. He used Sophia's loupe to peer intensely at indecipherable images.

"You really think it's a shoelace?" he asked not sounding like he wanted an answer.

"My gut?" She shot him a quick glance. He nodded. "Yes. My instinct tells me the guy is dead down in that quarry. In a way, it's the only logical explanation—unless he was kidnapped. But, if he'd been taken, don't you think Charlotte would have heard something by now, had a demand?"

"I guess so. It's been days now, right, since Thursday? So yes. Man, I hope you're wrong, Soph. But I seem to recall that your gut's pretty reliable." Martin rubbed his eyes, grabbed a hunk of sandy blonde hair and leaned into the Saab's headrest. Without thinking, Sophia reached over and massaged his shoulder. He relaxed under her touch. They passed the Three Angels statue along Kelly Drive. Martin gazed out the window. Sophia felt her knuckles tighten on the wheel at ten and two. She stared straight ahead;

30

bronze flashing, then trees and a lone rower on the Schuylkill. She was suddenly aware of Martin's smell again, apples and something spicy she still couldn't place. She was about to apologize for touching him, although she was not sorry.

"Thanks," he whispered before she could speak. "I just don't want it to be, you know?" he said almost to himself.

"I know Martin. I know." They were silent watching the city pass, safe as long as they were in the car and time stood still.

******

Martin spoke again as they drove along Midvale Avenue towards Chestnut Hill.

"I know Charlotte is a tough old bird—she's had a hard time though."

"She seems to have a pretty good life, I mean aside from this," Sophia said.

"That's just it, you'd think she had it made, but she's very sad and very lonely. She's already lost a son."

Sophia nodded, started to speak but something in Martin's voice made her hesitate.

"Clay was her baby. Clayton. He took after his father. I mean she loves Campbell, or loved him. Jesus Christ I cannot believe this."

"You have a soft spot for her," she said.

"I do. Don't get me wrong, she can be a real bitch."

Sophia flinched.

"But she's repressed, don't you see?" Martin asked.

"Does she remind you of someone?" Sophia ventured. Martin's relationship with his own mother had been complicated. She had died of breast cancer years ago and Sophia wondered how much of Martin's pain was really for her.

"My mom? I guess. I don't know. I mean—Charlotte's losing everything. First Clay, then Jackson. Jackson was her life. She was one of those women who completely dedicated herself to her husband. Things revolved around him, his job, his—everything. When he died I think she relived the loss of Clay. And now Campbell. And all of this without really being able to show it." Martin stared out the window, silent now.

Sophia was surprised and somehow vindicated. Selfishly, she had always wanted Martin to be a deeper person. It justified her passion for him; made her feel better about her own motives. Their love affair had been intense and powerful. It had also been frightening, the intimacy almost out of control. At the time, Martin had been wrestling with his conscience. The fast track won and he took a job with Whitehouse & Robbins, later marrying Christopher Whitehouse's debutante daughter, Regan. Sophia had rebelled by plunging herself into her art. She spent months with a camera glued to her eye, hidden, looking at the world in small chunks and with measured focus.

Years had passed since then. They had been young and young lovers rarely end up together. Yet something about their parting had deeply saddened Sophia. How could she have been so wrong?

She looked over at Martin who was still quiet. Her pulse quickened as she gunned the Saab.

6

July 6th, 9:07 a.m.

Frank Reynolds pulled into the quarry driveway next to Campbell's Jeep. Joe Rizzo sat in his truck, idling. Frank gestured to the Jeep as if to ask "Is he here too?"

Rizzo shrugged in response and shook his head. His truck died with a soft click and he gulped his coffee while gathering himself to join Frank.

Frank stepped heavily onto the gravel. He scanned the area. It sure looked empty. *You can't beat mornings at the quarry*, he thought. *Even in the summer, when the rocks hold the heat, there's something peaceful about the place.* He frowned as his eyes moved to the forklifts. *One of those is out of place*, he thought. He shook his head and motioned for Rizzo to join him in the office.

******

"It looks pretty busy for a holiday weekend," Sophia said as she gestured to the parking lot. She slid the Saab next to a shiny new pick-up truck. Martin was quiet and fumbled with his seat belt.

"Oh Jesus Christ," Sophia exclaimed as she almost stepped on someone's jeans-clad legs getting out of the car. A man slid out from under the pick-up grinning. She jumped. "I almost ran you over!"

"Well, I'm glad you didn't," the man said and stood.

So am I, she thought. He was deceptively tall with broad shoulders and luminous olive-skin. He stared at her; his brown eyes flecked with green. He wore faded Levis, work boots and a worn Phillies cap. Despite having been lying on the ground under his truck, his white-t-shirt was spotless and contoured against his chest.

Sophia noticed a small brown freckle on his lower lip and felt a stirring inside her.

"Something I can help you with?" he asked, his voice uncertain. "We're closed for the weekend."

"Oh, I'm—we're," she gestured haphazardly at Martin who watched them both intently, "looking for Frank Reynolds. Is he here?"

The man gestured toward the office, but held his other hand at his waist and snapped his fingers in mock disappointment as if to say, "Wish you were looking for me instead."

Martin missed the exchange from the other side of the car, but he caught the energy behind it. He said, "Good, thank you very much, we'll be going to see him now, Sophia?" He held his arm out to wait for her, protectively as a father would for his innocent, vulnerable daughter.

"It was nice to almost meet you," the man said winking.

"Likewise," Sophia replied, more seductively than she'd intended. "Sorry about the scare. Hope you're okay."

"I'm great, now," the man said and hiked his jeans up past his hipbones only to have them settle again low and loose around his waist.

"Sophia, let's go in now," Martin said through clenched teeth.

"Sophia," the man said with a whisper as if savoring each letter. With that, he turned to get in his truck.

"What the hell was that?" Martin asked as they walked toward the office.

"What the hell was what?" she replied, still savoring the moment. They were interrupted by another voice.

"May I help you?" The man's cigarette-ravaged voice boomed across the quarry floor.

"Man, this guy's been ridden hard and put away wet," Sophia wisecracked under her breath.

Martin glared at her, his cheeks pink with emotion. He shifted gears. "Hello. You must be Frank Reynolds." Martin met the man on the asphalt and extended his arm. They shook.

"I am," Reynolds answered warily. He had thick hair red hair shocked with gray and a bushy mustache. He was still Marlboro Man handsome, aged in the deep, rugged way that Robert Redford had. Sophia looked at his strong, gnarled hands. Reynolds eyed them both with caution.

"I'm sorry," Martin said. "I'm Martin Duncan, the Keats' family attorney. Charlotte Keats told us you might be here. This is my associate, Sophia Gold. Sophia, Mr. Reynolds has been with the quarry for over twenty years now." The smooth words spilled out of him like a tawny port.

Great acting. I bet he's amazing in front of a jury. She smiled and extended her hand, giving the full shake.

Reynolds almost grinned under his mustache. "That's a pretty good grip." Sophia smiled at him.

"What're you folks doing here? Is something wrong?"

Although she'd known Reynolds might be here, Sophia wasn't prepared to explain herself with anything but the truth. The long holiday weekend had given her a sense of stolen time. Martin gave her a reassuring look. Sophia realized then how impressed she'd been by Charlotte Keats and her reluctance to involve the police. After speaking with Martin in the car, she was beginning to understand not only the woman's power but also her weakness. Sophia wanted to protect her; she wanted to find her son.

"Yes, Mr. Reynolds," she started. "Something *is* wrong." She pursed her lips. *This man could easily be involved,* she thought. *He's a suspect, he's a suspect, he's a suspect.* The mantra ran in her head like a ticker tape. "Campbell Keats is missing. He disappeared on the Fourth."

Reynolds seemed genuinely surprised, although it was difficult to tell beneath the leathery mask his face wore. But though his eyes were a cool, pale green, they looked kind.

He hadn't known, Sophia thought. She decided at once that he was a good man, although she had been wrong before.

"Missing?" Reynolds cleared his throat. "Missing," he said again and patted his pockets as if looking for something. He pulled out a hard-pack of Camels and a lighter. He was wearing a canvas work jacket stiff with years of quarry dust. He seemed to just notice the heat and removed his jacket. He lit a cigarette and peered into Sophia's eyes. "Missing how?"

If this man had been at Keats Quarry for over twenty years, he would have also seen Jackson's recent death. And Clayton's. Apparently, the family had a Kennedy-like curse that humanized them despite their wealth. Reynolds would know that first-hand. Sophia's mind wandered. Were the Kennedy's really that cursed, or was their plight simply more public? Doesn't every family see tragedy? Sophia shook herself and came back to the present. She glanced at her watch—it was nearly noon and the day was heating up, the air collecting moisture and weight. "Something has happened," she said. "We don't know what yet."

His eyes bore into hers, then Martin's, cigarette smoke curling in front of him in thick white clouds. "Frank," he said definitively. "Please, call me Frank." He smiled without teeth, standing perfectly still, waiting.

"How about we go in the office?" Martin asked. "It's getting hot. We can tell you what we know, Frank."

The man nodded and motioned for them to follow. A warm breeze kicked in and stole the long ash of his cigarette. He took a long desperate drag and ground it on his shoe carrying the smoldering butt in his weathered hands. "Don't like to smoke in the office," he said quietly. "Helen." They nodded, saying nothing. Sophia recognized his chatter for what it was—comfort seeking. She had seen it before when delivering bad news to others. They focused on the mundane because the big picture was just too grim. Martin pulled up the rear as they filed into the office.

Several cups of coffee later, Frank Reynolds was up to date. Sophia felt sure Reynolds was hearing all of this for the first time. His reactions were too real.

"Frank, may I ask you a few questions now?" Sophia asked, softening her voice.

"Of course." He absently moved for a cigarette and lit it, then started. "Oh, I'm sorry, do you mind? Helen, well, she's not in, and under the circum—"

"No, really it's fine," Sophia assured him. She turned toward him and pushed her hair behind her ears. "Frank, how long have you worked here?"

"Twenty-five years next June."

"And Frank, I have to ask you this, what were you doing here today? Mrs. Keats said that although the quarry was closed, you might be working."

Reynolds stared absently toward the largest desk in the office. It was adorned with several picture frames, one held a portrait studio shot of Charlotte Keats, another a candid shot of a smiling Zoë with her arms around a giant Irish setter. Mother and wife vying for attention on Campbell's desk.

He nodded. "I had to meet with one of our sub-contractors to do some scheduling. We have a big week coming up and need to hit the ground running on Monday." His voice was distant.

"I see," Sophia feigned nonchalance. "Was that the man we saw in the parking lot, the sub-contractor?" She thought she heard Martin snort but didn't look his way.

"Joe Rizzo, yes," Frank said, then paused. "What was he still doing here? He must have left close to an hour ago."

"Looks like he was working on his truck. I—we found him under the chassis when we pulled in," Sophia replied, still avoiding Martin's gaze.

Reynolds smiled and nodded knowingly. "Man, he loves that new truck. Can't imagine there'd be anything wrong with it already, he was probably just tinkering."

They were all silent. A more serious topic was at hand.

"So, you finished up your scheduling with this Rizzo, and...?" Sophia continued.

"I was just wrapping up some paperwork. Guess Mrs. Keats knows me well enough by now to know I never leave paperwork sit." He pondered a long cigarette ash.

"Tell me about your relationship with Campbell," Sophia probed. She looked into Frank's eyes marveling at the depth of green and yellow. She smiled and they held a look—just long enough to build trust—and she relaxed her face.

"Well, I watched that little guy grow up, you know. He wasn't quite ready to take over the business when his dad died, well, the timing was... " Reynolds stopped, smoothed his mustache and rolled his cigarette against the walls of a large glass ashtray making a neat point with the embers. "I mean, I was sort of running things. I had to. He's so young. But he has an eye for business," Frank had shifted to the present tense. "He wants to get more involved on the project side. But I guess you didn't ask me that, did you?" Reynolds squinted at them across the desk.

"No, that's fine, whatever you can tell us will help."

"Well, since Jack died, things have been tough around here. Before, I ran the shifts, the projects, that sort of thing, and Jackson, he ran the business end, but he was plugged in, knew everything that was going on. When he died, Campbell took over for him—and he's good at the business side," Reynolds stopped himself. "What do you think happened to him? Where did he go?"

Sophia's limbs felt heavy. Her arms were like tree-stumps. She reached for the file from Martin. *It's easier to say with pictures*, she thought and fished for the shoelace shot. Reynolds looked confused.

He didn't see it.

"What does that look like to you?" Sophia pointed to what she thought was a shoelace. "Isn't that a grommet from a shoelace, or a boot?"

"Where is that? That's here." Reynolds gestured toward the office door. "When did you take that?"

"I was here yesterday. I took this picture yesterday." Sophia glanced at Martin who watched and listened patiently. They had come to the quarry because of that picture, and now were getting to it. Reynolds' presence had changed the dynamic of things; slowed the pace. He stood, screeching his chair across the office floor almost knocking it over. Sophia started, and then stood herself.

"Well, what're we waiting for?" He moved to the door. "C'mon we'll go see what that is. It can't be anything," he was mumbling now. "That poor woman, she's tough as nails but this… no, it's nothing, we'll see." They were out in the heat again, Reynolds swiftly moving towards the quarry's edge. He peered over and into the abyss glanced back at Martin and Sophia and started his descent. They followed. What else could they do?

7

July 6th, 1:00 p.m.

Cool clear water spilled onto the cobblestones, the splashes drowned out by shrieking children. Maria Rizzo sat quietly watching her son and other neighborhood children play in the fire hydrant's deluge. She held the Diet Coke to her cheek, closed her eyes and imagined she was on the beach and not sitting by the gutter on a tattered folding chair.

Matteo's black hair flopped in his eyes; he needed a trim. He ran circles around the other children like a long-limbed greyhound. Maria was in awe of him. He had lean muscles and was perfect with ten fingers, ten toes, shiny white teeth, and blue eyes like the ocean.

She had named him Matteo, meaning "Gift from God," because he was truly that.

At that moment, her Gift from God landed in her lap giggling and soaked. Now she was wet too, and covered in soda.

"Mattie!" She tried to put anger in her voice but instead it was playful. He giggled and ran off again into the arc of cold hydrant water as it sprayed across the small street.

South Philadelphia bubbled with tastes and spices like a well-simmered ragout. Today, Maria loved living there. Growing up, she had wanted to get out. She'd known her parents would never move; she would always have them as a connection to the neighborhood. But Maria had dreamed of being the first in her family to go to college.

Her grades had been scholarship-worthy, and she had saved all her tip money from waitressing at The Saloon. She had wanted to go to Saint Joseph's University, a small Catholic college on City Line Avenue. Sometimes on Sundays the family would go driving and Maria would beg her father to drive past the campus. And he had always indulged her. The school was just as Maria dreamed. There was a beautiful double-spired church and huge oak trees under which she imagined reading Shakespeare in the fall.

She would live in the dormitories and meet a boy from a good Catholic family. They would eventually marry and buy a house in the suburbs, but Maria would visit the neighborhood and would always go to church with her parents on Sundays. Her parents would have been so proud, boasting of their daughter's accomplishments and her dedication to family. Maria knew the fantasy so well she could see herself in cap and gown receiving a well-earned diploma.

A blast of cold water brought her back to today. She'd known even then that Saint Joe's was a fantasy. If anything, she would be able to afford part-time classes at Temple University. She would live at home and brave the subway to North Philly every day. But even that dream had died.

Her parents had been taking their first vacation in years to celebrate their wedding anniversary. In deference to America, their adopted home, Angelo and Lorena had been married on July Fourth. Twenty years later, Maria and her brother rented them a room in quiet, romantic Cape May to mark the occasion. They had set off in the dark in early July ten years ago. Angelo had mapped the entire trip and was convinced that they would miss the traffic if they drove late into the night before the holiday. It took one car to ruin those plans. They were driving the speed limit along the Garden State Parkway when a drunk driver hit them at such dizzying speed that they were killed instantly.

The police had come to the small South Philly row house—a kind, albeit misguided, gesture. When the state trooper had called in the accident, Angelo Rizzo's name was flagged. It happened all the time, people thought they were related to the infamous Frank Rizzo, Philadelphia's first Italian mayor. Typically, any connection their surname implied was unfortunate. On this night, it was a blessing. A police escort took them directly to the accident site. With sirens blaring, Maria and her brother were whisked across the Walt Whitman Bridge past Glassboro, Vineland and other parts New Jersey.

By the time they reached the area, her parents had been transported to a nearby hospital and were pronounced dead on arrival. Maria and her brother went into shock, both determined to go to the scene to pray for their parents' souls.

The police had obliged, still thinking Maria and Joe were descendants of former Mayor Frank Rizzo, once a Philadelphia police commissioner. In the 1970s, Rizzo had fueled racial unrest throughout the city; his attempt to change the city charter allowing him to serve a third mayoral term had been the last straw. The city rebelled against his law-and-order rule and four years later, elected the city's first black mayor. But, like for Mussolini in Italy, in certain circles there would always be an unspoken respect for Frank Rizzo.

Had the state trooper been a young African-American, the deaths might have been handled differently. Instead, a dedicated Pennsylvania State Trooper named John Lombardi had been called to accompany Maria and her brother to the hospital, accident scene and back to their small row house on Ninth Street. And after that night their lives changed immeasurably.

Maria was lost in the memory. Earlier that week had marked the tenth anniversary of her parent's death. Joseph came up behind her and kissed her forehead. She jumped. "Mamma mia, you scared me!"

"Sorry cara, how's everything? How's my boy?"

Just then Matteo caught sight of his uncle, ran towards him and landed in his outstretched arms. "Zio, you're home!"

"Yes, I am. How's my favorite man?" Joe hugged his nephew.

"Good. Did you see the fire 'drant, Uncle Joey?"

"Hy-drant," he corrected. "Yes, I saw it. Are you having fun? It looks like you got your momma all wet too." He shot a quick glance at Maria and smiled.

She smoothed her hair. "I must look a sight!" she said gesturing to her damp shorts and tank top, wet hair plastered to her head.

"You look bellissima, non preoccuparti."

Maria loved when Joseph spoke Italian around Matteo. She wanted her son to be proud of his heritage. Since he'd never known his grandparents, it was up to Maria and her brother to teach him where they came from. So far, it was working. Matteo was a proud little Italian, his vocabulary expanding daily. And he seemed well adjusted, despite the lack of a real father in his life. Maria was so grateful to her brother. Together, they were raising a wonderful little boy.

"Everything okay at work? I thought you had the weekend off?" Maria asked as Matteo ran in and out of the spray. Fire hydrants: the blue collar fountains of Philadelphia.

"Something happened and I had to go in. Let's not talk about it. Everything's fine."

"Okay, it's just that you seem tense. You've been working so much lately."

He sighed and cursed under his breath. "Puttana Eva Maria Angela, you sound like a wife. Like I said, everything's fine."

"Joseph! Don't talk like that in front of Mattie—he's learning the language quickly. Do you want him to learn those words too?"

"I'm sorry, it's just—it's so damn hot. And, I've been thinking about, you know." They locked eyes over Matteo's head, not wanting to mention their parents' death in front of him.

"I just don't want to talk about work right now. Okay?"

"Fine, I won't ask again, but watch your mouth." She looked up to see her son out of earshot. "Stronzo." She laughed as she whispered the last word, meaning "jerk" in Italian. Depending on the inflection, "stronzo" could be nasty or merely playful. All was forgiven and Joseph gave her a tap on the shoulder.

"Get some clothes on or Eva won't be the only puttana." He lifted her chair and carried her into the spray with the children.

"Hey, no fair!"

Soon they were all laughing and splashing together. As the other children were called home, the three of them moved to their stoop and sat for hours watching the sun finally set a brilliant pink, enjoying the smells of nearby barbeques and freshly lit cigars.

8

July 6th, 1:30 p.m.

Sophia stumbled behind Frank Reynolds who moved like a jackrabbit, surefooted along uneven terrain. He made it down into the quarry's abyss in seconds. Martin pulled up the rear again, his tennis shoes slipping against the rocks. As they reached the depths of the quarry, Sophia noticed a palpable change in the air.

It was cooler, and then like a force the smell assaulted them.

Reynolds didn't seem to notice at first, maybe years of smoking had dulled his senses. But Martin gagged behind her and tapped her shoulder. She turned to him and nodded grimly. Sophia had smelled a dead body before. There was no mistaking it.

They reached a flat area and stopped in unison as if on cue. Reynolds turned. He stood directly atop a smooth flat slab of limestone scanning the area, his nose slightly upturned like a hunting dog's. He ran his craggy fingers through his hair and sighed.

"Something smells, eh?" Reynolds' voice was light-hearted as if his tone could change the circumstances. The smell was overpowering now and Sophia had pulled her T-shirt up over her nose and mouth. Martin produced a stark white handkerchief and held it over his face leaving two tearing blue eyes peeking out.

Reynolds' nose seemed to catch up then and he moaned, moving back up the hill slightly. He took out a cigarette.

"Careful!" Sophia admonished. "Sorry. Evidence."

"Jesus Christ our Lord, evidence," whispered Reynolds. "Do you think?"

"I think we have to check it out. Smoke if you need to, just be careful of the ashes. It'll help though—you know, with the smell."

Reynolds smiled with gratitude—and fear. Sophia moved closer to the overwhelming odor. She glanced back at Martin, who stood more still than death itself. *Okay*, she thought, *I guess it's up to me*. She moved to a neat pile of rocks that looked out of place.

Her eyes were burning and she felt like throwing up. Then she saw it. The same grommet from the photo. It screamed out at her from beneath a huge slab of limestone. That's it, she thought. That's him. Just a few more seconds, then you can go throw up.

She moved in another step and knelt down to get a different angle, one her camera lens had missed from above. There was what looked like a leg, it was black though and moving. Flies. They lifted slowly, landing again in a wave, a blanket cascading through the air, settling again in uneven patches against their prey. They sensed her behind them, but did not abandon their post. Sophia steeled herself against the smell. In the seconds it took for the flies to lift and settle, Sophia saw a Timberland boot, a white monogrammed sock with the initials CWK. She felt her face flush, her stomach pumping adrenaline; CWK is for Campbell W-something Keats, certainly not Calvin "W." Klein. For a sick second, Sophia remembered the scene in *Back To The Future*, where Lea Thompson thinks Michael J. Fox's name is Calvin because he is wearing Calvin Klein underwear. *Not relevant right now Gold, you idiot, you are standing two feet from a dead body*.

She took a shallow breath, trying to avoid taking in any air, squeezed her eyes shut and then re-focused. If that was Campbell Keats, and Sophia knew that it was, his monogrammed leg was covered in a black carpet of flies. She had seen enough. The police could do the rest. She hopped backwards and catapulted into Martin, causing him to lose his balance. He grabbed her instinctively. They righted themselves quickly and locked eyes.

"Let's go back up now. Let's go, Frank." Sophia moved to Reynolds, who stood smoking and staring. "C'mon." She took his elbow to jolt him. Silently, they began their ascent.

9

Sophia flushed twice, willing her body to heave. Nothing. She stood, splashed cold water on her face and neck and turned off the bathroom light. The men sat at different desks in the large office, white as sheets, both sipping Cokes.

"That's a good idea," she said rubbing her belly. She moved to the refrigerator, removed one for herself and sat down at the guest chair next to Reynolds' desk. She looked over at Martin.

"Martin," she said his name forcefully. He started and his eyes focused somewhere past Sophia; she was in their path. "We have to call the police. I know Mrs. Keats didn't want them, but this—we have to call the police."

Martin started to speak, then nothing. He nodded. Sophia moved to another desk, sat and picked up the phone. As she was dialing, she noticed the desk was adorned with knickknacks and a photo of a little girl with blond ringlets holding a black Lab puppy. The girl had three or four teeth in her mouth and was smiling to show them off. This must be Helen's desk, she thought. Somehow seeing those innocent, Norman Rockwellesque photos brought everything to the surface. Her eyes brimmed with tears, her stomach flip-flopped. She took a breath and looked away, waiting for the call to engage.

"Homicide. Washington."

She heard the familiar voice on the other line and let out a breath she didn't know she'd been holding. "Tariq, it's Sophia."

"Goldie?" His voice still held pleasure on the other end.

"The one and only. Listen, I have a problem. Not in Philly though, I'm in

Plymouth Meeting. I'm so relieved to get you. You're working the holiday weekend?" Small talk was not at the top of Sophia's list at this point, but she knew he liked to chat, maybe because so much of his work was with those who weren't so chatty anymore.

"Yeah, I'm on duty. So, tell me."

"I found a body." she said. "You know the Keats family?" Tariq whistled softly under his breath. "I was hired to find Campbell, the oldest son. He went missing on the Fourth. I think I found him."

"The Fourth?" Tariq asked. He fumbled for something on his desk. "Let's see, today's the sixth—didn't they call the police yet?"

"No. That's just it. His mother was concerned about the press."

Tariq sighed into the phone. "These rich people—what the hell?"

Although the Keats family was not the city's most famous, or its' wealthiest, they were media magnets. Sophia was not surprised Tariq recognized the name immediately. Washington was the kind of man who knew a lot about everything and he was single-minded in his approach to life and death, right and wrong. He was a great homicide detective. Sophia could picture him, all 6'6" of his lanky frame dwarfing a tiny desk in the squad room, fingering the phone cord and shaking his head in disbelief.

Sophia had met Washington on her first and only other murder case. She had been hired to find a missing child. Before she even began to look for the girl, the Philadelphia police got an anonymous tip. They found the little girl, Grace, slumped against a jungle gym in one of Center City's few playgrounds just several blocks on all sides from City Hall; the city's financial center; the main subway line; up-scale condominiums; and areas of poverty and want. It was this juxtaposition of all things urban that made Philadelphia so rich— and so vulnerable.

The girl had only been dead hours. Sophia was with the girl's mother at the time. Wendy Bennett, a former art school classmate of Sophia's, was not the type of person to hire a PI, let alone be friends with one. Since Sophia was not a typical PI, it was a wash. It was a tough first case—personal and tragic, but somehow affirming of her new career choice. She would always be an artist, but she had opened the floodgates to another part of herself. She wanted to help people like Wendy. She didn't know if she could, but she knew she had to try.

The girl's father, Wendy's troubled ex-boyfriend, had been the prime suspect, but was never caught. Washington was convinced he had left the country, but had doggedly stuck with the case long after his colleagues and superiors had moved on.

At the time, Sophia had wondered whether Tariq's ego, or almost perfect clearance record, motivated him. She had come to know that it was his compassion and an unusual commitment to his work. Their friendship grew from there, despite the different worlds they came from and traveled in.

"I know, Tar," she replied. "Listen, I need some advice here."

"Okay, first of all, you have to call the locals. Let me know who it is. If I know 'em, I'll make a few calls, but you have to call them *now*. The longer you wait the worse it gets—for everyone. Maybe the family's already on their radar—know what I mean?"

He was right. It was possible that the local police were already acquainted with the Keats family's influence and penchant for privacy. *The relationship may in fact be adversarial*, she thought.

Or perhaps it was run-of-the-mill upper-class revulsion to all things common that kept Charlotte Keats from involving law enforcement. Whatever it was, it would likely ruffle a few feathers.

"Just call them," Tariq continued. "Family's the first suspect. The more you stall, the easier it'll be to look at them."

Sophia sighed, suddenly aware of both Martin and Frank Reynolds watching her intently. She had waited long enough. Tariq was gently reminding her of that, pushing her to act.

"Okay. Thanks, I'll call you later," she hung up.

"I'm calling the police," she said definitively.

"I'll call Charlotte." Martin seemed resigned to it. In the time Sophia had taken to call Tariq Washington, reality had set in. "Maybe she can get here before they do." He started dialing.

Sophia slowly reached for the phone again, paused. "No!" Martin and Frank both jumped. "Sorry," Sophia softened her tone. "What if it's not him? Let's not get Charlotte out here. She'll need to know, and she'll find out soon enough. Let's wait for the police, Martin. I think it's best."

Martin nodded. Frank turned a yet whiter shade of pale. Sophia wouldn't have thought that was possible. She punched in 911.

******

The Plymouth Township police arrived in a hot, spinning cloud of gravel and dust. Their bubble flashed silently—the siren would have been overkill. *How often did a patrol car get to race to the scene in Plymouth Meeting?*

Sophia wondered. *Probably more than you'd think*, her cynical side replied. Two eager officers leapt out of the car. *Rookies*, she thought, *on duty over the holiday weekend.*

The patrol officers approached.

One male, one female, both white, young, and fit. Poster children for law enforcement. "I'm Officer Gentry," the male officer began. "This is my partner, Officer McKenzie. We understand there may be a body." McKenzie unceremoniously whacked her partner, who immediately felt his error. Sophia knew why. It's not a "body." It's someone's spouse or child or parent. Gentry realized too late that the family might be among the group standing outside the quarry office.

"Officer McKenzie," the woman said. "What can we do for you folks?" Officer McKenzie was smooth despite her youth. Sophia thought how fortunate they both were to be women. Blessed, and sometimes cursed, with the urge to nurture. Women handle these kinds of situations differently— often better—than men.

"Sophia Gold." She held out her hand. They shook all around. McKenzie had a hard edge, her grip called and raised Sophia's, but she had warm deep eyes.

Gentry seemed a typical rookie cop, not that there's anything wrong with that. His expression was flat and he stood arms akimbo, drawing attention to his gun on one hip, nightstick on the other. "Tell us what happened Ma'am," Gentry spoke quickly, seemingly aware that he was losing top cop status. His partner had taken control.

It took less than two minutes to bring the officers up to speed. Sophia told them everything but in broad terms and with a small twist. "And, so you see," she wrapped up. "Mrs. Keats was sure this would resolve itself. She did not want to involve the police yet as her son had not been gone very long."

Gentry's brow furrowed as if he was doing math in his head. He was. "That's over forty-eight hours ago. For a missing person, a report should be filed after forty-eight hours." Sophia was ready for him; she had done the math in double time.

"Yes, Officer Gentry. Actually, it's been since late on the Fourth—he's been missing less than three days. It'll be forty-eight hours tonight, I think, actually."

The rookie grunted; at first blush, time did not appear to be an issue. But to save himself he said, "We'll see what homicide thinks."

Sophia was taken aback. But then she heard gravel crunching again and saw that both officers were looking over her shoulder toward the driveway. An unmarked American-made cruiser pulled in and two well-dressed detectives emerged slowly. Both tall, they unfolded out of the car with grace and experience in arriving at crime scenes.

A sharply dressed Ken doll-like man strode toward the group. He was too handsome for real police work. He looked like he'd just walked off the set of *Law & Order*. His next gig would be movies. TV is so ordinary. His partner rounded out the aesthetics, however, with a slight paunch, balding pate, and clip-on tie. He was wizened; the man had seen many a dead body. Ken-doll, on the other hand, Sophia was not so sure about. But, she'd been wrong about appearances before, so she shook hands and took in the scenery.

Ken-doll's real name was Buck Dallas. Sophia fought the urge to roll her eyes when she shook his hand, giving him the full-on Gold Grip. He didn't notice. *His name cannot really be Buck*, she thought, *I bet it's Bert or Barry or something*. Who knew this kid would grow into a hunk? His looks begged for a stage name and "Buck" was perfect. His partner, on the other hand, was Jack Webb. Sophia wondered if she had stumbled into a B-movie or a bad straight-to-cable deal. She'd heard Webb say his name and immediately the little wheels in her head spun with recognition. When it came to her— *Dragnet's* Joe Friday—she almost laughed out loud. Webb caught it, smiled and held up his palms as if to say, "What can I do? It's *really* my name." She liked him.

"What can you tell me?" Webb looked directly at Sophia, sensing that she was the one to talk to. Sophia would have liked to think it was her commanding presence. It could have been that both Martin Duncan and Frank Reynolds looked like a couple of nauseated deer in headlights.

She was the only one standing firm, at least for now.

She went through the same story again while the officers and detectives all took copious notes. Webb raised his eyebrows slightly at the end when she tried out her lie on him.

"Let's be honest, Ms. Gold. I know who Charlotte Keats is. She doesn't trust the police and she hired you to find her son with no intention of involving us, am I right?"

It was so obvious. Sophia had been lulled by the patrol officers' naiveté. Gentry was so mired in procedure, all he could think about was the 48-hour missing persons rule. Had he thought about who the missing person actually was, he might have understood.

Martin's attorney instincts kicked in. "I can address that, Detective Webb. As the Keats' family attorney, it was my responsibility to ensure discretion until such time as it had been determined that there was, in fact, a crime. Initially, it was our belief that Mr. Keats would return unharmed. His mother, Charlotte Keats, believed that this was a personal, family matter that could be resolved in time, with discretion, and with the help of a private investigator. That is how Ms. Gold became involved."

Now that's what I call lawyer-speak, Sophia thought

"Fair enough. Mr. uh, Duncan was it?" Webb replied. Sophia felt sure Webb had gotten Martin's name the first time. Martin stood tall and nodded at the detective. Buck Dallas meanwhile looked like the statue of David. Beautiful, stony, idle.

"Why don't we take a look and see what we have?" Webb directed.

Together, they walked to the quarry's edge, Officer Gentry like a puppy dog to a mound of kibble. Sophia pointed out where they had seen Campbell, or rather who they thought was Campbell. Then, as she had expected, Dallas and Webb instructed them to stay put while the officers filed down to the scene.

As they began bumbling down the rocks, the forensics team arrived, unpacked their gear and followed swiftly along.

Frank Reynolds peeked over the brim of the quarry.

"You can't go down there Frank—it's a crime scene. We may have already contaminated it," Sophia said.

"I don't really want to go down there again, Miss Gold. I've seen enough."

"Hmm," Sophia used a comforting tone and nodded. "Listen, Frank, if you're up to it, I'd like to ask you a few questions. I know the police will want to as well, so you'll have to get used to it. What do you say?"

Frank nodded, still ghostlike and wooden. "I suppose I'd rather talk to you, Miss Gold, than the cops."

What does that mean? Probably just that no one wants to talk to the cops. Probably. She smiled and took his elbow. "By the way, Frank, call me Sophia, or Sophie or something else. I keep looking around for my mother when I hear 'Miss Gold.'

"Let's go into the office where it's cool." She stole a glance at Martin that said, "Stay away." She wanted Reynolds alone. If there was anything incriminating to say about Campbell, the family, the business, or—reluctantly—Sophia admitted, Reynolds himself, a lawyer, especially one employed by the Keats family, might hinder that.

Reynolds looked expectantly Martin.

"You know what?" Martin jumped in, "I should really stay here and watch this search. As the family attorney, you know. You don't mind if I wait out here do you, Sophie?" *They were like a well-oiled machine*, Sophia thought and then shuddered at the double entendre. *At least there isn't a cartoon bubble above my head broadcasting my every inappropriate thought*, she mused.

"Thanks Martin. No, that will be fine, right Frank?" Sophia said. "We'll catch up when the police are finished. Frank, I'll meet you in the office, I need to get something from the car."

Frank obeyed and Sophia watched him light a cigarette as he walked toward the air-conditioned office. All bets were off for Helen and her no-smoking policy.

Sophia met Martin at the Saab and popped the hatch. He sat on the lip of the trunk and sighed. "This is unbelievable," he said.

"You know it may not be him." She was unconvinced. "Are you okay?" Sophia felt herself soften. She wanted to sit on his lap. She wanted to stroke his hair.

"I guess so. I mean, I will be. You're right. It might not be him, right?" Martin looked at her with the hope of a lost, abused child—courageous on the surface but somehow deeply tainted, knowing.

"Right," she stopped. "Listen, I actually *do* think it's him. You need to prepare yourself for that." And then silently she promised: *You are not alone in this. I'm not just going to work this case; I'm going to take care of you, too.* Instead she said, "Why don't you just hang out here for awhile, you don't really need to watch the police, do you?"

"I guess not, although as their attorney..." He was fading in and out of shock and professionalism.

"Martin, how well did you know Campbell?" Sophia asked. "You aren't just the family attorney, are you?"

He smiled oddly. "We went to high school together."

"What?! You went to Chestnut Hill Academy? You never told me that."

"Just for senior year. I graduated from CHA, I went to Central till then."

"Why didn't you tell me?"

"Because I thought you'd think less of me. You were so class conscious in college. I was afraid I'd be dismissed as a spoiled rich boy. I wanted to be with you."

"No, Martin, now. Why didn't you tell me now? Since the other day.

Were you friends? My God, you were friends. I am so sorry," Sophia paused. "Was I really that judgmental back then?"

"Back then?" Martin half-teased.

Sophia huffed. That stung, more because it was true than because it was hurtful. She was still vacillating between empathy for the Keats family's tragic history and disdain for their privilege and money. Was she a reverse-snob? It was not something she wanted to admit. She grabbed her backpack and turned to the office.

******

Martin smiled, watching her implode. As she walked away he noticed the thick ropy muscles in her calves. She was still captivating, annoying, exotic— he had missed her and was really feeling it. Seeing her again made him sad, nostalgic for simpler times. Maybe she was right. Wealth and fame were curses. Or were they? Surely it wasn't that simple. Sophia saw things in black and white, just like her photographs. There must be shades of gray. He had yet to find them, but they had to be there. He had worked too hard; had come too far. Yet his marriage to Regan was over. His marriage: a shallow and convenient union from which they both benefitted socially and financially. Martin couldn't live with the emptiness any longer. He marveled at his wife's ability to do so. He would not give up the law, however, nor would he relinquish his position at the firm. Granted, her family name had catapulted him far beyond where he might otherwise be at this age. But he had put in long hours, dedicated himself to his clients, and ameliorated himself as an officer of the court. That was his and his alone.

He took a deep breath and thought back to high school, senior year. When he wasn't caring for his mother, he had spent the summer after graduation with Campbell and his friends, drinking too much, smoking cigars, spending money, meeting girls and treating them poorly. He had started at Penn in the fall and met Sophia. He was so ashamed he'd never told her, or anyone, about his brief connection to high society, such that it was. The University of Pennsylvania was a big enough school for Martin to become anonymous. Campbell Keats went to Princeton and never took college seriously; he had a well-paying job waiting for him at the quarry. He went through the motions, mostly for Charlotte, and graduated with a liberal arts degree in something or other, Martin couldn't remember. Martin had been invited to the occasional Christmas and summer parties, never went and eventually the invites stopped.

When he married Regan and launched his law career, he'd come full circle. Now the Keats family was his client.

It all came back to him like a flood. The feelings of belonging, then of being a fraud; Sophia; law school and the romance of money, of finally being rich, really rich, not just posers like his parents; of being able to send his future children to good schools from day one, not just for one year to fool the college admissions offices. He could do it. He was a smart enough lawyer; he could play the part. He loved being a lawyer and having money. But something was missing, something so deep and real that it ached. He looked up again to see Sophia's silhouette against the office window.

10

Frank Reynolds had opened two more Cokes and put them on coasters at Helen's desk. He smiled at Sophia as she sat down, pulled up the desk chair and got out her notebook.

Reynolds dropped his cigarette in an empty soda can, stood, went for the glass ashtray and lit up again.

"Frank, listen, I just have to ask you a few questions," Sophia said. "The police will need to talk to you too, that won't be a problem will it?"

"No, no. I'm just, I mean it's just—I don't know what to say."

"Just tell the truth. That's all you have to do."

"Wait a minute," he stopped, "am I a suspect? Why wouldn't I tell the truth?" Reynolds incredulity was convincing.

"No reason, Frank. Don't worry about it. Mrs. Keats hired me to find Campbell. I need to do that job until I hear otherwise. We don't know for sure that Campbell is down there." She gestured toward the quarry.

Frank sighed. "What can I tell you?"

"Well, when did you last see Campbell?"

"Late on Wednesday—the third, I guess. We were here finishing up before the long weekend. The crew was on OT." Sophia nodded for him to continue. *Overtime, okay,* she thought, *go on.* "The guys from Red's were here. McDonald, Rizzo, Gonzalez. You met Rizzo this morning, right?"

Sophia nodded. *Hmm,* she thought, *he left just in the nick of time, didn't he?* "Campbell was in the office doing paperwork," Frank continued. "Working the phone, that sort of thing. I sent them home around 7:30. He was still here."

Sophia waited until Reynolds took a breath. "What's Red's?" she asked.

"Red's Construction. A sub-contractor we hired for the Abington project. We needed a few extra guys to team up with us. I guess we hired them about a month ago, something like that." Frank inhaled deeply and blew smoke over his shoulder away from Sophia.

"What were their names, Rizzo and who?" Despite the man's physical presence—Sophia could still feel his energy—the name Rizzo would stand out to any Philadelphian. Former Mayor Frank Rizzo had made quite a name for himself in the 1970s.

Frank stood, went to his desk and returned with a clipboard. "Let's see William Gonzalez, James McDonald, Joseph Rizzo. You see—there's the time sheet." He handed her the clipboard.

"And, you met just with Rizzo today, not the others?" she asked.

Frank nodded. "He's the project manager."

"Was he here when you got here this morning?"

Frank cocked his head like a curious animal. "I guess he was, yes. He was waiting in his truck." Frank gasped. "You don't think...?"

Sophia held out her hands in protest. "I don't think anything at this point Frank, I'm just asking questions."

Just then Buck Dallas blasted in the door, long legs spread wide, hands on hips. With him came a cloud of hot humid air, a sweet sick smell.

"We've recovered the body, can you folks come with me please? We'd like to make a preliminary ID if possible." Dallas was like a caricature.

Reynolds pushed himself up and moved to the door. If either of them could identify Campbell Keats, it would be Frank Reynolds. Sophia followed. Martin lumbered over from the Saab to join them.

They were assaulted by the heat, dust, smell and noise. The quarry grounds had become overrun with police vehicles, officers and forensics teams. The medical examiner had arrived; the black coroner van sat ominously next to several unmarked American model cruisers. Instinctively, Sophia reached for Frank's elbow to guide him towards the fray. She started at her presumption. The man knew the quarry as well as his own home; he might even be involved in the crime, yet somehow Sophia wanted to protect him. She wondered if he was a father and if so, if he had a daughter. He was probably in his mid-fifties, although he looked younger and smoking hadn't curbed his energy, although Sophia imagined his lungs were black and shriveled like prunes. She stopped herself and simply waved her arm in the direction of the quarry.

"We're bringing it up now," Webb stated firmly, although his voice was kind. "The ME had to do some work down at the scene, but we're ready to have you take a look if you can. We'll still need a positive ID from a family member, but maybe you can tell us what you think." Jack Webb must have said those words a thousand times at a thousand different crime scenes. Somehow he managed to make them sound unique, uttered just for them. Frank and Martin nodded.

The body was already in a bag. In a sick flash Sophia thought how hot those black bags must be in this weather. She was again relieved that her thoughts did not broadcast themselves in cartoon bubbles above her head. She'd never make it in civilized society that way. Buck Dallas barked at a pair of hefty forensics officers who exchanged an annoyed glance but who jumped to attention and set the body down next to their feet. Dallas gestured toward the top zipper, indicating for one of them to open the bag. Sophia bet that he was purposely not wearing gloves so he wouldn't have to touch anything. Classic. Webb on the other hand, had been peeling off a pair of gloves as they'd approached and now donned a new, clean pair.

Bulky Officer #1 unzipped the body bag several inches. A man's face appeared bloated and pasty white. His eyes bulged wide and glassy. Beneath the film of death they were Paul Newman blue. The smell was overwhelming. Frank Reynolds stifled a cough. Martin moaned and looked away. It was Campbell Keats—that was clear from their reactions. Reynolds continued to stare, unable to draw his attention away from the grotesque scene. Dallas looked impatient. Webb, on the other hand, waited, watching both men carefully. There was silence except for the sound of the forensics teams gathering evidence in the depths of the quarry.

Webb bided his time. He glanced at Sophia. She had gained the man's respect; she could feel it. Charlotte Keats would likely keep her on to investigate Campbell's death; the matron making it clear she did not trust the police and Sophia had done something right with Webb. She did not know what, but she'd take it—it always helps to make friends with the police. She nodded at him with as authoritative a nod as she could muster. He grinned at her as if to say, "I know this is the biggest fucking case you've ever seen—don't worry, I won't tell."

"Well?" Dallas had held back as long as he could. Self-restraint personified. "Is it our guy?"

Webb glared almost imperceptibly at his partner. "Mr. Reynolds, do you recognize this man?" he asked delicately.

Frank nodded unable to speak.

Martin stepped forward. "It's Campbell," he whispered.

"You knew him as well, Mr. Duncan?" Not surprised, Webb turned his attention to Martin.

Dallas stood stiffly, a smug expression on his chiseled face. Sophia noticed his forehead had an odd bronzed hue. *He must fake-and-bake*, she thought. *His tan is too smooth, and slightly orange.*

"Yes, I'm the family attorney." Martin's voice was weak. He cleared his throat and shot a glance at Sophia. "We were also classmates in high school senior year at Chestnut Hill Academy."

"I see." Webb was cool. Sophia could almost see Dallas' internal dialogue do a quick "well la-de-da" when Martin mentioned the elite private institution. She hated him already. Then she realized she had had a similar reaction to the same knowledge about her former lover.

"Well, if you gentleman are sure about this, the next step would be to contact the man's family. We do need a positive ID from them. We will also need to question you both, of course." Webb removed yet another pair of latex gloves and opened a small notebook. "We don't need to be here anymore. Is there anyone else here?" Webb asked.

Sophia hesitated and glanced at Frank. He wasn't going to implicate a co-worker. Much as she hated to do it, she said, "Someone was here earlier, a sub-contractor. He met with Frank this morning, guy named Joe Rizzo."

"Rizzo." Webb wrote a note to himself. "Do you have his contact info?" He looked at Frank who nodded. "Okay, we'll need to talk to him too."

"What say we all go to the Keats' residence? I imagine we can question you there just as well. We'll need to bring the mother or the wife to the morgue, however."

Sophia looked up at Webb. Keats was surely a household name in Plymouth Meeting if not in all of Philadelphia, but Zoë? How did Webb know Campbell was married? He caught her eye, smiled and touched a hand to his left ring finger. She nodded.

No one said anything. Dallas huffed, probably itching to whip out the handcuffs and arrest someone, anyone. Sophia knew Webb considered them all suspects, including Rizzo and even herself, although it was a long shot. But he was playing it cool, playing it right. He had no evidence against anyone and he'd get nowhere antagonizing them; combined their connection to the powerful Keats family was impenetrable.

"Shall we go?" Webb asked, guiding them all towards the bank of cars. "Mr. Reynolds, why don't you ride with us?" Frank glanced at his truck. "Someone will make sure you get back here later. It'll be easier this way. You've had quite a shock—I'd be negligent if I let you on the road alone."

Webb turned to Sophia, "Ms. Gold, I take it you and Mr. Duncan are together? You'll be driving." Had he said "together" that way intentionally? She was beginning to realize with all of his delicacy, Webb was a wily man. She could learn something from him. She looked over at Dallas. *So could he*, she thought. He was straightening his tie and smoothing his already slicked back hair against a perfectly shaped skull, readying himself to meet the infamous Charlotte Keats.

11

Charlotte Keats answered the door herself as if she had been waiting for them. Sophia supposed she had—her son was missing.

She was remarkably composed in greeting Sophia, Martin, Frank Reynolds and the two detectives. They had descended upon the large door together, jockeying for position. The detectives clearly wanted to be first to see Mrs. Keats and to gauge her reaction to their presence. They were up against a formidable opponent. If Charlotte Keats had anything to do with her son's disappearance, she was covering nicely. However, Sophia had spent enough time with the woman to recognize one quirk. As she stepped aside and allowed passage to her unexpected guests, the woman put a hand to her thin neck, stroking the pearl necklace that lay against her skin

They stood nervously in the oversized entryway. Webb and Dallas introduced themselves. Charlotte Keats paled as Webb said the words "homicide detective." She silently motioned to the group to follow her. They filed into the same sitting room Sophia had seen the day before. It was still spotless. The sofa cushions were taut as if no one had ever dared place their weight upon them. The cherry end tables gleamed. Perfect yellow roses sat in a shimmering crystal vase atop the mantelpiece.

Webb spoke first. "Mrs. Keats, we have reason to believe we have found your son. We need you or his wife to positively identify him, his body. We may be wrong. We hope we *are* wrong."

Charlotte clutched her neck. She was impeccably dressed in subtle yellow silk—Talbots or Ann Taylor. She matched the roses, Sophia realized. Her skirt covered her knees but revealed shapely stocking-clad calves as she sat in a high-backed Queen Anne chair. A simple yet elegant cardigan draped her shoulders, revealing its cashmere twin beneath. Sophia, Martin and Frank took one sofa. Webb sat on the edge of the other. Buck Dallas stood spread eagled by the pristine fireplace. Charlotte locked eyes with Frank, then looked down at her Ferragamo pumps and crossed her ankles behind her.

"Mrs. Keats," Buck Dallas jumped in with a surprisingly gentle tone to his voice. "Both Mr. Reynolds and Mr. Duncan believe in fact that we found your son—your son's, uh body." The whites of Charlotte's knuckles gleamed against the soft folds of her sweater. Dallas moved towards her and sat next to his partner. They watched Charlotte absorb the words.

"Unfortunately, Mrs. Keats, we do need you to come down to the morgue with us; we need an actual positive identification before we can move forward. We'd be happy," Buck corrected himself, "We'd be willing to contact your son's wife if you'd prefer."

Charlotte looked up at Dallas with bitter eyes. Her hands shook slightly as she moved them to her lap. She exuded antipathy for the man delivering this news to her, perhaps wondering why it might be her son at the morgue and not this man, not someone else, anyone else.

"My daughter-in-law is expecting a baby anytime now. She mustn't be upset unnecessarily." With that, Charlotte rose. "I do not believe that you have found Campbell, but I will do this identification, and I will do it now. The sooner we determine you are mistaken, the sooner we can get on with finding my son—alive."

Martin started to speak, but both Sophia and Frank stopped him, gently sandwiching him between them. The detectives rose, and everyone ceremoniously filed back into the entryway. It happened that fast.

At the entryway, Charlotte called down the hall. "Zander! Will you join me please?" Sounds were heard from a room nearby, a chair moving against the floor, the soft click of a door, leather soles on hardwoods, and then a man exited. Sophia thought she heard Martin gasp. If she hadn't known better, she'd have thought it was the man's movie star-like presence. He was wearing custom-tailored slacks—they had to be—a crisp striped shirt and had a soft, light sweater grazing his shoulders. With his height, build and coloring, he was a show-stopper. *What was it with this case and good-looking men?* Sophia wondered.

"What're you doing he—" Martin stammered.

Charlotte interrupted him. "Detective Webb, Detective Dallas, this is

Zander Jarvis, a friend of the family. Campbell's oldest friend. I would like him to join me." It was not a request. She went on, "I must ask for discretion. As I said, I do not believe you have found my son; you cannot have found my son dead but, you do now know that he is missing. You must know my family, my husband's family. Please," her throat caught, as if the pearls were tightening their grip. "The media." That was all she could get out, and Jack Webb saved her.

"Of course, Mrs. Keats." Webb was nothing if not politically astute. He nodded at the movie star. "Mr. Jarvis." Sophia was sure he would consider Charlotte Keats a suspect in her son's disappearance and in his death, but Webb also knew the power of the name Keats.

If he had been unsure before, certainly being in the woman's home, being in her controlled and domineering presence had turned him around.

"Martin," Zander said. They shook hands but exchanged no other words.

Sophia thought she could feel Zander staring at her and she wanted to crawl out of her skin. What was he staring at? Who was he? She shifted gears and looked over at Buck Dallas.

He was silent now, having surprised her earlier. Sophia shook her head against her own thoughts and followed the group out of the house to the curved driveway. Charlotte Keats waited for Webb to open the rear door of his cruiser and got in. Her companion followed. Charlotte acted as if she had done this before, either that or she was used to being chauffeured. Both, Sophia decided with sad acceptance. The woman had seen a lot of death in her family. She had also seen the backs of a lot of men's necks, oblivious to traffic, stop signs, overturned semis, parking. Sophia nodded at Webb as he went to the driver's side. She got in her Saab, Reynolds and Martin scurrying along after her.

12

The coroner's office for Montgomery County is in Norristown. Jack Webb drove through Plymouth Meeting with Sophia following close behind. The Plymouth Township Police had jurisdiction, as Tariq had predicted, but no medical examiner.

Sophia wondered how many murders they saw in a given year. Certainly more than when I was a kid, she thought, noticing familiar landmarks from her school days. She'd bused from Center City to this area for private school and summer day camp. At that time, it felt like being in the country. Now it was different with pockets of office parks and strip malls, and more traffic than ever. Plymouth Township was in Montgomery County and the county's sheriff, coroner and other offices were all housed in Norristown, just a few short miles away. The drive felt long though as they drove out of the city proper and into spacious Montgomery County.

Sophia pondered at the Keats' commitment to Philadelphia; they lived just inside the city limits. With their money, prestige, and quarry location outside the city, why hadn't they moved west or north, to a larger home with more acreage, to a more suburban area than Chestnut Hill? She speculated it had to do with Jackson Keats—she had heard he was down-to-earth, although having met his wife, she found that hard to believe. *Besides*, she thought, *the Keats' home is in fact a mansion on a quiet street in a wealthy and prestigious neighborhood. So, there are more elite neighborhoods—there's the entire Main Line—but Chestnut Hill is nothing to complain about. Still*, she thought, *there is something in that choice.*

The morgue was like any other morgue—cold, gray, sterile—pretty standard.

Sophia and the gang waited in the abandoned lobby while Webb and Dallas guided Charlotte Keats to identify the body. Zander was at her side, gliding down the hall in silent support. Martin seemed to want to join them but Webb waved him off. No one spoke. They were like automatons.

In what seemed like seconds, Charlotte Keats returned to the lobby, her lips pursed tightly. She looked like a yellow ghost in flowing silk against an unnaturally thin body. Her bony hands clutched at her neck and her eyes were hard but moist.

She did not look relieved.

She wanted out. Zander and Dallas ran after her out the door and into the steamy parking lot. Sophia watched them at the car as Dallas graciously unlocked the door and Charlotte folded herself into the seat.

Webb took Sophia's elbow, startling her. "It's an ID," he said unnecessarily.

They all nodded, the weight of awareness settling on them like a crashing wave. "We need to notify the wife. Mrs. Keats wants her sent for, thinks she should be at the house since she's pregnant and all," he lowered his voice to speak directly to Sophia. Both Martin and Frank were staring, glassy-eyed, past them and into gray space. "I do need to conduct an investigation at the same time." Sophia nodded. "Mrs. Keats seems to trust you. I'd like to ask you to go with Buck to pick up the wife, Zoë is it?" Sophia nodded again. "And you do know Zoë Keats?"

"We've met, yes."

Webb sensed something in her face, maybe the thought of spending time alone with the likes of Buck Dallas. "I need Buck there to gauge her reaction, you understand. I thought about having her come to the house, telling her there, but under the circumstances, with the pregnancy and all, the stress of not knowing could be worse. When my wife..." his voice trailed off.

Webb was right. The stress of not knowing could be even more harmful to Zoë and the baby. But, Sophia thought, that isn't his only motivation. Zoë could easily compose herself in the hour it would take to arrive at the Keats Mansion, and formulate a story before having to answer directly to the police. "That's fine Detective," she said. "What about the others, Frank, Martin, Zander?"

"I'll take them. I think Mrs. Keats should have her lawyer with her," he said the words without feeling. Sophia got the implication. Family members were the usual suspects, no matter how rich and powerful. "And," he continued, "I need to question the others."

******

Parking in Center City is a bitch, unless you're Buck Dallas. As Sophia rounded Rittenhouse Square, Buck reached in his tailored jacket and pulled out a piece of cardboard. He placed it on the dash. It read "POLICE BUSINESS" and was embellished with some sort of official-looking seal.

"Just double-park in front," he said definitively.

Sophia hated that she was impressed. She busied herself scanning the addresses, although she knew exactly where the house was, and pulled alongside a well-kept Mercedes station wagon and engaged the emergency brake.

They both ambled to the front door, putting off the task at hand.

And before the bell could echo throughout the house, Zoë stood bleary-eyed on the steps before them. A wave of recognition hit her, as she looked at Sophia then at Dallas, a stranger in a slick suit, arms akimbo, revealing the hint of a badge clipped to snakeskin and gabardine.

Sophia felt sick. Twice today she had brought death to the Keats family doorstep. She stood across from Zoë, so young, fragile and pregnant. She wanted to run away.

How would Zoë or Charlotte ever be able to answer their doors again without overwhelming dread and despair? A million welcome mats couldn't erase this. A thousand years couldn't take away this pain. And Zoë knew. How could she not know? It was palpable.

With a twisted irony, the afternoon sky had turned gloomy. Philadelphia summer storms will suffocate you. Even on a good day, the heat intensifies with the coming rain. They stood paralyzed as cool air-conditioned air wafted into the street.

Zoë stepped aside and crumbled against the doorjamb, losing consciousness.

Buck was quick, and strong. He scooped up Zoë and carried her into the house. She was very pregnant, large in the way only a pregnant woman can be, but also so petite as to seem like a doll. As if they'd partnered before, Sophia followed Buck into the house and moved instinctively to the kitchen.

The large hallway swallowed her as she sought a stream of fluorescent and the hum of a refrigerator. Dallas had made a left into the first room he saw and found a couch where he placed Zoë's limp body.

He was reaching for the phone when Sophia returned with a wet towel and a glass of water.

"Paramedics?" he said with the hint of a question in his voice. Sophia nodded dumbly. This was getting worse by the minute. Sophia knew nothing about being pregnant, but fainting couldn't be good. Dallas punched in 911. Sophia mopped Zoë's clammy brow with the dishcloth. A faint whining sound seeped into the room. Dallas was absorbed with the 911 operator, but started when he heard it. A sharp bark punctuated the air.

Sophia sighed so heavily she snorted and leapt to her feet. "The dog, they have a dog. She has a dog. I'll go…" Sophia ran back toward the kitchen, grateful to have something to do, grateful to not have to stare at Zoë's motionless body. Sure enough, a beautiful but agitated Irish Setter paced restlessly in the yard, occasionally clawing at the back door. Undoubtedly, he sensed something was wrong and wanted his owner.

Sophia remembered Zoë mentioning the dog. "Here Max." She unlocked the door as one hundred pounds of golden red came barreling at her. Max sniffed her briefly then made a quick beeline for the front room where Zoë lay, gradually coming back to consciousness, moaning.

The dog went right to her side, whined some more and started licking her feet.

Buck Dallas looked worried; he'd begun to sweat despite the air-conditioning and had loosened his tie. Before Sophia could say anything, sirens wailed outside and within seconds paramedics pounded on the front door.

By the time Zoë arrived at Graduate Hospital's Emergency Room, Dallas had notified Jack Webb and he, Charlotte Keats and Martin were in the cruiser, lights flashing.

Webb had sent Reynolds and Zander Jarvis home, despite their protests. They'd been questioned already and weren't family—or lawyers. There wasn't much more they could do. Webb had promised them he'd be in touch.

Emergency room waiting areas reek of disease, death and pungent cleaning solution. While doctors attended to Zoë, Sophia and Buck sat silently among weeping family members, some inadvertently bloodied by their charges, all blank-faced and weary. *This case really sucks*, thought Sophia. *If she loses that baby, I don't know if I can handle it.* Tears and bile welled up in her throat. She stared past Buck Dallas, who seemed equally struck by the enormity of the day.

They waited.

13

July 6th, 3:00 p.m.

Joe Rizzo watched from his car as his teammates warmed up, pelting ground balls back and forth, tossing the occasional fly, grinning ear-to-ear. Life was good—South Philly, summer, softball, the weekend. Rizzo spied Jimmy's red and white cooler under a tree. There was no shade today, not in this heat, but that was where the cooler went. *Everything in its place*, thought Joe. That damn cooler must be twenty years old, there were groves in the ground under that tree; the cooler slid easily into its spot.

Joe scanned the bleachers. *Jimmy's hot girlfriend is here, damn that girl is good looking,* he thought. *Jimmy is one lucky SOB. I wonder when she's going to bring her sister*. Jimmy kept promising he'd set Joe up, but the sister was still a ghost.

A sleepy voice broke into his thoughts. "Are we there yet, Zio?" Mattie was waking up in the cab. Joe caught a glimpse of him in the rearview; the kid was growing like a fucking weed. Still staring in the tiny mirror, Joe saw deep lines etched on his face, graying temples. He was getting old. Where the hell had the last ten years gone? His head swirled with emotion, love, bitterness, regret.

"Uncle Joey, are we there yet? I wanna play catch." Matteo sat tall, his mop of black hair skimmed long-lashed shocking blue eyes, a hint of chocolate stuck in the creases of his mouth. Oreo crumbs scattered the back of Joe's truck.

"Yeah, kiddo, we're here. And, what did I tell you about eating in the truck?"

Mattie looked sheepish and then grinned. "Food on the seat will get you some heat."

"That's right. Now wipe your mouth and you can clean the crumbs up when we get home. There's girls here, we want to look good."

Mattie was excited and swiped the back of his hand across his face. Joe shook his head and laughed as he watched in the rearview mirror.

He reached for the glove box where Maria had stocked Handi-Wipes, Kleenex, cough drops, Advil; the woman was a regular Rite-Aid.

"C'mon up here with Uncle Joey—I'll clean you up." Matteo scrambled out of his seatbelt and leapt over the seat, crashing into his uncle. "Or, you could use the doors," Joey mumbled. He went to work on the chocolate face.

"Who's that?" Matteo pointed through the windshield.

"Stay still a minute, you're a mess," Joe worked on the crusted chocolate in the corners of his nephew's mouth.

"Zio, look!" Mattie was pointing excitedly, jumping up and down on the seat as if he had to go to the bathroom.

"Mattie." Joe glanced up briefly, unable to resist his nephew's zeal, "Holy sh—" he caught himself as Matteo giggled.

"You almost said a bad word, Zio."

"Yeah, yeah, sorry bud." Joe was fixated now. Maybe Jimmy did bring the sister after all. Jimmy, his girl and another gorgeous creature were all standing together talking and looking in the direction of Joe's car. Jimmy caught Joe's eye and jerked his head back. The customary cool-guy salute. Joe nodded, smiled.

"Let's go find out who she is. You ready?"

"Yeah, Uncle Joey, I'm ready!" He bounded out of the car while Joe slowly folded his frame out of the driver's seat, reaching in the back for the sports bag. Matteo expressed Joe's excitement for him. *Kids,* Joe thought, shaking his head. He swaggered over to the bleachers. By the time Joe reached the group, Matteo was holding the strange girl's hand and smiling broadly.

"Jimmy, Teresa, how you doin'?" Joe slapped his friend playfully, kissed Teresa on the cheek. She was anchored to her boyfriend's side as always. Good-looking, but the chick was clingy. Jimmy never complained though. Why should he with that pressed up against his body?

"Joey, this is my sister, Christina. Christina Genovese, Joseph Rizzo," Teresa said, her voice thick with South Philly.

"Tina," the girl cooed. "You can call me Tina. It's nice to meet you."

"Yeah, you too. Call me Joe." *What a dork. Duh, call me Joe.* The air was heavy with humidity and sexual tension. Matteo watched the adults in awe.

"Zio, let's play catch, c'mon." He tugged on his uncle's pants. Joe looked down at him and was thankful he had worn his new baseball pants and not a pair of ratty shorts. This was a big game. It felt even bigger now. The adults laughed as Matteo's energy infected the air.

For a second Joe wondered if Tina would think Matteo was his son. He'd called him Zio; Joe was sure Tina was Italian, but she might not get it. He felt a flutter in his stomach. Surely Jimmy would have told her about him, about his situation.

He needn't have worried. "Uncle Joey, c'mon! Let's play catch." Clearly, Matteo wanted to show off for Tina as well.

"Okay, let's go." Joe put his arm around Mattie's shoulder. "Yo, Jimmy, we better warm up," he said jerking his head in the direction of the outfield where the other team had arrived.

"Gotta go babe." Jimmy planted a sloppy kiss on Teresa and swatted her ass. She giggled.

"See you later, Tina." Joe tried to be cool without sounding like a chump. She waved and smiled at him. Life was very good

******

Maria was relieved to be alone in the house.

Joe and Matteo would be gone for hours. And, if Joe's team won tonight, they'd go out to celebrate after the game. Maria often worried about Mattie going to bars with his uncle, but Pat's was the neighborhood haunt. Everyone looked out for Mattie there. Pat and her father Angelo had been friends years ago. The neighborhood had rallied around Maria and Joe when their parents were killed. The local priest had forgiven Maria's pregnancy; only he and Joe knew the truth and no one asked questions about Matteo's paternity. Maria knew they talked about it. What neighborhood didn't gossip, especially a close-knit one like South Philly? Everyone knew she'd confessed to Father Domenica, and that seemed to be enough. Maria had held her head proudly and never faltered, never allowed the question to be asked, and never offered an explanation.

Maria went to the kitchen and made a bag of microwave popcorn. In minutes she was curled up on the couch, romance novel in one hand, Diet Coke in the other, alternating popcorn with page turning until she was completely relaxed and lost in the world of fantasy. A late afternoon nap was pure luxury and Maria planned to indulge.

She took in the room, every wall covered with photographs of her parents, her with Joey growing up, and now Matteo. Three generations of Rizzos. All things considered, they were doing all right for themselves. She missed her parents but was lucky to have Joey, and Matteo was the best thing that ever happened in her life. She stretched out on the couch and closed her eyes, drifting in the twilight that comes before sleep.

She dreamt of her communion, the pride on her father's face, the food her mother had cooked that day—homemade gnocchi and tiramisu. Joe and Matteo flitted into her mind, playing like father and son as she watched from a place far removed, and then her parents were there too, all of them were there sitting at the cramped dining room table, saying grace, eating gnocchi, laughing, together.

When she woke up she was sweating, the afternoon heat having baked the tiny house sandwiched between brick neighbors. She shook off her dream—the sadness of truth threatening to overwhelm her. She turned up the air-conditioning, cranked The Boss and got out the cleaning supplies. Maria worked furiously for two hours, a whirling dervish buzzing through the small row house leaving gleaming chrome and perfectly matted carpet in her wake. She finished in the living room and the house was peaceful. No one needed to be fed and no one needed a beer. She popped the La-Z-Boy and flicked on the TV. She couldn't remember the last time she'd watched television in peace.

The familiar anchor's voice filled the room, his face grave. Maria sat up straight when she saw the inset on the screen. It was a small picture of poor quality, but its subject was unmistakable. Across the bottom of the screen the words "BREAKING NEWS" screamed in her living room.

"In an Action News exclusive, we have an unconfirmed report that Campbell Keats, son of the late Philadelphia limestone baron, Jackson Keats and philanthropist Charlotte Keats, has been missing since July Fourth and today is presumed dead. The Montgomery County coroner has not confirmed this report, but sources say the Keats family has been to the Norristown office and positively identified the body of Campbell Keats. We take you live to the scene, Jim…"

His voice trailed off as he passed the baton to a street reporter. Maria was paralyzed. Campbell Keats was dead. She felt sick. She barely made it to the freshly scrubbed toilet.

14

July 6th, 7:00 p.m.

"She's stabilized," announced a scrub-clad genderless ER doctor. A palpable sigh filled the room. From behind a paper face mask, the doctor revealed warm brown eyes, a thick mustache. "Are you the father?"

The doctor looked directly at Martin, assuming that he was Zoë's husband. Everyone looked startled, even the unflappable Jack Webb. Dallas had left earlier to chase down the forensics team. Charlotte stood alone by the window.

Martin stammered. "No, I'm the family attorney—I'm a friend of the family, actually." The doctor took in the scene. Any ER doctor worth his salt can identify a cop when he sees one. Plain-clothes detectives stand out more than uniforms. Webb was no exception. They were an odd bunch.

Charlotte strode decisively toward the doctor. "I'm Charlotte Keats, Zoë's mother-in-law. How is she? Is the baby all right?"

"Mrs. Keats," the doctor paused silently, letting a moment pass for the unspoken "*The* Mrs. Keats?" "I'm Dr. Zimmerman," he said finally. "Do you know the name of your daughter-in-law's Ob/Gyn?" He removed a hospital-green paper hat revealing dark curly hair.

"Oh my God, what is it, is it the baby?" Charlotte's interest heightened exponentially.

"Please, Mrs. Keats, I don't mean to alarm you, but I do think Zoë should be examined by and released to the care of her own physician. At this point in her pregnancy, with what happened, she should be monitored closely. The ER is not the best place to do that," he paused pulling on his mustache. Sophia noticed it was flecked with gray and red, despite the doctor's full head of brown hair. "Where is the baby's father? He needs to be notified." Was there something Dr. Zimmerman was not telling them? He kept asking for Campbell, naturally as he was Zoë's closest next of kin, but there was something odd in his voice. Maybe they just learn that in medical school, she thought. "Doctor as God 101: Maintaining the Aura."

"Doctor, what has happened to Zoë? Is my grandson all right?" There was something in Charlotte's voice too. It was: I am Charlotte Keats—answer me or you'll be sorry, damn you. "Dear God," she whispered. "This I cannot bear." Recent events seemed to weigh on Charlotte; Sophia watched her visibly weaken.

Jack Webb stepped in, "Doctor, Detective Jack Webb, Plymouth Township police. Can we count on your discretion here?" Dr. Zimmerman folded his arms across his chest. Webb did not wait for an answer. "Good. We are conducting an investigation into what appears to be the recent murder of Zoë Keats' husband, Charlotte Keats' son. A detective of mine was informing Mrs. Zoë Keats of this when she fainted."

Dr. Zimmerman pulled harder on his mustache, making an "O" with his mouth. He sighed. "You mean to tell me that—in this heat—you told a woman in her eighth month that her husband was murdered?" No one spoke. Sophia thought of jumping in but figured Webb could be the bad guy. There was no reason to add to her mounting guilt.

"With all due respect Doctor, Campbell Keats had been missing since Wednesday evening. We found his—" Webb looked around and lowered his voice. They were still in a secluded waiting area. People buzzed around them, but no one was in earshot. *Although*, thought Sophia, *you never know with reporters.* "We found his body today, and have reason to believe there may have been—" Webb shot a glance at Charlotte who was in a full-blown trance. "Well, we believe he may have been murdered, doctor. We had to tell his wife."

Dr. Zimmerman continued to pull on his mustache. Sophia stole a glance at Martin, who had paled considerably since bounding into her apartment that morning, hair still gleaming from the shower, fresh clean-Martin smell permeating the air.

Tragedy engulfed this family to the point of suffocation. *We expect the elite to have good lives, no matter what*, she thought. *If one should fall, well, there but for the grace of God go I, we think. Any moment now, I'll be in that ditch too, and no one will even know it.*

Sophia sighed heavily and stood. It was something to do. The group was silent, no one wanting to advance time. Any next step would be difficult—there was no silver lining—who knew if there would ever be one for this case.

15

Zoë's private suite at Pennsylvania Hospital was a stark contrast to Graduate's utilitarian emergency room. She was moved swiftly—doctor's orders. Barbara Horowitz, M.D. boasted a long waiting list of potential patients. Women signed up when they hit puberty; when registering for china patterns; before tossing the bouquet—all in anticipation of the good doctor's golden forceps. Doctor Horowitz had descended on the emergency room whisking her patient to other quarters. Webb caught Sophia's eye across the waiting room. "Welcome to the fishbowl," he said with a look.

Zoë was groggy, her eyes vacant. Sophia wondered what drugs, if any, she had been given. She may have been sedated—there might be drugs that wouldn't affect the fetus. Or she's in shock, Sophia reasoned. That would make even more sense. But, she couldn't shake the notion that, medically, there was something else wrong. She'd have to question Zoë directly.

Charlotte was obsessed with the baby. She was unyielding, latching onto Zoë's unborn child like a rabid bulldog. Sophia had never seen anything like it. All of the woman's hope was riding on this child, so close to joining the world, yet still in danger. Sophia's heart ached, thinking of Charlotte's future pain when Campbell's death would come home to her. She had now lost all of the men in her life. Her husband and both sons were gone. And rather than grieve for Campbell, she appeared to have shifted her attention to her grandchild—this new life, a clean slate. Clearly for Charlotte, perhaps for any woman, her grandchild-to-be meant more to her than her daughter-in-law. But what about her son? Sophia wondered if any of this was normal.

She cursed her lack of maternal instinct. She knew though, from something in the depths of her belly, that Charlotte's devastation would be complete were Zoë to lose the baby. She found herself praying against it, to what or to whom she did not know.

The media vultures swarmed. Perhaps an orderly had let it slip or someone had spotted the reputable Charlotte Keats. The word was getting out.

Sophia and Martin had passed an Action News van as they zipped through Center City. They had circled the hospital in search of parking karma, and by the time Sophia had given up and pulled into the hospital's lot, a news crew lurked. Although Zoë was nestled comfortably—as comfortably as she could likely be in her private suite. The entourage of Charlotte Keats, Martin Duncan, Jack Webb and Sophia had attracted a crowd, one that would be hard to shake.

Charlotte eyed the press stonily and then shut herself away in Zoë's suite. Whether by choice or force, the reporters kept their distance from the private rooms, but it would not be long before the entire city knew both of Campbell's death and of Zoë's hospitalization—assuming the story was still under wraps. Sophia wondered what else there was to know.

Webb conferred privately with Doctor Horowitz. Sophia watched from expensive leather side chairs, amazed that she was in a hospital.

Doctor Horowitz crossed her arms tightly against her chest. She widened her stance, braced against Webb's argument. Their facial expressions were intense, rigid. Webb flashed his badge, holding it inches from the woman's face. She took a step back, swept her arm open in a mock welcome gesture and strode off down the corridor.

Webb knocked lightly on the door to Zoë's suite. Charlotte opened it in an instant. She glared at him. Sophia couldn't hear them, but saw from Webb's facial expression that he had toned down since talking to the doctor. Charlotte shook her head firmly. Webb was insistent, although gentle. He was good. Charlotte glared again, and shut the door in his face. He stood, back to Sophia. *Hmm, this is getting interesting*, she thought. In two seconds, Charlotte was back, purse in hand. She flew past Webb and into the corridor. He held the door for her, long after she'd exited, nodded and entered the room.

"That man," Charlotte swept past Sophia to stand at the window, "that horrible man is going to upset the baby." She corrected herself, "He's going to upset my daughter-in-law and in turn hurt my grandson. Where is Martin?"

"He went to get us some coffee. Listen, Mrs. Keats, I know this must be very difficult for you. I trust Detective Webb though, I spoke with him and he's aware that Zoë's health is in danger. He's just doing his job. He does have to question her."

Charlotte looked at Sophia, her eyes brimming with tears, her gaze unwavering. "You spoke with him? What exactly did you speak with him about?"

They locked eyes and turned as Jane Howard ran toward them, her freckled skin red with exertion.

"What happened?" She gulped for air.

"What are you doing here, Jane?" Charlotte asked. "On second thought, where have you been? Zoë's collapsed."

Jane blanched and looked pointedly at Charlotte Keats. "I was at the club," she said and paused. "I have a tournament coming up and my caddy is in town. Zoë was fine when I left," she went on defensively. "Oh my God. What? What happened? I got home—to Zoë's—and no one was there. I panicked. I called your house. Ginny finally told me where you were. Is she alright?" Despite the tailored golf ensemble replete with visor and pristine white bobby socks, Jane looked like a wild animal, her eyes dilated and darting around the waiting area. "What happened?"

Charlotte Keats looked at her evenly. "Zoë is *fine*."

Interesting, thought Sophia, *she's not really fine*. She'll be okay, but "fine" wouldn't have been my choice of words.

"She had an incident," Charlotte continued. "However, Campbell, my son, is dead. That's what happened. My son was brutally murdered and Zoë fainted when she heard. Now, if you'll excuse me." She needn't have said the last part as Jane pushed past them to the nearest room, which happened to be Zoë's, and burst in.

Sophia heard voices as Webb's interrogation was interrupted.

Shortly, Jane came out of the room, covering her nose with a cloth handkerchief. She walked back over to Charlotte and Sophia. "I'm going back to the house to get some things for her. They'll keep her overnight. And, I need to walk the dog." Her eyes bore into Charlotte. "Excuse me." And she was gone.

What was between the two of them? Sophia wondered.

And, like water off a duck's back, Charlotte turned and spoke to Sophia. "I asked you a question, Miss Gold. What did you say to the detective?"

"Nothing specific, Mrs. Keats. You are my client. My allegiance is to you." Charlotte stared at her. "But, you do realize that a police investigation has been launched? Mrs. Keats, they believe Campbell has been murdered, and they have to investigate. Do you still want me to work on this case? Even if I do, the police will be involved."

Martin approached, catching Sophia's eye. "Charlotte, are you all right?" He took her elbow and handed Sophia a cardboard tray with several steaming cups. One had a tea bag hanging over the side.

"Oh, Martin, that detective is questioning Zoë. Will you go in there, be with her?"

Not a bad idea, thought Sophia, *the man is the family lawyer.*

"Of course I will. I do trust this detective though, Charlotte. I believe he will treat this case fairly, and he is concerned for Zoë."

"Miss Gold said the same thing. I suppose you're right." She composed herself. "If you'll both stay here I need to go home for a few hours. There are arrangements to attend to."

"Would you like me to drive you somewhere?" Sophia asked, realizing she was the only one at the hospital with a car. Charlotte would not likely want to ride with Jack Webb, although she was sure he'd question her soon enough.

"No. I'll call someone—a car. Stay for a few hours, Martin, would you please? If she's resting, we can leave her alone. I will return this evening though, if I can. Please, beware of the media." She motioned toward the busy corridor where several people had been milling about since Zoë had arrived. "I may have to issue a statement. But, I'll do it my way. They'll just have to wait."

"That's fine Charlotte, I'm happy to stay as long as you need me to."

"Thank you Martin." Charlotte took his hand in hers, and turned to leave. "Miss Gold. I do want you to stay on this case. I cannot imagine that Campbell was murdered. But if he was, I don't trust those police to find out what happened. They always blame the family. We need you to protect us. I will not have our good name tarnished in any way. Investigate those awful competitors of Jackson's—they've always been up to no good. I'm sure they're involved in this somehow. Martin will fill you in." And she was gone.

"She seems in control," Sophia said picking imaginary lint off her sleeve.

"That's her style."

"Well?" Sophia asked, reaching for the tea. "Is this for me?" He nodded. "You remembered. Thank you."

Martin smiled. "There's quite a lot I remember." He stood quickly. "Let me just get in there before Webb finishes up, okay? Will you wait here?"

"Hey, why not? I have no life." She grinned. Sophia took out her notebook and wrote down a chronology of the day, observations she wanted to make sure she didn't forget, people to question, and concerns. By the time Webb and Martin came out of Zoë's room she'd stumped herself and was making a grocery list.

"So, throwing your weight around Webb?" Sophia asked, a hint of compassion in her voice. Martin sat down next to her.

"I have no choice," Webb replied. "The ME's in the process of ruling Campbell's death a murder. You know as well as I do—"

Sophia held up a hand to stop him.

He smiled, shook his head. "This is bad—for the family, the city, politics. These damn doctors though, they should know better, they know we have to do this."

"You're just doing your job. I wouldn't worry about Horowitz; she's concerned about her patient. And, she's posturing. Charlotte Keats can make her life miserable if she wants to—speaking of politics."

"I imagine you're still on this case," he said. "I know Mrs. Keats doesn't trust the police. Never has, never will. I can tell I like you. But, I don't know you. You work *with* me and we'll be fine. I'm a nice guy, most of the time."

"I'll do my best, Sergeant Friday. I'm sure you'll tell me if I fuck up."

"Sergeant Friday, now that's a new one. Smart ass." He shook his head. "Here's my card." He handed Sophia a business card after handwriting a number on the back. "That's home. Call at three in the morning if you have to. But only if you have to."

Sophia fished out one of her business cards and handed it to him. He took it, winked and dead panned, "Remember, just the facts ma'am, just the facts." And he was off.

16

So, tell me about the competitors," Sophia said. She and Martin settled into guest chairs in the waiting area. Zoë was worn out from talking to Webb. Martin said she had fallen asleep as soon as the interview was over.

"About three years ago, Jackson had a heart attack," Martin began.

"I thought he died of a heart attack last year."

"He did. This one was his first. Really minor, went on medication, seemed to recover fully, the whole nine yards. It was so small the press didn't even get wind of it. But the competition did. Must have been a disgruntled worker, someone who knew someone at the quarry, we don't know. Anyway, they found out." Martin took a pull on his coffee.

"And, they took advantage of it."

"A hostile take-over bid came in. It was an incredibly lowball offer, by whom, I can't even remember. There were rumors that Jackson Keats' poor health would ruin the business. It may have been Whitemarsh Rock & Limestone spreading the rumors, but no one really knows for sure."

"Not much to go on," Sophia said taking notes.

"Nothing overt. But you see, Keats Quarry has always been the darling of the industry—the 'Microsoft of Rocks.' The implied threat, and I stress that word 'implied,' was that the quarry's reputation would crumble under mounting suspicion that Jackson Keats was dying and running the company into the grave with him."

"What happened?"

"Jackson was too smart for them. I wish you'd known him, Sophie. He was a shrewd businessman, incredibly clever, and frankly, not to be fucked with. He cut them off at the knees. He used the media before they could."

"And?"

"This was amazing, I'm telling you. He hired a publicist, some New York firm, and used his own connections too. He got himself a front-page deal in *Fortune* magazine. What corporate big shots give a shit about rocks, right? Well, Keats made them care. They sold *Fortune* this story on the Keats family legacy and running a family business. The employees stepped up to the plate, and he came clean about the heart attack. He even had big-time cardiologists pronounce his recovery complete. It was a public relations extravaganza. He won."

"Huh. Then why does Charlotte hate the press so much?" Sophia asked. "It sounds like they saved her before."

"She doesn't hate them. She's justifiably leery though. Remember, Jackson choreographed the *Fortune* story. The family drove the whole thing. Charlotte is only comfortable with the press if she's in control. With something like this," he motioned to Zoë's room, "and a murder, control is hard to come by. Also, a strange family runs Whitemarsh. They are supposed religious fanatics, undercut prices and do less than stellar work. Interesting combination." He grinned, all dimples. "But Keats, Keats is the Cadillac of rocks and Jackson was a Philadelphia Golden Boy.

"Someone had delusions of grandeur and thought they could manipulate Jackson Keats. They thought he was weak. He was old and quite unpretentious really. You wouldn't think he'd be such a cunning adversary."

"Unpretentious? I find that hard to believe knowing Charlotte," Sophia said.

Martin smiled. "They complemented one another well, Jackson and Charlotte. She's the socialite, although it was Jackson's family that made her one. They were really good together."

They sat in silence for a moment watching the hospital go by. The place was eerie. Sophia noticed there was much going on, but somehow, after several hours in it, she was immune to the sounds: gurney wheels squeaked on spit-shined floors; the soft patter of running shoes and clogs race-walked through the corridor; the occasional cough, moan, cry of someone in physical or emotional pain.

"This is a decent lead," she said. "I should get to work on finding out more about this other company. Can you hang here on your own?" She looked at Martin, wanted to touch him. His eyes were rheumy and dark circles gutted his cheekbones. He nodded.

"Actually, you know, I really should talk to Zoë first, if she's up to it," Sophia added.

"I suppose," Martin replied. "Charlotte would kill me, but let's go."

Sophia squeezed his arm. "I meant alone. She might not be comfortable with you there. I need honesty." He was too tired to argue, but Sophia could see he was filing it away, wondering what she was thinking. He nodded and turned back to his coffee.

******

Zoë was awake and crying softly, surrounded by huge down pillows. Her hospital bed sat next to a large window and she stared past her own reflection in the glass. The sun was setting in brilliant blazes of pink and orange as if on fire.

"Zoë?" Sophia moved across the room. Zoë turned toward her voice. "How are you feeling? It's Sophia Gold."

Zoë nodded as sloppy tears rolled down her cheeks. She reached out her hand. Sophia was taken aback but took it and sat gingerly on the edge of the bed. "I'm so sorry, sweetie. I'm so so sorry."

Zoë cried silently, squeezing Sophia's hand. "I just can't believe it," she said softly, "I can't believe this is happening. Campbell's, Campbell's go—" Her voice filled with tears.

"I know Zoë, it's horrible, it's just—" Sophia was suddenly overwhelmed by loneliness and knew it was more for herself than for Zoë. "How can I help? I mean—I am going to help. Charlotte wants me to work on the case still, to find out what happened. Can I get you anything now though?"

Zoë shook her head. Somehow she was still beautiful, her hair a soft yellow halo around her face, her smallness accentuated by the oversized hospital bed. She looked like a child, her pregnancy all but hidden beneath a mound of blankets. "But, aren't the police—? I don't understand."

"Well, the police are of course working on it, but Charlotte wants her own investigation; it's fairly common." Sophia winced at her own words. Zoë didn't need to hear that her tragedy was common. Zoë didn't notice, or if she did, she took the comment in stride.

Zoë sat up a little, gaining strength as she spoke. "Of course, typical Charlotte. You know, I think she cares more about this baby than she does about me."

"Zoë, where is your family?"

"Nepal."

Sophia looked shocked.

"My dad runs expeditions for National Geographic. He's always off somewhere. He was in Greece when I was born, on some remote island. Zoë's a Greek name. Anyway, my mother travels with him now. They're not even reachable. Guess she figured she gave birth alone, why shouldn't I?"

"Punishing you for your father's actions?" Sophia blurted out before she could check herself.

"Something like that," Zoë said with a knowing look. "Besides, we're not close. Campbell was my family. Oh my God, what am I going to do?"

"Is there anyone I can call for you?"

Zoë shook her head. "Jane is here. She's been a good friend. She practically grew up with Campbell."

"I thought she was from D.C." Sophia said.

"Oh, she is, but her father and Jackson were close in college. They rowed together. Growing up, Jane played amateur golf tournaments up and down the Eastern Seaboard. She spent a lot of time at the Keats Mansion, she was like the daughter Jackson never had."

"Really?" Sophia said, buying time to think through the dynamic she had witnessed between Charlotte and Jane. "Is there a rivalry between Charlotte and Jane? I sensed something."

Zoë sighed. "Charlotte doesn't like women. She was the only woman in the family until Jane, and now me. Jane wasn't around all the time, but when she was, I think there was some tension. Charlotte likes things her way. I guess I shouldn't be saying this to you. After all, you're working for *her* aren't you?" Zoë's coloring was returning, her voice getting stronger.

Sophia nodded. "She's the client, yes. But Campbell was your husband. What you say to me is confidential—unless of course it's something illegal." She smiled and then stopped herself. Was Zoë above suspicion?

Zoë snorted. "Believe me, the last time I did anything illegal was in art school and it involved a bong. I'm a good girl now. Maybe not blue blood like the Keats family—" She hadn't made the leap to being a murder suspect.

"Not many of us are," Sophia replied. "Zoe, did the detective already talk to you?" Just because she said she was a good girl didn't make it so.

She nodded. "Why?"

"Well, I need to ask you a couple of things too, okay? I mean I know this isn't a good time, but I want to figure out what happened, I know you want to know, right?"

She nodded. "It's my fault." Her cheeks were tear-stained but dry. Something akin to shock had come over her; she looked numb. She buried her face in delicate, un-manicured hands; the right wore an angry IV needle. "I didn't want—" Zoë looked up at Sophia with scared eyes. "I didn't want the baby," she whispered.

And the tears returned in a wave. Deep sobs wracked her tiny body and Sophia wondered what monitors were being set off at the nurse's station. From what she could see, Zoë was hooked up to both fetal and heart monitors. To Sophia's untrained eye, the screens looked normal; they were beeping along at an even clip. But what did she know?

Sure she'd be kicked out any second, Sophia pushed forward. "What do you mean? What happened?"

"I want him now. I want the baby now, oh God, it's all my fault."

"What Zoë? What's your fault?"

"Everything. I don't know, I wanted—" she closed her eyes tightly and whispered, "I wanted an abortion." Her voice was barely audible. "But then I changed my mind. He found out," she said quickly, "and now, he's gone."

Now I'm getting somewhere, Sophia thought. *Maybe this has something to do with the doctors' demeanor.* "Zoë, it's normal to be confused about pregnancy." Isn't it? She was winging it. She needed to hear more. "Tell me what happened." She sat on the edge of Zoë's hospital bed, ready for the story.

With a rush of cool antiseptic air, Dr. Horowitz and a strapping young male nurse swept in the room. Martin stood in the doorway looking as lily-livered as Sophia had ever seen him. Barbara Horowitz's patient was distraught and she did not like it.

"Who the hell are you and what are you doing interrogating my patient?" she demanded.

Sophia started to speak and realized that the good doctor didn't really want answers. She turned and barked at the nurse, "Check the monitors, and get a temp. And you," she glared at Sophia, "Get out. Now. Visiting hours are over."

17

July 8th, 11:10 a.m.

Sophia parked along the quiet, tree-lined Benjamin Franklin Parkway. For a Monday, the Parkway was quiet, the city still languid from the holiday

The infrequent taxi sped, horn blaring for no reason but the empty road and lack of July Fourth weekend law enforcement. Officers on horseback were typical on the Parkway, in part to awe tourists, but not today. If you were visiting the city, you'd eventually make your way to the Parkway, past Logan Circle, The Franklin Institute, and then, of course, to the steps of The Philadelphia Museum of Art. Sadly, Sylvester Stallone's *Rocky* had done more for those steps than any Chagall exhibit ever would. Fans worldwide had made that same Rocky Balboa run. Countless photo albums bore pictures of children and adults, arms held high, fists pumped, *Gonna Fly Now* soaring in their memories.

By Monday, even the tourists were scarce. Philadelphia was not an ideal place to spend July Fourth weekend—Betsy Ross or no Betsy Ross—especially when the Jersey shore was so close, and so inviting. The city was deserted.

And this was Sophia's favorite way to see Philadelphia, especially the museums. Her love affair with art was life long. Even as a child she found solace in the cool marble corridors, otherworldly masterpieces, and less than famous works at The Rodin, The Philadelphia Museum of Art and other local museums and galleries. Today, The Rodin was closed and she didn't want to risk running into any errant tourists at the art museum. While Sophia could block out quite a bit looking at art, she did her best thinking in the silence of a temperature controlled room with high ceilings, low uncomfortable benches and unobtrusive security guards. She settled for The Rodin Museum's garden, replete with several sculptures, a few marble benches and privacy.

Campbell Keats' Memorial Service had been organized in a hurry. Sophia was due at the Cathedral of Saints Peter and Paul at noon. Zoë was to be released for the service and then sent home, assuming her vitals checked out after the funeral. Dr. Horowitz was coming to the service, little black doctor's bag in hand.

When Martin had phoned with the details she heard exhaustion in his voice. She too was feeling overwhelmed and hoped an hour with *The Thinker* might do her some good. She sat down by a shady tree near the museum entrance. The bench was still cool with morning air. Sophia was wearing a thin, sleeveless sheath and had a matching suit jacket in the car for the service. She sat gingerly, avoiding splotches of white that could only be pigeon shit. She looked up at the sculpture and in mock salute, copied the pose. She closed her eyes to the world.

The case was still like a developing photograph—unfolding at random, on its own time in its own murky way. Only instinct would tell Sophia whether to poke at the image or to simply let it unfold. She knew in a day or so she'd have something to go on, whether or not it would turn out to be the right path. In the beginning, when you don't know where you are going, you have to let the art take you. And, it will.

Was something behind Zoë's hospital bedside admission? Logic told her that the woman was simply distraught; her husband had been found murdered. But Zoë's tearful, albeit nonsensical, ramblings along with her doctor's vehemence did not add up. Sophia would talk to her alone, after the funeral, when she might be more stable.

There were other connections to investigate, including that of Whitemarsh Rock & Limestone. Sophia was going back to the Keats mansion after the service and imagined she would gather useful information as the day went on. A warm breeze hit her eyelids and Sophia looked up to see several pigeons roosting above in an oak tree. She checked her watch, stood up and walked to the church.

******

Campbell's death had been on the Saturday evening news, the front page of the Sunday *Inquirer* and God knows where else. Sophia left the Saab parked at the museum and walked along the Parkway, her jacket folded neatly over her arm. You can see the cathedral from The Rodin and Logan Circle; it's a nice walk under other circumstances.

Today, media vans, huge chauffer-driven limousines, and an occasional gleaming Mercedes swarmed the streets, leaving well-wishers at the cathedral steps. Police vehicles outnumbered civilian. Cops were everywhere—a sea of dark blue and polished chrome shone against the otherwise black and gray attire. *No wonder there were no officers on the Parkway*, she thought. It made sense of course—Campbell's killer was still on the loose. And, if anyone merited Philadelphia's finest it was Charlotte Keats.

Despite the overwhelming presence of law enforcement, decorum settled in the air like so much humidity, whether in deference to Saints Peter and Paul, to the deceased, or to his powerful mother. Sophia wondered how long that would last.

The short service was tasteful. Influential Philadelphians spoke of the Keats family's longevity and dedication to the city—a tenure fraught with tragedy that no amount of clever speech writing could hide. Campbell's eulogy was almost an afterthought, demeaning his death and thus his life. Rather, it was the Keats' legacy that was mourned. And the sheer volume of death befallen on Charlotte Keats overwhelmed the congregation. It seemed most respectful not to say too much, to pray in whatever way such an eclectic group can, and to get out.

Professionally, Sophia was disappointed. Despite her fantasy the killer did not, in fact, throw himself on the mercy of the church and confess. She'd have to ferret him out. Or her, she allowed, although statistics were against the killer being a woman. Out of the corner of her eye she saw Dallas and Webb, gave a quick nod and imagined she'd see them both at the house later.

Martin waited for her at the church exit as promised. "I cabbed over, you?"

"I'm parked at The Rodin." Sophia gestured toward Logan Circle.

He smiled. "Still doing the museum thing?"

"Helps me think. You want a ride to the house?"

He nodded and they walked in silence watching the hordes disperse. There would be no cemetery service and only a select group was invited back to the Keats Mansion. The masses had paid their respects and were going home.

The air was sticky and Sophia removed her jacket. Martin loosened his tie. Walking with him felt like the most natural thing in the world, although the circumstances were anything but. They reached the car and Sophia immediately turned on the air, full blast. They sat idle for a moment.

"Why the cathedral? The Keats family has WASP written all over them," Sophia said.

Martin shook his head no and lit a cigarette.

"What the hell are you—? Open the window at least. I thought you quit like a decade ago."

"I did. Today doesn't count."

"Okay, damn it, give me one of those too. If you're going to smoke in my car, I might as well get as much out of it as I can." He handed her his already lit cigarette and took out another for himself. They were both awkward, like teenagers just learning to smoke, billows of thick white smoke escaping from their mouths. "So, who's Catholic?"

He coughed. "Charlotte. She's *really* Catholic. Actually, kind of toned it down for Jackson, but never really let go. She does a lot of work for the Cathedral, sits on the board I think. Jackson's funeral was there too, and Clay."

"Huh, curiouser and curiouser." They smoked in silence. Sophia's head buzzed with the hit of nicotine; it'd been ten years since she'd felt that familiar high. It tasted good and horrible at the same time. She took one final drag and tossed the butt out the window.

"Ridiculous," she said. "I cannot start again—I'm like a junkie with those things."

18

They drove in silence and arrived at the house early, having missed the traffic at the church. There was no way to tell if those already milling about the Keats home had been at the earlier service. It had been like a cattle call.

This would be more intimate, relatively speaking, and—Sophia hoped—more evocative. Charlotte was in the kitchen talking sternly to someone about crab puffs. Zoë sat below a Monet—an original—in the large, open living room. Sophia's breath caught when she saw the telltale crooked signature and heavy gilded frame.

Bouquets of richly aromatic freesia, white roses, multicolored tulips and other mixed flowers adorned every available flat surface. The occasional funeral wreath stood upright against a shelf or overflowing vase.

Zoë's presence had obviously been approved of and was being monitored by Dr. Horowitz, who sat next to her patient, looking demure and didactic at the same time. On Zoë's other side was Jane Howard. She was still and stared down at the floor. Zoë appeared tired and sad, having recovered only some of the color in her cheeks.

Martin and Sophia paid their respects to Charlotte as she entered from the kitchen. She thanked them for coming and eyed Sophia. "Miss Gold," she whispered, "What have you discovered about those horrible Whitemarsh people?"

"I'm working on it, Mrs. Keats. I was hoping to meet some people today. Will people from the quarry be here, anyone from Whitemarsh Rock, contractors?"

To Sophia's surprise, Charlotte nodded. "Jackson was a shrewd man. He knew the power of business relationships and passed that along to his son. He would have wanted them here. Besides, the press would certainly notice their absence. We wouldn't want that." She looked around. "I haven't seen the Whitemarsh people, but Frank is here and others." She waved absently at the crowd.

Sophia made a note never to cross Charlotte Keats. Her son was dead and she was running a public relations campaign at his memorial service.

"Hmm," she said, hoping her tone did not betray disdain. "Well, Mrs. Keats, I really am so sorry for your loss." Charlotte nodded and reached her hand to Martin.

Sophia moved on to Zoë. Dr. Horowitz glared at her like an eclipse.

"How are you today?" she asked. Zoë shrugged. Tears streamed down her face. "I'm so sorry. Will you be going home tonight or back to the hospital?"

"Home, I think," Zoë whispered. She looked across the room at Jane who now was carrying drinks back from the kitchen. "Jane offered to stay with me so I won't be alone." Zoë's doctor had averted her eyes and was people watching—looking for someone to impress, or to be impressed with her.

"How about if I come by tomorrow, just to see if you are okay? I'd like to talk to you and I live so close by." Zoë nodded. "I'll come around noon." The doctor was at attention again looking quizzically at Sophia. "Dr. Horowitz," Sophia acknowledged. "Zoë, my condolences."

"What was that about?" Martin was at her elbow seconds after making his way down the grief assembly line.

"Oh, nothing, I just need to talk to Zoë alone, and that doctor is watching her like a hawk. Now is not the time anyway. I hate these things," she admitted.

"I know, me too. We don't have to stay long you know." Still the caretaker.

"Oh, but we do. I'm working, remember?" she lowered her voice. "Ten-to-one the killer is here. I'm supposed to figure out who that is, you know. Earn my keep."

Before Martin could answer he was slapped on the back with an almost angry force. Sophia had seen it coming but not before she could warn him.

"What the—?" He turned to see who the offending party was. Standing behind him was Charlotte's companion from the morgue. He was a true Adonis. Sophia hated that she thought that, but there it was. The man looked like a Greek god, an Italian statue, someone she'd like to touch all over. That is until he opened his mouth.

"Marty!" he bellowed in a voice too loud for his surroundings.

"Keep it down, Jarvis. Don't you get where you are?"

"True, true. Ol' Martin Duncan always kept us in line." He eyed Sophia. "Why haven't we met?" he purred.

"We have," Sophia said. "I found your friend, Campbell Keats, you know, the reason we're here today." The jerk had been trying to pick her up.

"Ri-i-i-i-ght."

"Sophia Gold, you remember Alexander Jarvis," Martin sneered.

"Call me Zander, everyone does."

"Thought maybe you'd grown out of that."

"Marty, c'mon now, is that any way to talk to your old high school buddy?"

"I prefer Martin now."

"So, Zander," Sophia started, "I take it you went to high school with Martin and Campbell. Did you stay in touch with Campbell much after that?"

"Like a brother," he said. *Interesting word choice,* Sophia thought. *What was it that Zoë had said about Charlotte surrounding herself with men?*

"We all hung out in high school," Zander went on, slapping Martin on the back again, "and summers, plus some other guys. Then Marty here," he grinned, "sorry, *Martin,* was a little homebody and went to Penn. I went to Princeton with Campbell. We were like this." Zander crossed his fingers.

"You seem real broken up about your friend's death, Zander," Sophia said.

Zander gave her a quizzical look and grinned, bicuspids gleaming. "We all grieve in our own way now, don't we?" He turned to Martin. "I never did understand why you stayed here and went to Penn, dude. Didn't you want to get away?"

Martin had stayed close to home because his mother had been diagnosed with end-stage breast cancer. She was dying and his father was taking it badly. Not many people knew that. *Besides*, she thought defensively, *I went to Penn. It's an Ivy for Christ's sake.* More importantly though, why did she care what this jackass thought of her alma mater?

"So, Soph, what about you?"

She smiled at him with thin lips. "Actually Zander, I prefer Sophia. And, what about me what?"

"Excuse me, *Sophia,* where did you take your degree?" Zander was an unpleasant cross between a spoiled child and a pompous adult. Richie Rich all grown up—with attitude.

"Oh, me. I went to Penn."

"Huh, well touché or whatever." Zander recovered quickly. "Oh, so you're the feisty Italian." He punched Martin lightly on the arm.

"Jesus Zander." Martin blushed. "How about something to drink, Soph?" Martin asked, emphasizing the use of her nickname and ducking away toward the food leaving Sophia alone with Zander. They stood still for a moment, Sophia wondering if she could subject herself to more Zander, even for the sake of the case.

He whistled softly under his breath. That's it, she thought, this is the last straw. She looked up to give the guy a piece of her mind, and then saw he wasn't even looking at her.

So much for my ego, she mused.

"Holy Shit, I cannot believe that guy is here."

Sophia's interest piqued. "Who? Frank Reynolds?"

Zander was looking at Reynolds, who was talking to several men in their Sunday best, all looking slightly uncomfortable. "Reynolds? No, that guy." He gestured toward the group again. One of the men turned and Sophia caught his profile. It was Joe Rizzo, the sexy, unnerving sub-contractor she had almost run over at the quarry. She felt suddenly warm, jittery.

"Rizzo. Man, Campbell wouldn't believe it."

"Why, what's wrong with Joe Rizzo being here? He works at the quarry now, doesn't he?"

"What are you talking about?" Zander finished off his drink in one shot. It had been Scotch on the rocks long ago diluted by melted ice. He didn't seem to notice. "Why would he work—how do you know him?" Zander asked, suddenly bolstered by his drink.

"Oh, I met him the other day with Frank. Martin and I went by the quarry, he was there working. What's the big deal?"

"Nothing," Zander said. "There's, uh, no big deal." He glanced around and then held up his empty glass. "Well, it was nice to meet you. Please excuse me." Zander gave a surprisingly gracious exit, leaving Sophia baffled.

The house was filling up and Sophia went off in search of Martin. She caught a glimpse of him in a far corner of the room. He was talking with Zander and a woman. She saw the shapely heel of a sensible but expensive black pump. A guest blocked her view. When the guest moved to the buffet Sophia saw Charlotte Keats. She was in deep conversation with both Martin Duncan and Zander Jarvis. They were huddled together against the crowd— plotting almost. *The Three Musketeers,* Sophia thought.

Frank Reynolds came up behind Sophia and tapped her on the shoulder.

She turned. "Oh, Frank, you startled me! How long have you been standing there?"

"Long enough to see you lost in thought. What's wrong—besides the obvious?" Frank asked. His green eyes were dark today and filled with a deep and knowing sadness. He'd combed his mustache carefully; Sophia could see vertical stripes from the comb tines.

"Mostly the obvious," she replied shaking Frank's hand. To her surprise, he leaned in and modestly kissed her cheek. His mustache was scratchy and he smelled of cigarettes and Old Spice cologne. Finding Campbell's body, although gruesome, had bonded them in a way only tragedy can.

"Frank, I need to ask you something," Sophia lowered her voice. "Remember we were talking the other day about Joe Rizzo? He was standing with you earlier. Any reason Campbell might have known him in the past?"

"Rizzo?" Frank pulled on his mustache. "I wouldn't bet on it. Rizzo's from South Philly—he's a working guy," Frank stammered. "I mean not that Campbell didn't work—"

Sophia smiled, "I know what you mean, Frank. So they just met recently?"

"I guess, I mean I don't even know if they crossed paths at the quarry, probably did come to think of it. Far as I know, he knew Campbell as the boss and that's it. Why do you ask?"

She'd keep her reasons to herself for now. "Just curious. So what about the others you were talking to—who are they besides Joe Rizzo?" Sophia knew Frank would weave a good yarn once he got going.

"Well, Rizzo, I'd never seen him before last month. He came on as a project manager, pretty experienced guy. The other two, Jim McDonald and Bill Gonzalez, they've been with Red for years. And the last guy, the redhead, well, that's Red, he's the owner. I was telling you about them the other day. It was real good of them to pay their respects."

"Red? That's original," Sophia teased.

"I know it," said Frank shaking his head in mock disgust. "Heck, in all my years at this, I have always known him as Red. Finally found out the poor guy's name is Fergus, Fergus O'Brien. Think maybe he's Irish?" Frank's eyes sparkled and then went cloudy. "Red was an old rowing buddy of Jackson's. More the blue-collar type than Jackson Keats, that's for sure, but Jack, he was salt-of-the-earth. You'd be surprised. They were in a rowing club together, started talking business one day and been working together ever since," he stopped. "Well, the company's have anyways."

Sophia held back, saying nothing. She had more questions but needed to figure out what to ask, and of whom. What, if anything, was behind Zander Jarvis's intense reaction to Joe Rizzo? Maybe nothing. Frank didn't seem to know.

On the other hand, she could ask Frank more about Red, his company, employees and about Whitemarsh Rock & Limestone. Charlotte had implied the competitor was involved in Campbell's death. Sophia knew better than to take Charlotte at her word, but she had to look into it. Frank suddenly seemed nervous; his fidgeting brought Sophia back to the room.

Martin came up to them as if to join their conversation, but quickly began stargazing. "Excuse me," he mumbled, "I need to talk to...." His voice trailed off as he moved toward the fireplace and a dapper gentleman holding some sort of highball. Martin's target had silvery-slicked back hair. His suit, although clearly summer weight, was a dark, respectful charcoal and he wore an understated but expensive gray tie with flecks of yellow. A monogrammed cuff peeked from under the sleeve of his suit jacket. Even from where she stood Sophia could see the fine embroidery and a faint glimmer of gold at his cuffs. And she knew who he was. Martin was quickly engulfed in conversation with Christopher Whitehouse, senior partner at the law firm, Martin's boss, father-in-law and all around influential guy.

Frank pulled on his mustache again and tapped his right foot, and Sophia had another wave of awareness. "Need a smoke?" she asked gently.

"Sad, isn't it? I've been smoking so long now, I don't even think I could quit if I wanted to. Will you excuse me?" Frank was reaching for his inside jacket pocket.

"May I join you?" She wanted to talk to him, and the fewer people around the better.

"Sure, but you don't smoke do you? It's awfully hot—but I'd love the company," Frank added.

"Actually Frank, I take the occasional drag now and then, but really, I'd just like to ask you some questions, and get some fresh air." They opened the door and exchanged a knowing glance. There was nothing fresh about this air. The afternoon had settled just below a sky of buttermilk clouds, the heat trapped beneath their thickness.

Frank lit up, inhaling gratefully and then offered the pack to Sophia. She shook her head no—although she meant yes—secretly wishing for a gin and tonic, a cool room and a freshly lit cigarette. They spied a teak bench peaking out from under a weeping willow tree and went to claim it. Frank beat her to it and gallantly wiped the seat with his handkerchief.

"Frank, tell me about Whitemarsh Rock & Limestone," Sophia said.

"Whitemarsh? I thought you wanted to know about Red."

"I do, in fact I want to know anything you can tell me about his company and those guys who were standing with him. But I also want to hear about Whitemarsh. To be honest, Charlotte thinks Whitemarsh might be involved in what happened to Campbell. I need to find out as much as I can about them, as quickly as possible. By the way are they here? I need to talk to them," she rambled.

He stubbed out his cigarette and lit another. This time Sophia took one. He started to talk.

19

Three cigarettes later, Sophia and Frank split up. They had been sitting by the driveway watching guests leave. No one on Sophia's interrogation list had passed them to leave yet and although she was grateful, she wondered why there were hanging around. As she entered the dining room, she saw that Charlotte's earlier kitchen admonitions had given rise to an impressive buffet.

Maybe that's why everyone was still here. Sophia was hungry herself and pleased to see Joe Rizzo making his way through the hors d'oeuvres, one canapé at a time.

She approached him. "We meet again," she said instantly hoping it didn't sound too much like a line. She inadvertently glanced over at Martin who was locked in major ass kissing.

"Yes we do. I'm Joe Rizzo.

"Sophia Gold." They shook hands.

"Sophia, are you Italian by any chance?"

"Half," she said.

"I should've known. The hair, the eyes." He regarded her with awe. "You're the kind of girl a guy brings flowers to," he said and somehow settled into his hips so as to seem both menacing and sexy.

Wow. "Rizzo wouldn't happen to be an Italian name now would it?" *How coy can I be and get away with it?* she wondered.

He nodded, grinning. "Just don't ask me if I'm related to Frank." He moved closer to her and she could smell his aftershave, a subtle but powerful scent.

"So, you get that a lot? I take it the answer is no?"

"Right, the answer is no. So, what brings you here, Sophia Gold? It's not exactly a happy occasion."

"I, uh, I work for Charlotte Keats." *Might as well come out with it,* she thought. *Campbell's no longer a missing person—he's dead.* "I'm helping Mrs. Keats find who out what happened to her son."

Rizzo looked quizzical. "Don't tell me you're a cop"

Sophia shook her head no.

A wave of awareness came over Rizzo. "You're a PI aren't you? That's why you were at the quarry the other day. Unusual job for a woman, isn't it?"

Great, this again. "Not really," she said. "So, what about you?" she asked shifting focus. "How well did you know Campbell?" *And, more importantly, do you know Zander?*

"I didn't *know* Campbell. I met him at the quarry," Rizzo said. "What a terrible loss," he said without feeling. No one at funerals ever knows what to say. "I'm sorry" is trite; "My condolences" causes syllabic stumbles. You just say something to have it said and move on.

"So, you don't know his friends from high school?" she asked and then winced fearing she'd pushed it with the question.

He looked startled. "Why would I know—no, I don't," he said recovering quickly. "I work for Red O'Brien," Rizzo continued with the cool-guy head jerk toward Red who stood talking to Frank Reynolds and several other sturdy types.

"How long have you worked for Red?"

"Curious or working?" he asked with reserve. Yet, his body language was still open and inviting.

"Curious mostly. I mean c'mon, it isn't often I almost run over a guy and then hook up with him again at a funeral. Pretty intriguing way to meet someone." She was all over the map—flirting, interrogating, flirting, interrogating.

"It certainly is," he said, brushing her hand as he reached for a napkin. "I've been with Red several months now. Before I was on my own, doing construction. Working for Red is better money, better hours, you know, security." He smiled.

"So, you like the work?"

"Yeah. I like to be outside, working hard. I play softball all summer and hockey in the winter. I'm a real outdoors type," he paused, reached for something to eat and then jerked his hand away. He was out of his element.

"This food, it's kind of ritzy," she said, leaning into him. He smelled of clean laundry, cologne and new, raw sweat. "Between you and me, I like a good cheese steak." She blushed. She was out of her element too. A cheese steak would have hit the spot about then.

A faint muffled ringing sounded. Sophia noticed several men pat their suit jackets—it was a cell phone. Rizzo reached in his jacket and the ringing assaulted her.

"Sorry, excuse me." He looked at the display and rolled his eyes. "I thought I'd turned this off," he said turning toward the door. "Si?" He whispered into the tiny phone. A combination of hushed tones and Italian words peppered the brief conversation. She heard the words "Keats" and "casa" and "presto." He hung up and stashed the phone back in his jacket, but not before turning it off.

How sexy was that? Speaking Italian. "Your wife?" Sophia asked innocently.

"Oh, no, I'm not married," he said locking eyes with her. "That was my sister. My nephew is sick, she wanted to know when I'd be home."

"I hope it's nothing serious."

"No, just a little virus. I need to pick up some medicine, no big deal. He's a strong little guy."

"Sounds like you're close to your sister. Is she married?"

"Why, you interested in her now?" he asked his voice flirtatious.

Sophia laughed. "No, just curious again."

"Occupational hazard?"

"Maybe, maybe not," she replied. And, it was her turn to stare at him with open wanting eyes.

He smiled easily and looked kind. "I help my sister take care of Matteo—she's not married. It's a long story. My parents were killed before Mattie was born, so we kind of stuck together. We live in our family house. You should know about that, being from an Italian family and all."

"Hmm," she said. *I'm not your traditional Italian girl, Joe Rizzo, but never mind about that*, she thought. "So, do you have a picture of your nephew?"

"Do I have a picture? I have a whole album." He winked and took out his wallet. The boy was beautiful. He had straight black hair and rich olive skin, his eyes a surprising, piercing blue.

"Wow, a future lady killer," Sophia joked. "Look at those blue eyes, where'd he get those?"

"Yeah, he's a good looking kid, isn't he?" he said, not answering her question. "Listen, Sophia, I gotta go. It was nice meeting you, again. It would be great if—" he stopped himself, looked around the room.

He was asking her out. "I agree." Sophia blurted softly.

"Great. We could go to Pat's for a steak or something?" He winked. Pat's Steaks was a Philadelphia landmark with the best, greasiest, cheesiest cheese steaks around. They were guaranteed to harden your arteries and stay with your taste buds until your next meat-and-onion based meal.

"Or something," she said. What the hell had come over her? She reached in her purse for a business card and handwrote her home phone number on the back.

"So, I'll call you." It was a statement not a question. She'd have to wait and see if he meant it.

******

Martin came up to her as Rizzo was leaving. "Did I see you just give your number to that guy? Wasn't he the guy from the quarry the other day?"

"Martin, good. Did you see him?"

"Did I see him? I saw you flirting at a funeral for Christ's sake."

Was he jealous? "Martin, keep your voice down. Did you recognize him? Joe Rizzo—I mean from besides the quarry."

"No. How would I know him?" Rizzo was a name you don't forget.

"Zander does. He was pretty surprised to see him, actually a little freaked out. Any idea what that might be about?" she asked.

Martin glanced around the room quickly. Was it posturing or something else? "Freaked out how? What did he say?"

"He said—" she regarded him slowly, "Listen, Martin do you know something about this guy?"

"Just tell me what Zander said." He was impatient. "The name *is* familiar, and not just because of Frank."

"He seemed surprised to see him. Said Campbell would have been too. Do you know him?" Sophia probed.

Martin scrunched his eyebrows into a frown. "The summer before college—I don't really know what happened—but I might have heard the name Rizzo. I never met the guy though. I wasn't around much, Mom was doing bad. Remember how I was at the start of freshman year? Well that summer was worse, I've told you that. Anyway, I stopped hanging with those guys. Plus, half of them were gearing up for Princeton or Yale. I was the loser staying home to go to Penn." He took a deep breath. "Can you imagine?

"Look Sophie, Zander was cocky. Campbell too with a few drinks in him. They'd go downtown, some other guys too, wave around a lot of cash, smoke cigars, drink, go to JC Dobbs or The Saloon, hang out on South Street. That Rizzo guy, he looked like a South Philly type, am I right?"

She nodded.

"Probably just got into a shouting match or something, maybe even a fist fight."

"So, how'd Zander know his name? Rizzo denied knowing Campbell, except from the quarry."

Martin nodded. "They probably didn't know each other. I'm telling you, there were stories all the time. I cannot tell you how many guys they supposedly 'scared the shit out of.' What a laugh, because Zander is scared of his shadow, and Campbell, well, he was scared of his own mother."

"And you think somehow Zander and Rizzo shook hands, nice to meet you, I'm Zander Jarvis, I'm Joe Rizzo?" she asked in disbelief.

Martin shook his head, "No, if I know Zander—and unfortunately I think I do—he'd try to guess the names of these guys. Whose going to guess Zander, even Alexander or Campbell? We all have slightly 'above average' names to go with our above average breeding." Sarcasm dripped from his every word. "I mean, Martin is boring, but of course they all called me Dunc or Duncan. That was more elite. Anyway, Zander played this game where he'd taunt these guys. He'd bet them drinks and stuff that he could guess their names, but that they couldn't guess his. How hard is it to guess someone Italian is named Joe?"

"Hey. I'm Italian," she protested. "But I know what you mean. Joe's a fine name, but certainly more blue-collar than Duncan. Zander seems like a real ass."

"That he is," Martin agreed.

"And Rizzo—I mean Frank—people were still talking about him even then," Sophia said, "Maybe Zander teased him: Oh, you're Italian, so I bet you're related to Frank Rizzo, something like that?"

"Didn't take you long to read Zander," said Martin, "not that he's a tough read."

"Well, I guess I'll go out with him, close the loop."

"Zander?"

"No, Rizzo."

"You're going to date that guy?"

"I'm not going to date him Martin, I may go on *a* date with him. He might not even call me," she said. "Oh, relax. How could you possibly think I would be interested in him? You'd think you were jealous or something." As soon as she said it, she wished she hadn't. She wasn't ready to address their relationship, lack thereof, or future thereof. Besides, she was also interested in Joe. Whatever was happening again between her and Martin would have to take a back seat to the case, Martin's marital woes and the search for world peace.

"I guess I am a little jealous," he said. "I'm also worried about you. If this Rizzo guy had a beef with Zander or Campbell... I don't know. I feel protective of you. Also, I miss you."

"I miss you too," she whispered, "And thanks." What was she doing? They didn't say more as the world swirled around them. Sophia heard tears, dishes clattering in the kitchen, Charlotte Keats' forceful voice. They'd get to it eventually, Sophia thought. For now, knowing he missed her was enough.

20

July 9th, 11:50 a.m.

Sophia took the scenic route through Rittenhouse Square.

The lunch crowd gathered, staking out benches around the park's perimeter. The Square, in an elite neighborhood, was a miniature model of the city's diversity. The edges were rough, the seams splitting; everything bled together.

Some of the city's homeless had become permanent residents on the occasional park bench. Every ten feet, another bench sat frozen to the ground with thick concrete legs. Sharply dressed businessmen chatted on cell phones; babies in strollers were rocked to sleep, their mothers and nannies pushing back and forth across uneven ground; artists sketched oversized oak trees and bronze statues of frogs, goats, lions; all without disturbing those sleeping, ensconced in creative tents of blankets, cardboard boxes and shopping carts.

Sophia paused at the Square's edge by the Curtis Institute of Music. Someone practiced their scales, a cello echoed into the streets joined by a flute.

She turned onto 19th Street and made her way toward Delancey Place. Just two blocks separated the park, music school and Spruce Street from Zoë's home, but it felt like miles. Sophia looked down at her feet. Concrete blocks became well-paved brick and multicolored cobblestone. Oaks towered over the street, their enormous trunks protected by freshly painted black iron rails. A hush whispered through the leaves. Sophia raised the gleaming brass knocker and let it fall against the door.

Jane Howard appeared wearing a short khaki golf skirt and a fitted white t-shirt with a little blue polo player on the breast pocket. Her long hair exploded uncharacteristically around her face in a blaze of orange and gold. "May I help you?" She stepped out onto the front step and pulled the door closed behind her, taking care not to catch the lock. Her left arm snaked behind her back to hold the doorknob, revealing well-toned shoulders and sinewy biceps. Her right arm went to her hip making a sharp triangle.

"I'm here to see Zoë."

"Zoë's not seeing anyone today. There's been a death in the family. Is there something I can help you with?"

"I know there's been a death in the family. And I'm very sorry to disturb you. Jane Howard, right? We've met—I was at the funeral." Sophia took out a business card. "I know the timing is bad but I need to speak with Zoë. She's expecting me."

"She didn't tell me you were coming." Jane paused with authority. "Wait here," she ordered once they were in the cool marble vestibule.

Sophia heard muffled voices on the other side of the thick door. "Not a good idea without an attorney." The response was softer, weaker, probably Zoë.

She couldn't make out the words. Then the forceful voice again. "Be careful what you say …works for Charlotte… don't like it… suspect the family.… "

She pushed open the door. "Hello." Both women looked surprised. "First of all, I can hear you. If anything, you're making it worse for Zoë. I appreciate you feel you're protecting her, Jane, but it sounded like you were advising Zoë to withhold information from me. I do work for Charlotte Keats. But, we're all after the same thing, aren't we? Catching a killer." Sophia paused. "A suspicious mind might think you two were lying about something." Sophia smiled at them with every tooth in her mouth.

"I did not tell her to lie," Jane protested.

"Okay. Well, it sounded like you did, at least by omission. Look, I need to talk with Zoë. The police will too again, if they haven't already, and, if you can believe it, they'll be even less civil than I."

Jane crossed pencil-thin arms across her chest, her fiery hair tumbling across her shoulders.

"I know. It's hard to imagine. Look Jane," Sophia continued, "You seem to really care about Zoë, but it won't look like that to the cops. Don't keep them waiting while you coach their witness. Really makes it look like you've got something to hide. So, unless Zoë wants to confess to killing her husband right now," she paused wondering where the bold accusation had suddenly come from. Why was she so antagonized by these women? It had hit her like a truck. After all, they were just being cautious, weren't they?

Zoë gasped, stammered, "I didn't ki—"

"You know damn well she didn't do it," Jane said.

"I don't think so either. So, why don't we sit down and have a little heart-to-heart?" Sophia softened her tone and moved toward the front sitting room.

"Why don't we go in the kitchen instead?" Jane asked.

"No, Jane, why don't *you* go in the kitchen instead." Again with the attitude, hers and Jane's. Sophia took Zoë's elbow, looked into her eyes. "We need to speak alone."

Zoë found her backbone. "It's okay, Janey. I've got nothing to hide. I want to know what happened and if I can help, I will."

Jane stood firm, arms akimbo.

"Go." Zoë said. Jane went.

Sophia made a production of sitting down, taking out her notebook, letting her silence guide Zoë to talk.

"She's just so protective of me. Especially since Campbell—they were like brother and sister, you know. She's been a really good friend," Zoë explained.

"She seems to really care about you," Sophia said. "Zoë, I know I was tough on you just now. And I am so sorry for your loss, but I have a job to do. I don't believe you had anything to do with your husband's death. But the police might if you and Jane act at all suspicious. If it seems you have something to hide, they will assume that you do."

"I know."

Jane crept into the room. "I thought you might want some water, or lemonade." The quintessential *Town & Country* woman—back to decorum in two minutes flat. She put a tray down with two glasses of each.

"Thanks, I'm okay now. Go on." Zoë reached for the lemonade. Sophia did the same. Jane made a quiet exit.

"Zoë," Sophia asked leaning gently forward. "I have to ask you some general questions, the same as the police. Did you know of anyone who would want to hurt Campbell? Did he have any enemies?"

She shook her head. "No, I can't imagine, I mean he had so many friends, even at the quarry, everyone loved him."

"Why 'even at the quarry'?"

"Well, I mean he was the owner's son, you know—but he worked hard, he earned his place there. He was really conscious not to take advantage of his father's name."

"Has he always been like that?"

"What do you mean, well-liked?"

"No, I mean conscious not to take advantage of his father's name."

"Well, yes." Zoë looked taken aback. Either she was lying or she hadn't known her husband the way Martin had. "Why do you ask that? Campbell was not a snob, he was very down-to-earth, not like Charlotte at all." She crossed her arms across her belly.

Sophia changed tacks. "How are you feeling, by the way?"

"Much better. I slept really well last night, which is hard to do with this," she grabbed her sides with both hands. "The doctor said the baby is okay, thank God."

In her mind, Sophia replayed Zoë's hospital bed ramblings. "I bet you're relieved. It must be so amazing being pregnant."

"Oh, it is. It's hard though, physically and, I mean your emotions all are over the place. At first," Zoë stopped.

"At first what?"

"At first, I wasn't sure if I wanted to have children, it was so hard for me growing up. My parents never seemed to want me; they were always on a trip. We were never a *real* family."

Whatever that is, Sophia thought, flashing to her own mother in beaded hippie garb dragging her to anti-war demonstrations.

"I worried I'd repeat their patterns, you know how they say you do that, repeat patterns?" Zoë gazed at Sophia who nodded. "Anyway, Campbell changed my mind—convinced me. He was right." Her eyes brimmed with tears. "And now, well, it's a blessing, you know. It's a boy. I'm going to name him Campbell, Jr."

"Charlotte will love that," Sophia said. In fact, maybe it was her idea. "Zoë, at the hospital the other day you told me you wanted an abortion. You said Campbell found out. What was that about?"

Zoë looked down at her belly, put her a finger to her lips. "Nothing."

Sophia waited.

"I mean, at first I wasn't sure, that's all. We'd only been married a year.

I'm so young, you know, my work was going so well. But Campbell made me understand it was fate."

"What kind of art do you do?"

"Sculpture." She laughed. "Nothing since this, though." She palmed her belly like a ripe melon. "I can't fit on my chair, and the smell makes me sick. Everything does, stone, clay, everything I used. I guess once the baby's born I won't have time either. Oh well." She gave nonchalant a try, but as an artist herself, Sophia knew it was an act.

"You could always get child care, you know. There are lots of ways to make a family, to make a child feel loved." *Like I'm some kind of an expert*, Sophia thought. "I'm an artist too—photography—I would be miserable if I couldn't work. No family wants that."

Zoë nodded. "I suppose I could get a nanny. Anyway, I can't really think about that now." She took a drink.

"You said you and Campbell had only been married a year when you got pregnant. How did you meet?"

"We met at an art opening at The Pennsylvania Academy of Fine Arts Gallery."

Sophia nodded.

"Anyway, one of my pieces was in the show. It was a really big deal for me. He said it was the first art opening he'd ever been to. He swept me off my feet."

"I didn't know Campbell was interested in art. I thought that was Charlotte's deal."

"It was. It is. Charlotte was there too, at the opening. Keats Quarry had just become an academy corporate partner. Charlotte was in public relations mode. Campbell only came because Charlotte made him. Jackson was out of town and I think she was lonely."

"Charlotte 'made' him?" Sophia lifted her eyebrows. "Campbell was a grown man. How could she 'make' him?"

"Oh, you don't know Charlotte very well, do you? She had a hold over him, even more so after Jackson died. I never knew Clay but—Campbell hated to disappoint her or to make her angry because she really made him suffer for it."

"How did Charlotte feel about your marriage?"

"Subtle." Zoë flashed a look over her glass, drank more lemonade, wiped her mouth with the back of her hand. "Well, lucky for me, Jackson was still alive when we met, although not for long. He could see how happy we were.

But Charlotte wasn't crazy about the idea. I'm not the right stock, you see. At least I wasn't. Then I became pregnant with a boy." Zoë smiled weakly.

"I thought you said your father ran National Geographic or something, that seems like pretty good stock to me." Sophia wanted to relive the hospital conversation, this time with Zoë lucid.

"No, he runs expeditions, not the Society. There's some prestige there but more with artists and environmentalist types. We're not blue blood enough for Charlotte, and my Dad's Jewish. Not practicing, and it passes through the mother anyway."

Sophia nodded and said, "My mom…."

"Okay, so you know. We're from D.C., like Jane, but not a well-known family like hers. I moved to Philly for art school, got an MFA. I was in my second year here when I met Campbell. It was a whirlwind romance."

"So for Jackson's sake she pretended to accept you, but really came around when you got pregnant?"

"Sort of. After Jackson died, Charlotte hardened, if you can believe it, but not to Campbell. It was like he was ten years old again—the apple of her eye. She doted on him, but was mean to me. She took me aside one day and told me that Campbell had only married me to rebel against her, that he wasn't really in love with me. She said that now that his father was gone, he would realize his mistake and make his way back to the family. She said Campbell had always been the good son but occasionally he'd flex his muscle, you know 'boys will be boys' and all that. She said it would never last."

"Ouch," Sophia said. "That's a pretty big rebellion—to marry a woman you don't love. What did you think of that?"

"Oh, I lost it. I was really upset at first and confronted Campbell. I know I shouldn't have listened to her, but our relationship was so new. I was insecure. He wasn't at all surprised, didn't make any apologies for her, just told me this was how she could be sometimes and to ignore her. He said: 'Daddy is gone and she's lashing out at you. I married you because I love you, and you're nothing like her.' He told me not to worry about it."

"Seems kind of strange, his reason for marrying you is that you're nothing like his mother," Sophia ventured.

"He loved me. We loved each other." Zoë seemed suddenly offended. "What are you getting at?"

"It's just an odd thing to say."

"Well, you weren't there. He didn't mean anything by it; it was a compliment. Can we talk about something else?"

"Sure, why don't you tell me about not wanting the baby," Sophia said.

"I told you, I do want the baby. You do realize that I buried my husband yesterday?" She stood slowly, pushing herself up from the sofa.

"I'm sorry Zoë." Sophia's was on guard again. "Some things just don't make sense though. It's my job to figure them out. And, you did say something about not wanting the baby." What was she hiding?

Zoë turned quickly, agile for a pregnant woman, her nostrils flared. "I told you. I wasn't sure at first. I didn't think we were ready. I changed my mind." As if she read Sophia's mind she added, "Obviously, I did not have an abortion."

"But you wanted to, didn't you?" Sophia asked.

"At one point, yes." Her face was bright red.

"And Campbell didn't like it."

"He told his mother I was pregnant. We hadn't even talked about it, I was still unsure. Once she knew, it was too late. She got involved, I had no choice."

"You must have felt trapped. Were you angry?"

"Yes, of course. Wouldn't you be if your husband ran off to Mommy and shared intimate details about your marriage? Why would I kill him, especially now? It's too late for me to have an—besides, I want the baby—I've changed my mind."

"Zoë, I assume you're the beneficiary of Campbell's estate."

Zoë shook her head and almost laughed. "I figured you'd get around to that, the police already did. Yes, but I signed a pretty limiting pre-nup. Charlotte insisted on it. It's ridiculous, I don't want their goddamn money." The anger boiled at the surface. Just what did Zoë want then? The image of a *real* family? She'd certainly been off-base there.

"Campbell Jr. is taken care of, and so am I really. Of course there are some provisions. I don't care anyway. I just want my husband back." She wept, absently rubbing her belly.

"Okay, Zoë, I think I've tortured you enough for now. I really am sorry." Still wary, Sophia went and sat next to her on the sofa. "You know, Charlotte is my client, so I have to do this. But don't think I'm not reading between the lines. She sounds like a difficult woman to have as a mother-in-law."

Zoë nodded and sniffled. They sat together drinking lemonade for a few minutes. Much was unsaid. What was germane to the case?

Sophia stood. "I'm going to go. Please call me if you can think of anything that might help, even if it seems trivial. Okay?" Sophia stood to leave. "Take care of yourself."

Jane was sitting on a hand-carved bench in the hall. She appeared to be reading a fat paperback but her dark red eyebrows made round arches above the page. She had been watching the closed door.

Sophia said, "She's all yours. I'll just be using the powder room, then I'll see myself out."

"Good."

Behind her Sophia she could hear the sitting room door burst open.

"Everything okay? Are you alright?"

Zoë's voice was strong and Sophia heard her reassurances as she made her way down the long hallway.

******

Sophia opened the door to a tastefully done quarter-bath. The sink was a beautiful green glass bowl that appeared to be suspended in mid-air. Above it was a mirror framed in chunks of brightly colored glass. Her dark eyes, wild hair and full lips were at home there. She wondered how Campbell's reflection played there, or Charlotte's. Did refined grace mix with modern art? Small sculptures adorned the top of a rattan chest of drawers that looked Burmese or something else equally expensive and rare. Sophia picked up one of the sculptures. They were signed "Z. Cohen." They must have been pre-marriage. Or Zoë still used her maiden name for work. Sophia caught her reflection in the teak-framed mirror. *What the hell*, she thought. She opened one of the drawers. It was filled with neatly folded hand towels. The next with cotton balls, Band-Aids, Q-Tips, Tylenol—a well-stocked powder room for the pampered guest. She moved to the bottom cabinet—pulling too hard on the handle—it slipped of its hinges and flew out to the floor. The drawer held rolls of toilet paper. At the very back of the drawer was an open box of tampons. Sophia would have never seen it had she not pulled the drawer off its hinges. Zoë hasn't needed these for months, she thought. There was something sticking out of the box, a sheet of paper, it looked like directions. Every box of tampons comes with directions, yet no woman needs them past the age of fourteen. They get tossed as soon as the box is opened.

Sophia looked in the box. Not a single tampon in sight. The paper was a print out from an Internet search. The site was aptly called: www.NOT-2-LATE.com. The blurb was on the Copper-T IUD as Emergency Contraception. Sophia read the words:

The copper-T intrauterine device (IUD) can be inserted up to five days after unprotected intercourse to prevent pregnancy. Insertion of a copper-T IUD is much more effective than use of ECPs or minipills, reducing the risk of pregnancy following unprotected intercourse by more than 99%.

And the page went on about sexually transmitted disease and pelvic infection. Inside was another, smaller purple box.

Sophia took a deep breath. The back of the box was covered in medical language. The familiar but indecipherable pharmacology, indications for usage, contraindications, Sophia turned it over. It read:

PREVEN™ Emergency Contraceptive Kit Rx Only

1 Instruction Book

1 Pregnancy Test

4 Emergency Contraceptive Pills

Take two blue pills within 72 hours after unprotected sex and two more blue pills 12 hours later. Each dose contains 0.25 mg of levonorgestrel and .05 mg of ethinyl estradiol.

Next to the purple PREVEN™ logo was a silhouette of a woman. She was jumping for joy. Two of the little blue pills were missing.

21

July 9th, 8:00 p.m.

"She wanted an abortion," Sophia said.

"Are you sure?" Martin stopped pouring the wine. They were on their second bottle.

"That's what she said." Sophia sat down at the kitchen table. "It wouldn't be such a big deal except that I found something in her bathroom."

Martin raised his eyebrows.

"Don't look at me like that, this is a murder investigation," she said. "If you're uncomfortable knowing this stuff, I won't tell you. I'll just work on my own."

"No, I want to know. What did you find?"

"What the hell are we doing anyway?" Sophia waved her arm in the air. Cardboard pails of steaming food from Happy Buddha littered the table, packets of hot mustard and duck sauce the centerpiece.

"We're working," Martin said.

"Bullshit. This feels like a date, like it used to," she said. "Are you even divorced yet?"

"Why, do you want to marry me? I'm one of the few men my age who owns his own tux." He grinned, drunk.

"Amusing."

"Look, Sophie, why are you getting so wigged out here? We're old friends having dinner and we're working together, what's the problem?"

"I don't know, maybe that you're married. And, how this feels."

Martin leaned against the counter. "Regan has been in France since May. I haven't even talked to her." He took a sip of wine. "Mmm." He put a glass in front of her. "Have some."

"So you're really getting divorced?"

He took a healthy slug of Chardonnay. "As far as I know." He finished his wine and went to refill his glass.

"Aren't you sad? I mean this is your marriage."

"Sure, but you know, let's talk about something else. Like how about the fact that there's still something between us." He looked at her hard.

"I feel it too," she blurted. "Now what?" Sophia was shaking. *The damn wine*.

"Well, we could be together, that'd be one option." Martin was drunk enough to be confident. At least one of them was.

"But we disagreed on so many things. Life things. Remember?" She didn't know if she was making sense. Did *she* remember their differences? Where was that bottle?

"Yes, but we were younger then." He stood. "I'm not happy with Regan. It's mutual."

"Marriage of convenience not so convenient anymore?"

"Again, I would love to change the subject. Have I told you how sexy you look?" He grabbed her waist. She had a fleeting thought of pushing him away. And it was gone. "Mmm, it's been so long. You smell good. Exotic. I've missed you."

"Me too." She took a sip of wine. "This is good."

"Yes. At the rate I'm going we'll need another bottle or four."

Sophia handed him the corkscrew. "Why do people even go to therapy?" she asked. "You have a few glasses of wine, you say what you really think, boom, you're done."

Martin grinned. "Sophie, I am a little lit, but I would tell you this sober too. I still love you. Do I think the timing is off? Yes. Do I feel cautious? Yes." He Houdini-ed another cork out of a bottle of wine. Impressive technique. "Can we just see what happens? Maybe we were right for each other all along."

"Okay," she said, "but no sex yet." Hah.

"Oh, absolutely. The thought hadn't crossed my mind. What makes you think I want to have sex?" Martin moved a chair next to hers. His hand went to her cheek, toyed with an errant curl. He held her face for a moment. They kissed.

Sophia could feel herself smiling. A huge goofy smile so few ever got to see. *What the hell am I doing? I'm an adult*, she thought. *He's an adult. Life is too short.* Other clichés.

Slowly, Martin lifted her and carried her into the bedroom. She let him.

For hours they swam in memories and wine, making love with the frenzied lust that comes from long absences and familiarity. Sophia's head spun with the potency of passion and alcohol. After, she drifted to sleep on Martin's chest, his heart beating in post-orgasmic lullaby.

Leave it to a feline to ruin the mood. Luigi broke the silence when he landed on the kitchen table, his head in a carton of food. He'd knocked the shrimp over and was ripping into it when Sophia jumped out of bed and ran naked to the kitchen.

"Hey, you're not allowed on the table, get down."

The animal turned, flicked his tail—ass-proud—and raced under the bed.

"Well," Martin said behind her, "I suppose we should eat this before he does." He was nude and looked beautiful. He'd been working out, probably to combat the stresses of a rough marriage and a law partnership. It didn't matter why; it looked good on him. Sophia ran her hands along his stomach. He kissed her neck and moved to the sink.

"I'll just get my robe," Sophia said and padded to the bedroom.

He yelled over the faucet, "Will you grab my boxers?"

Sophia wrapped herself in the only sexy lingerie she owned, a short red silk robe that skimmed her thighs. She stepped over shoes and crumpled sheets finding the pile of Martin's clothes. His wallet had fallen out of his back pocket. A business card or piece of paper worked its way out of the leather folds.

Sophia saw handwriting, not typeface, and fought the urge to read it. She averted her eyes and grabbed the boxers. As she lifted them, the wallet shifted, the paper more visible. What could she do? It said:

Regan in Paris 011-33-

Her stomach dropped. *So he has his wife's phone number in Paris. Almost ex-wife. So what. He needs to know how to reach her.*

"Soph? You coming?" Martin called from the kitchen. "You still like to singe the roof of your mouth? I'll put yours in the microwave." He appeared in the bedroom in all his naked glory. "Hey, you okay?" he asked, grabbing her ass. "Yum, you look delicious. I love this red thing."

Sophia handed him the boxers. "Here you are. Ralph Lauren, I presume?" She was still rattled.

"Very funny. What can I say, I buy them in bulk," he joked.

"Right." She smacked him.

"Ow," he winced. "You want to go again, baby?"

"Move it, let's eat." She led the way to the kitchen. She could feel Martin ogling her ass as she walked. She was glad he couldn't see her face.

Martin went to the counter and began spooning mounds of food onto plates, then popped one of them into the microwave. "Your's'll be right up, soon as it's hot enough to peel away a layer of skin. So, what were we talking about anyway, some murder case or something like that?"

Sophia forced a laugh. "Right, I knew it was something important." She poured more wine, tried to put the phone number out of her mind. "I was telling you about Zoë. I went to see her today. Have you met her friend Jane?"

He nodded. "She was at the funeral. She's an old friend of the family. Big time D.C. family."

"So I've heard. Well, she seems to be the only one concerned for Zoë in all of this. Maybe too concerned. In fact, she tried to get Zoë to lie to me."

Martin scrunched his eyebrows in a frown. "That doesn't sound like a Howard."

"Doesn't matter, I set her straight. At the hospital Zoë mumbled something about an abortion. I got her to tell me more today. Apparently, she wasn't ready to have a baby. Campbell told Mommy before they could make a decision about it, and then, voilà, Zoë was pregnant, and stuck."

"Let me ask you something," he took a bite of food, "as a woman."

"I *am* a woman Martin. That's the only way you can ask me something."

He grinned. He had plum sauce on his teeth. She was sorry she'd made the joke. "So, could you see having an abortion, even if you were married?"

"I don't know, maybe. I mean they had just gotten married. It sounds like she didn't know if she even wanted kids. The point is the decision is not his to make. By telling Charlotte, he essentially made it. Zoë was trapped."

The microwave beeped three times and Sophia reached for her steaming plate. "Ow, Christ that's hot." She reached for a towel. "Not a word out of you," she said wagging a finger at him.

"A toast: To some things never changing and some things staying the same." Martin clinked her glass.

"No more wine for you either," Sophia said. She dug into her food, blowing on it madly and swallowing fast. The heat deadened her tongue.

"So what's the problem with Zoë then?" Martin asked through a mouthful of moo shoo pork.

"The problem is, I went to the bathroom and found a box of emergency contraceptive pills, and some information about IUDs."

"You snooped in her medicine cabinet?" he asked.

"No, that's the thing, I was in the powder room. There was this really cool chest—Burmese or something. I was checking it out. Okay, I was snooping, but in the powder room—easy access for anyone. There was a box of tampons in the cabinet. She hasn't needed those lately, right?"

Martin shrugged.

"I was curious, saw something sticking out of the box. The rest is history."

He didn't need to know about the drawer coming off its hinges. She'd had a hell of a time getting the thing back in. She'd even been afraid she'd broken it at one point. Details. They ate in silence for a minute. Luigi's protests finally secured him a shrimp.

"The thing is, Campbell would never have looked in that box, not in a million years. When have *you* ever opened a box of tampons?"

"Good point," he said.

"Oh, I didn't tell you the best part."

"Oh, great, there's a 'best part.'" He wrapped another pancake.

"Two pills were missing."

He looked confused.

"The emergency contraceptive pills. Two were missing. I'll show you." Sophia pushed her chair away from the table.

"You'll show me? You took them? Tell me you didn't take them."

"Of course I took them. I'll put them back." She tossed the package on the table. "Don't touch!" She handed him a napkin.

He rolled his eyes but took the napkin. "So, what does this mean?"

"I don't know, it means she went ahead and tried to have an abortion anyway, or almost did, or something. I don't know what it means." Sophia picked up her plate. It was still hot, the food steaming. "Follow me." She moved to the computer and turned it on logging on to Planned Parenthood's web site. Within minutes she and Martin were experts in the use of emergency contraceptive pills and the ultimate weapon, the copper IUD, a combined arsenal that increased chances of pregnancy termination to 99%.

"So what happened?" Martin was pale in the monitor's glow.

"What do you mean?"

"Well, it looks like she didn't go through with it," he said, "She changed her mind, right? What's the big deal?"

"She changed her mind," Sophia shoveled chopsticks full of kung pao in her mouth, "or somehow, she got caught."

22

Sophia's red message light blinked furiously. She and Martin had turned the volume down on the answering machine and the ringer off on the phone.

After three—or was it four—bottles of wine, lots of Chinese food and unpleasant speculation about the case, they'd moved back to the bedroom and crashed, locked like spoons in a kitchen drawer. They woke up to Luigi chasing his tail around the apartment. Little did he know he never left home without it.

"Oh shit. I have a meeting in an hour." Martin shot out of bed while fumbling with his watch on the nightstand.

"What time is it?" Sophia rolled over and read the glowing numbers on her alarm clock. 7:03. Luigi had shown great patience. Usually the wakeup call came at 5:30. Maybe the wine and conversation got to him too.

"You'll make it." She snuggled into her pillow.

Martin stopped rushing and looked at her, black curls swirling around her head. They'd fallen asleep so suddenly she had neglected to put her hair up and her locks were wild. He bent down and kissed her cheek. "You are beautiful."

"And you are a very wise man." She sat up and hugged him then she pushed away. "I just realized—I dreamt about Zoë, and babies—unwanted babies. Awful dreams."

"I'm sorry. All that wine and food couldn't have helped. What's on the agenda today?"

"I think I'll give Zoë a break; she's not off the hook though. I need to talk

116

to Whitemarsh Rock, and my gynecologist." Martin raised an eyebrow. "To ask about the pills, Zoë's pills. Horn-dog." He snapped his fingers in mock disappointment. Sophia yawned. "She'll probably make me have an appointment anyway, it's been awhile."

The answering machine's red light screamed from the other room. Martin was already in the bathroom giving himself a quick sponge bath in lieu of what he really wanted, a long slow hot shower with Sophia. Sophia padded towards the kitchen, Luigi on her heels. She hit the flashing button and cranked the volume as she passed her desk. The first two calls were hang-ups. The caller had sat on the line though, waiting before hanging up, breathing into the receiver. A wrong number? Twice?

The machine beeped, signaling the third message was about to begin. "Hi, Sophia, this is Joe Rizzo, from the other day." He sounded nervous. She lunged for the machine just as Martin came in from the bedroom. Too late— they listened together. "I was wondering, I know it's short notice, but I'm in this big softball tournament Wednesday night. Thought you might want to come. Just hang out, you know, drink a few beers. It's seven o'clock at Wilson Park, near Smith Playground. Hope you can make it. Oh it's field number two, we're the Snyder Slammers. Okay, see ya—uh it's Joe, Joe Rizzo. Okay, bye." The machine was on autopilot, beeping loudly and then whirring to rewind the tape. Sophia scrambled to write down what she'd just heard.

Martin stared in disbelief. "What the hell are you doing?"

"I'm going to a softball tournament," she said and went to the hall closet for her Phillies cap. She plopped it on her head. "How do I look?" She looked down at herself then, short ratty T-shirt and leopard print underwear. "Hmm, maybe I'll wear this outfit."

"Sophie, I'm serious, you're not going out with this guy. What the hell did we just do?" He motioned to the bedroom.

"No, I'm not going out with him. I'm conducting an investigation and he might know something. My God, the jealous boyfriend already, that was fast. I thought we were going to just 'see what happens.'"

"Right, right. But what could he possibly know? Plus, you know what he really wants. I don't like it."

"Of course you don't like it. It's me doing my own thing. You've never liked it." She sat on the sofa's arm and looked at him hard. "You'll have to get used to it, again."

"Okay. I know that, I mean I know that issue, whatever. But this worries me. What do you know about him? Besides, what could he possibly know about Campbell's death? Why do you need to interview him? Could he be the killer?" He stopped. "What if he's—"

"I don't think he's dangerous, I really don't. But Zander really lost it when he saw him and then tried to pretend it was nothing. There's something there."

"Be careful," he said with genuine concern.

She kissed him tentatively. "Not that we've complicated matters at all, getting back together?"

Martin looked at his watch. "I gotta go. I'll talk to you later?" He stopped at the door. Turned back. "Maybe we should—"

"I agree," she said, beating him to it. "We keep this under wraps for now. Until the case is over anyway." He grinned and shook his head in disbelief. She could hear him chuckling as he clomped down the stairs into the street.

23

July 10th, 10:45 a.m.

Sophia sat in the Saab at Whitemarsh Rock & Limestone. Dense July air muffled the sounds of men yelling, machines beeping, and gravel crunching under work boots. She'd been distracted by Rizzo's phone message and by Martin's presence while she listened to it. And then there were the hang-ups. Too much going on for her to absorb it all.

Being with Martin again was effortless, and yet everything felt different too. He was still married, although how married she couldn't discern. And, he had become immediately jealous of Joe Rizzo. By now, Martin had to know how independent she was. Regan Whitehouse, on the other hand, would have honored and obeyed. She would have whined while doing it, but she'd have done it. Martin had said he didn't want that. But had he meant it?

She got out of the car and strode decisively to what looked like the main office. Several oversized metal desks were strewn about the room all covered with piles of paper. She approached a miserable-looking woman at the first desk. Her expression said she was making seven bucks an hour. Tops. *At that*, Sophia guessed, *I'd be miserable too.*

"Good morning," she oozed.

The woman sized her up. Sophia could see the wheels turning. Nice suit, clipboard, looks official, better be nice to her. "What can I do for you ma'am?"

In the spirit of Jekyll and Hyde, she switched personalities and beamed at Sophia.

Sophia made an exaggerated point of looking at the nameplate on her desk. "Yes, Mrs. Johnston, I'm from the Pennsylvania Aggregates and Concrete Association in Harrisburg. May I speak with Mr. Scott?" She'd done enough homework to get the owner's name and a plan was formulating as she stood there, amazed that anyone would choose to have their nameplate identify them as *Mrs. Johnston*. Was *Mrs.* her first name?

"He's not in at the moment, would you like to talk to Ronald, his nephew? He's Mr. Scott too. I'll get him." She didn't wait for an answer. Mrs. Johnston seemed impressed by Sophia's outfit, which was amusing; she'd only ironed the tiny triangle of her blouse and collar that stuck out over her jacket.

Sophia hoped her claim wouldn't backfire. It was too late now. Chances were, no one from the Harrisburg-based organization had been here before. She knew from the on-line membership directory that Whitemarsh was not a member. Keats Quarry was.

A small plaque from the industry association hung on the wall of Campbell Keats' office, next to an old black-and-white photo of the quarry pit with the caption "Established 1890." Sophia figured the industry association set guidelines, drove standards, printed state directories, and ultimately, and by affiliation only, elevated members' status.

She took the place in. The office felt familiar. Keats Quarry's offices had a similar layout: a large open space with individual desks scattered about, a small makeshift kitchen at the back. But here there was considerable disorder. Sheer sheets of pink paper, invoices or receipts, floated in and out of piles. The room had a baked-in odor of years of cigarette smoke. She was lost in thought when she heard voices approaching. Mrs. Johnston's already familiar whine had announced Sophia's presence.

"Are you sure?" a deep voice asked.

"Yes, Ronald, that's what the lady said, she's from the Harrisburg office. Maybe it's about membership."

The third voice sent a chill down Sophia's spine. "Well thank you for your time, Mr. Scott. As I said, these questions are all routine, nothing to worry about. Please let your uncle know I was here. When you come to the office you may wish to notify your attorney. Nothing to worry about sir— just routine." Buck Dallas turned to see Sophia staring at him with pleading deer-in-headlights eyes.

She jumped. "Mr. Scott, pleased to meet you, I'm with the Pennsylvania

Aggregates and Concrete Association in Harrisburg. We're just talking to some local companies about membership, if this is a bad time...."

The young man looked relieved. Dallas had obviously been questioning him, and he wasn't finished. Someone at Whitemarsh was a murder suspect and by the looks of Ronald Scott, he was scared. While fear is not an admission of guilt, it can certainly fuel the fire for an eager detective.

"No, Miss, uh you're fine. I believe we're done for now. Detective Dallas?" Scott arched an eyebrow at Buck, hoping for a break. The last thing he'd want was for the state's industry association to know Whitemarsh was involved in a homicide investigation.

******

Buck Dallas sized up the situation. This damn PI was everywhere. But, with her cover, maybe she'd get more out of Scott than he had. And, maybe he could get her to share, in fact, he was sure he could. Whatever the outcome, there was no harm letting Ronald Scott think he was meeting a cheerleader from some industry association.

"We'll see you tomorrow at nine a.m. then, Mr. Scott?" Dallas left some force in his voice and managed a well-camouflaged wink at Sophia as he left the office.

******

Sophia sighed as relief washed over her. She hoped it was invisible. "He seemed like a serious fellow," she said with a cryptic look.

Ronald Scott nodded. Now that Dallas was gone he could say whatever he wanted. "Yes, he did didn't he? I'm sure you've heard about the tragedy at Keats Quarry. Well, the police have come to us for assistance, you know, as the leading quarry in the area, to see if we can help them figure out what happened."

Leading? Sophia wondered what "area" Scott was referring to. She let it go. "Did I hear him say something about an attorney?" She was playing the excited kid who'd happened upon a car wreck—simply fascinated by the human condition—nothing more, nothing less.

"Yes, well, you know that's a formality." Scott did condescending well, and fell easily into the role of Tarzan to Sophia's Jane. *This might be a fruitful meeting after all*, she thought.

"Oh, of course. Oh Gosh, I haven't even introduced myself." Sophia stuck out her hand. "Sophia Gold, Membership Committee."

"What can I do for you Miss Gold?"

"Well, Mr. Scott," she said with a touch of coy, "PACA is working on increasing membership, but I'm not here today to solicit you to join. This isn't a sales call. I just wanted to ask a few questions about how we might serve the industry better, get an idea of what kinds of companies are out there, that kind of thing. Would that be okay, Mr. Scott?"

"Ronald, please." Scott seemed open to the idea of talking about himself and his business with, presumably, no strings attached. "Why don't we sit down in the kitchen, would you like some coffee?"

"Yes, thanks." She followed him to the kitchen, which was a battered table in the corner of the same room as the office and the waiting area.

Ronald Scott was an easy mark. After one probing question about his uncle's business, he talked for fifteen minutes about the company, its history and mostly, himself. His speech was rambling and disorganized and he seemed nervous again. Sophia wasn't sure why, maybe standard run-of-the-mill sexual tension. She listened as intently as she could, took notes where she made sense of things and nodded at the appropriate times.

"You know, we've been meaning to join." He looked down at his hands.

"Well, we hope you do, but only if membership meets your needs," she paused. "I believe that Keats Quarry has benefited from membership. You might want to talk to the folks over there. Oh, goodness," Sophia put a hand to her throat as if to stop the words. "I suppose now wouldn't be a good time for that."

"Yes, it's really tragic what happened." Ronald Scott's expression was flat and he sat very still. A hint of a smirk appeared on his face. "That family just can't seem to hold it together," he added, unable to hide his disdain.

"What do you mean? I'd heard the Keats family was one of the city's most prestigious."

"You would think so." Scott leaned back in his chair, tempting the worn plastic with his bulk. He was a big man, muscular in a *Grapes of Wrath* sort of way, thick, stolid. "You have to wonder about a family with so many deaths—the father, both sons, you know, it's really a shame. Wonder what they are being punished for."

Sophia leaned forward. "Punished?"

"Oh, I don't know, it just seems strange, you know."

Sophia waited.

"They just got this huge contract, stole it from us really, right out from under us. And now this happens. I wonder if they'll be able to finish the job."

That sounded like motive.

"Well, I know we are all very sorry for their loss," she said. "It sure would be a shame though if, because of a personal tragedy, the industry gets a bad name."

"Well, it just goes to show that money can't buy everything," Scott replied.

Sophia adopted a shocked look. "Mr. Scott, are you implying that something unethical occurred? If that is the case, and you have information about it, PACA would be very grateful if you could share it." She was purposely flustered; this was the most horrendous thing she had ever heard.

Ronald Scott averted his eyes and allowed them to flit about the room. He settled on his cuticles, completely absorbed. "I have no evidence, of course. And please, Ronald." He smiled a one-dimensional smile and said, "You just have to wonder about that family. Everyone seems to die," he whispered, leaning forward. Sophia could smell the coffee on his breath. There was something hidden in his eyes. "I heard the wife, Campbell's wife, is in the hospital. Something about losing the baby." He shifted his gaze. "The Lord works in mysterious ways."

This guy was creepy, but she didn't think he was a killer. He was being too forthright, even with someone whom he thought a stranger to the case.

Sophia feigned outrage. "Ron-ald! It sounds like you relish in their misfortune. I can't help but feeling sorry for them. Is his wife okay? Did she lose the baby?" Sophia forced herself to pat Scott's arm and cluck disapprovingly. "You're terrible, really."

"Oh, I know." He was sheepish. "I suppose it is too bad. I do feel for them, but you know the company has hurt our business, and not because they're better," he added hastily, "Because they use their influence, their money." Now he sounded like a bratty child blaming his siblings or friends for not making the team, not getting a date to the prom, missing the pop fly in left field. Ronald had his back to the room and was so absorbed in sulking that he did not hear his uncle approach.

Sophia watched as an attractive, weathered man moved toward them.

"I'm Bill Scott." He shoved a large paw across the table to shake with Sophia. She stood and returned the pump.

Ronald looked caught. He stood and almost overturned his coffee. "Oh, Uncle Bill, this is Miss Gold, from PACA. The membership committee."

"Yes, Gertie told me." *Ah, Mrs. Johnston, a.k.a. Gertie. No wonder she didn't advertise her first name.* "It's very nice to meet you. What can we do for you?"

"Actually, Ronald was just telling me about the Keats family, giving me some inside scoop on their business practices." She winked at Ronald. He blanched faster than an almond, beads of sweat exploding on his upper lip.

"Excuse me?" Bill Scott turned to his nephew. "Son, you have got to get over this. I will not have you bad mouthing the Keats' family business. They have been through enough." He lowered his voice, "Miss Gold, I don't know what my nephew told you, but the Keats family has done nothing to us. Ronald here thinks our business suffers because of them. Our business only suffers or prospers because of what we do." He sounded like a preacher. "Ronald? We've talked about this. Have you been doing your affirmations?"

Affirmations? Was this Bible Study?

"I knew Jackson Keats," Bill Scott continued, "God rest his soul, for over thirty years. He ran his business fair and square. Nothing wrong with that. Oh sure, he mingled with the hot shots. But, I'm not ashamed of Whitemarsh Rock & Limestone. We do just fine."

"Could do better," Ronald pouted.

"Yes, we could do better. We can always do better, can't we Miss?" Sophia watched the two men lob back and forth. "But let's not criticize others to avoid facing our own demons," Bill Scott said, crossing his arms across a broad chest.

"Amen to that," Sophia heard herself saying. She was rewarded with vigorous nodding from the elder Mr. Scott. *Where'd that come from?* she wondered.

"Well, I suppose I've taken enough of your time. Why don't I go ahead and send you an information packet on PACA membership when I get back to the office?"

"That'd be just fine, Miss Gold. No promises of course, we like to run our own show here, but I'll take a look at your information just the same." Bill Scott was polite but dismissive. He would never join PACA, not that Sophia cared. He was on his own and proud of it and content with his company's success, or lack thereof. He wasn't hungry, maybe never had been. Sophia realized something else that was different from the Keats Quarry office. It hadn't registered earlier—there were no computers on any of the desks.

She rose to leave. Mrs. Johnston tapped away at a typewriter, filling out forms in triplicate. Ronald dragged his feet behind his uncle as they walked

Sophia to the door. "Thank you again for your time, gentlemen." Sophia moved to shake their hands again. Bill Scott took hers and shook. Ronald, oddly enough, waved like a child as she walked away.

24

Buck Dallas slouched against the Saab smoking a cigarette, hidden from view. Sophia started when she saw him.

"Jesus! You scared the crap—what are you doing?"

He grinned through a cloud of cigarette smoke, stubbed the butt out under his Cole Haan's. There were several fresh butts in a pile by Sophia's front left tire. "I'm waiting for you, what does it look like I'm doing? By the way, nice cover—did they buy it?"

She nodded in disbelief at her luck. "They did, I think your friend Ronald was so relieved I wasn't another cop, he'd have bought anything. You scared him."

"Yeah, well he should be scared—guy's got a record," Dallas said.

"What did he do?"

"Can't tell you that."

"Can't or won't?" she asked

"Really doesn't matter 'cause either way, I'm not telling you."

She let it pass. "Well, he's an odd guy."

"Odd how?"

"Can't tell you that," she said.

Dallas stood tall, stretched his limbs, and gave a quick glance toward the office. "Look, why don't we spar somewhere more private?" Sophia gave him a questioning look. "Your cover won't be good for shit if they see you talking to me."

"True," Sophia said, "But don't forget, my client is Charlotte Keats."

"Right." Dallas pulled up to his full height. He was a human tree. "And my client is *Campbell* Keats." He moved for his car keys and in so doing revealed a Glock gleaming in its holster. "There's an IHOP around the corner. Meet me there."

******

Buck Dallas filled up the entire side of a booth at the IHOP. He sat back to the wall, facing the restaurant, scanning the crowd. A cup of steaming coffee sat in front of him. Two glasses of water. Sophia slid into the seat across from him. He pushed one of the water glasses toward her.

"Odd, how?" Dallas repeated his question.

Sophia sighed. "At first, he was sort of morbid. Almost seemed to be enjoying the news about Campbell and Zoë. He said something about the quarry stealing business from them, or rather 'buying' contracts. When I pressed him though, he backed down."

"I thought you were supposed to be a cheerleader from an industry organization," Dallas said.

Sophia took a gulp of water. "I was. We were talking about membership benefits, I casually mentioned how much Keats Quarry got out of membership and oops, silly me, I brought up the dead guy." She grinned. Dallas raised his eyebrows and took a swallow of coffee.

"It was like taking candy from a baby at that point. He really hates that family. Doesn't seem to have a good reason to and he seems like too much of a wimp to do anything about it. He's got victim written all over him. I don't like him." Sophia looked up, embarrassed at her presumed authority, use of cop-speak. "But then, what do I know, I'm just a lowly PI."

Dallas chuckled.

"His uncle came back, you know," she added.

"I must have missed him hiding behind that foreign heap of yours."

"Heap? Jesus Christ, Dallas. Let me guess, you drive a Camaro."

"No I don't drive a Camaro, but I sure as hell don't drive foreign. What is that, Swiss or something?"

Sophia stifled a laugh. "Swiss? Yes, it's Swiss, they're known for their chocolates, watches and cars. It's a Saab. It's *Swedish*. One of the safest cars on the market, by the way."

"Whatever." Dallas smoothed his hair back against his skull. "You said the uncle came back. We're bringing them both in for questioning tomorrow."

"Well, you won't get much, he's practically born-again. I have more motive than he does." Sophia took another drink.

"Should I be checking out your alibi, Ms. Gold?" Dallas teased.

"Very funny. You know what I mean. Seriously, I don't think the uncle was acting. He seemed genuine. Weird, but genuine. He scolded Ronald for not doing unto others, that kind of thing. A lot of borderline God-talk. Ronald was like a whiny little kid with him." Sophia looked up at Dallas. "What did you think of him?" she asked.

"Oh, not much. He hid his hatred of the Keats family, tried to at least, but I noticed something off about him. We'll check his alibi. He says he was watching fireworks all night with friends. In Jersey." Dallas motioned for the waitress to refill his coffee. He pointed to his cup and asked Sophia if she wanted some.

"No thanks, I'll just have this." She took his water glass and drained it.

A waitress came over with a coffee pot. "Will there be anything else?" she asked. Dallas shook his head. He put a five-dollar bill on the table. She started to reach into an apron pocket that bulged with change.

Dallas shook his head again. "No change. We're good."

The woman looked at the five, shrugged her shoulders and pocketed the bill.

"By the way, what do you drive?" Sophia asked.

"Ford Explorer. It's American."

"You don't say, Tex. A Ford is American? So, any other suspects?"

"You know I can't tell you that. And don't call me 'Tex.' What about you, who else are you talking to?"

"Why I'm surprised at you." Sophia did her best Southern belle imitation. "You know *I* can't tell *you* that."

"If you find something, remember, there's always obstruction of justice. When's your license up for renewal anyway?" Dallas asked. He might have been teasing. Sophia wondered what his jacket looked like, if there were any citations for excessive force, or inflated ego.

"Chill, Dallas. I'm not going to impede your investigation. I'll let you and Webb know if I find something. I want this killer found as much as you do."

"Do you? I thought you said your client was Charlotte Keats."

"Well, if she did it, and I find out, I swear," Sophia put her right hand on her chest, "you'll be the first to know. I'll flush client confidentiality down the shitter. Thanks for the water, big guy."

Her exit would have been truly great had the backs of her thighs not stuck to the vinyl seat. Philadelphia in July. She could hear Dallas laughing softly as she waddled away, her underwear creeping stealthily up her butt crack.

25

July 10th, 6:45 p.m.

Sophia made it to Wilson Park by dusk and found the softball fields. She imagined them from an aerial view, well-groomed field after well-groomed field anchored together like pieces of a puzzle. To the east was the Smith Playground building, a beautiful relic long stained with green streaks of copper residue. Philadelphia had many similar pockets of history and nostalgia and, as always, Sophia was amazed at the city's beauty.

There was something wide and expansive about Philly, especially in its parks and common areas. It was like a wistful family farm, replete with wrap-around porch and giant front yard. The reality had never been quite so idyllic. She parked the Saab among a slew of American-made pick-up trucks and sedans, and thought of Buck Dallas. Damn him. She grabbed her camera bag and hopped out of the car.

A camera was the ultimate sidekick. Photography could, if you let it, protect you from the experience of the moment, allow you to stand back and be an artist without being a participant. She didn't know what to expect with Joe Rizzo, and when she didn't know what to expect, she brought her camera.

She saw him by the bleachers. Rizzo was oddly sexy in black baseball pants and a T-shirt with the number six emblazoned on the back, a "Snyder Street Pub" logo on the front. He tossed a ball back and forth with a little boy. Sophia recognized him as Rizzo's nephew from the photos she'd seen at the funeral. Rizzo's female double sat on the bleachers nearby. His teammates, identifiable by the green T-shirt uniform, were already warming up in the field.

Sophia caught his attention and waved. Rizzo ran toward her, scooping up the child as he ran. "Hey, you made it," he said with reserved pleasure.

"How's it going?" The air was thick with musky male odor, sweat mixed with deodorant. Sophia was surprised to feel a thrill inside her.

"And who is this?" she asked, smiling at the beautiful dark-haired boy. His eyes were an almost icy blue, light and clear like a Siberian Husky's. He had two pronounced dimples and a killer smile.

"This is Matteo, my nephew. This is Sophia."

Matteo stood tall and proud next to his uncle. "Pleased to meet you Miss Sophia." The boy held out his hand.

"Very pleased to meet you too, Matteo." He ran off calling for his mom. "Wow, he's more polite than most adults I know."

"He's a great kid. My sister raised him right."

"Where's his—?" Sophia's question was interrupted.

"This is Miss Sophia, Mom."

"Hi, I'm Maria." She was as beautiful as her brother was handsome. They both had glowing olive skin and dark brown eyes. To a stranger, they could be married, Matteo their son but for the blue eyes. "How do you know Joey?" she asked.

"Oh, we met at the quarry and then," Sophia paused, "at the Keats Memorial." Said aloud, the words were jarring.

"I see." Maria's eyes changed and she put her arm protectively around her son's shoulders. Matteo sensed his mother's discomfort and stopped smiling, kicked the dirt beneath his feet.

"It sound's terrible, I know, to meet at a funeral," Sophia said.

Joe lunged at Matteo with his softball mitt, tickling his belly. "It's no big deal really, we just started talking. Sophia's Italian too." Joe's voice was lighthearted. He used his nephew to cut the tension. "So, whaddya' say bud, should we show Mom and Sophia how you catch pop flies?"

"Yeah, c'mon Mom," Matteo was easily coaxed out of his grim mood. "You gotta watch. Hey, what's the camera for?" Matteo directed his question at Sophia.

"Mattie, that's not polite!" Maria chided her son.

"Well," she said looking at Maria and then at Joe, "I'm a photographer.

Maybe, if it's okay with your mom, I could take some pictures of you and your uncle playing. Then when I develop them I could give you copies, what do you think?"

"Cool, like baseball cards," Matteo said.

"Is it okay?" Sophia turned to Maria. Most people love pictures of their children, no matter where they come from. And yet, Sophia felt compelled to ask.

"Of course, but only if it's no trouble for you," Maria answered.

"Not at all, it's my life's work," she said, "And with subjects like these...." She winked at Maria.

Joe blushed.

Matteo beamed.

Matteo ran efficiently, little brown muscled legs carrying him into the field. He caught his uncle's fly balls one after another, grinning at his mother after each one.

Sophia had her zoom lens and captured the essence of childhood in Matteo's determined expressions, intense gazes and huge smiles. She took a few shots of Joe as well. He was even easier on the eyes than his nephew.

Sophia joined Maria on the bleachers. "He's a really great kid," Sophia said.

"He sure is, and his uncle is so good with him."

"They seem really close," Sophia paused, "Does he see his father much?"

Maria kept her eyes facing front. She clapped once as her son ran for the ball. "No, " she said softly.

"I'm sorry, that was rude. It's really none of my business." Sophia was embarrassed, although asking personal questions was par for the course in her line of work. It was Maria's opening, but she said nothing. They sat in silence, the softball whizzing back and forth past the bleachers and landing with soft thuds against the leather of well-worn mitts.

"Jo-ey, let's go!" A deep voice came from the outfield and they all looked up to a sea of green T-shirts, barely discernible against the lush grass of the field. Joe tossed the ball one last time to his nephew and then ran towards his team.

The afternoon bled slowly into evening, the sunset a deliberate burn across the horizon. The air was still thick with humidity and Maria shared a Diet Coke with Sophia while Matteo drank from a juice box. An awkward cloud hung over them; the child was a welcome buffer. Joe played well and Sophia was sure he was showing off for her. He was athletic and well-liked, drawing cheers and hoots both at bat and in the field.

Several other spectators had joined them on the bleachers. Matteo charmed everyone, but always came back to his mother, who watched his every move. By the sixth inning, Sophia was ready to leave, wondering if she'd wasted an evening. Had she advanced the investigation? Had coming tonight been ego masquerading as instinct? And what of Martin? Joe Rizzo found her attractive, made her feel sexy, coveted, and surprisingly feminine.

She hadn't known men like him, men who worked their bodies for a living, who believed in old-fashioned but simple rules of the world, for whom feminism might be a dirty word, while female the most beautiful ever uttered. She shivered against a chill that no one else felt. And yet, she stayed.

When the game was over, Rizzo swaggered over to the bleachers, resplendent in victory. Matteo had fallen asleep on his mother's lap but awoke to his uncle's bellowing voice and hugged the man with pure love, uninhibited as only a child can be.

"We're going to Snyder's for a beer," Rizzo announced.

"I need to take Mattie home, he's exhausted." Maria held her son close as if someone had threatened to snatch him away. "Can you get a ride?" Maria held out her hand. Rizzo fished a set of keys out of his gym bag.

"Sophia? A beer?"

"Sure. I can at least give you a ride." It was high school all over again. The air suddenly felt cool and Sophia wondered if this time the chill was real. She wasn't sure what she was doing. *No good can come of this*, she thought. *I'm leading him on. Besides, what could he possibly know about Campbell's death?*

26

Sophia circled the park twice before finding a spot on 24th Street. She wedged the Saab against the curb and took the short cut through Fitler Square back to her apartment. Martin Duncan sat under a pillar lamp on a park bench rummaging through his briefcase. She sat down, startling him.

"Oh Jesus, you scared me." He jumped.

"That's what you get for sitting alone in a park at night," she teased. "Were you waiting for me by any chance?"

"Yes, I was waiting for you. How was it? Did you have fun?" Martin had one hand still flailing about in his briefcase.

"What are you looking for?"

"Oh, I don't know." He laughed nervously. "I was just waiting for you and getting worried."

"Martin, I was working."

He looked at his watch. "Until midnight?"

"We went out for a beer after the game," she said, defiant.

"And?"

"And, for the second time today, someone implied that Campbell Keats may have gotten what he deserved. By the way, you'll be happy to know that the police questioned Rizzo."

"And…."

"And nothing. He's got an airtight alibi and no motive as far as I can see." Martin buried his head in his briefcase.

"You know, I'm wondering what Campbell did to make so many people,

people who supposedly didn't even know him, think he got what he deserved." She stood. "Of course, his killer hated him the most. Are you coming up?"

"Do you want me to?"

"No, that's why I asked." She shook her head, laughing and grabbed his briefcase.

The stairway was dark and Sophia fumbled with her keys. She flicked the light switch several times. "Must be burned out," she said running her hand along the wall to guide her. "Ouch. Damn it. Something stung me or pricked me. Shit."

"Are you all right?"

"I guess. Ow! Let's just get into the apartment. Can you see at all?"

"No, I'll just let my fingers do the walking." Martin had his hand on Sophia's ass as he followed her up the stairs.

"Very funny. Okay, here we are." She fumbled again with the key, leaned on the door and it swung open. "What the hell?" Her door had been closed but unlocked. The latch barely caught so that with her weight, it opened easily. She turned on the light. "Holy shit. My hand!" Sophia's hand was bleeding and a piece of opaque white glass was stuck in her palm. She removed it, wincing.

"Oh my God, are you all right?" Martin ushered her to the kitchen sink.

"Luigi, where is he?"

"The cat? I'm sure he's fine. I'm worried about you."

"No, the door was open, someone's been here." She was frantic. She grabbed a dishtowel from the counter and ran into the bedroom. Luigi was hiding under the bed, spooked. When he heard Sophia's voice he came out and rubbed against her leg a few times, then trotted into the kitchen.

"See," Martin said.

"Martin, someone was in my apartment. Someone tried to hurt me. My door was unlocked."

"That's ridiculous. Are you sure you didn't forget to lock it? You know, in your excitement to go the softball tournament?" He said the last words with a sneer.

"I'm serious Martin, someone's been here. Look at this." She shoved her bleeding hand into his face.

"Well, that we can do something about. C'mere." They went back to the kitchen and Martin kissed her on the forehead. "Rinse. I'll get a Band Aid."

Sophia inspected the glass while Martin went to the medicine cabinet. It was a cloudy white and on it was the number "75." Under that she read the letters "WA." It came from the light bulb in the hall, a 75-WATT bulb. The hall light was always on, and in the years Sophia had lived there, had never been burned out, even for a day. Sophia's landlady was especially concerned for the safety of her single female tenants.

Someone had broken the bulb in the hall, to cause Sophia trouble getting in or to have darkness in which to work. Or both. They'd been in her apartment. She could feel it.

Martin was back with gauze pads, Band Aids and hydrogen peroxide. He went to work on her cut.

"I need to look around." Sophia tried to pull away.

"Relax. It's okay. Let me just fix you up first."

Sophia started to cry, but she was angry. "Fucking hell," she said. "Who did this? First the hang ups, now this."

"What hang ups? What are you talking about? Soph, calm down."

"Don't tell me to calm down. This fucking killer, someone is trying to get me off this case." She sniffled. "I'm scared. I'm pissed off, and I'm scared."

"Look, just tell me about it," Martin said. "We'll figure it out." He finished bandaging her cut.

"First I have to check the place," she said, wandering around the apartment, picking things up and putting them down again.

"Is anything missing?"

"I don't think so." She fumbled on her desk, touching the keyboard. Her computer whirred, awakened from slumber. "This isn't good," she said.

"What?"

"I turned my computer off this morning." She stared at the screen as the colors revived.

"Are you sure?"

"Yes I'm sure. Why are you so quick to discount this? God damn it Martin." She was breathing hard.

"I'm sorry, honey, okay. You're scared. There are probably good explanations for all of this. You could have left the computer on. Did you leave in a hurry? And the door, maybe you thought you locked it but it didn't catch."

"And the hang ups?"

"Telemarketers."

"But they were on the line, like they were waiting."

"Computers make those calls. They're programmed—it's not even a human on the other line." He was explaining it all away.

"What about the light bulb, this?" She gestured around the apartment.

"Sophie, you're way too suspicious. Nothing's missing, you're safe. Louie's safe. How about we cuddle up and go to bed?"

Martin was treating her like a child. And she felt like one, a frightened one. *For tonight*, she thought, *I'll just let myself be coddled. Martin's here, no one's going to come back tonight, if someone was here at all. Denial isn't just a river in Egypt.* She followed him to the bedroom where within minutes they were tucked in.

But she couldn't sleep and started filing away every coincidence since she'd taken the case, including Martin waiting for her in the park. When she got up, he asked sleepily where she was going. "To get a glass of water," she said. But instead she checked the lock again. In the living room she stood at the window for a long time. Fitler Square was dark. She shivered, then took out her notebook, tried to remember the times and dates of each incident. She left a light on, burning bright in the window and out into the street. When she crawled back into bed Martin was asleep.

27

They were drinking coffee and easing into the morning. Neither had said a word about the events of the night before, the break-in, the distance between them, Martin falling asleep while Sophia worried in the other room. Yet, Martin insisted on going with her to the Keats mansion. Sophia was due at Charlotte's by eleven.

"Don't you have other clients?" she asked as they finished breakfast.

"Nothing now." Martin said.

"How's your hand by the way?"

"Fine." She waved her bandaged palm in his face. "Okay, suit yourself, we have to leave at ten."

"If I didn't know better, I'd think you were trying to get rid of me." He looked at her hard until she returned his gaze.

"It's not that. I'm just not sure if Charlotte will be completely honest in front of you."

"I disagree. She's protected by attorney-client privilege with me. I've known the family forever. Jesus, I'm the only person in her life even resembling a son."

"You know, that said, I can't help but wonder if you know more than you're telling me."

"About what?" Martin shifted in his chair. His cheeks were suddenly bright, his thick eyebrows tightened across his forehead. "Are you calling me a liar?"

"No," she said, although she wasn't sure if she meant it. "Just that you have insights into this that you may not even realize, you know being so close to it. For example, why does Ronald Scott—granted he's strange—think Campbell deserved it?"

"I don't know. You said it yourself; the guy is a little off. I wouldn't be surprised if he's spent time 'resting' somewhere. Somewhere in a nice hospital with padded rooms."

"Are you serious?"

"I've heard some talk."

"See, that's what I mean. I need to know these things," she said rolling her eyes. "It would be good to find out for sure." Sophia moved to the phone. "Besides, why did Joe Rizzo imply the same thing?" She stopped. "You already told me about the stuff in high school. I guess that could be Rizzo's excuse. He was a little drunk when he said it."

"Exactly. Besides this Rizzo guy, he's a pretty macho type right? Maybe he was showing off for you." Martin finished his coffee. "What did he actually say anyway?"

"Well, I said how it was a shame about Campbell and how the family seemed to have a lot of bad luck, like the Kennedys. He said something like maybe they had it coming. He asked me if I really thought Michael Skakel was innocent, you know Ethel Kennedy's nephew?"

Martin nodded, encouraging her to continue.

"He said he'd seen some *Dateline* show about him. He said that family, with all that money, could get away with anything, but Skakel was paying now, wasn't he?" She shook cat food into Luigi's bowl. He came barreling out of the bedroom. "He makes a good point, actually. About Skakel I mean. Seems he got away with whatever he did for a hell of a long time." *What did Campbell get away with?* she wondered.

"Campbell was nothing like Michael Skakel. Besides, whatever happened to innocent until proven guilty?" Martin asked.

"Right, and O.J. was innocent," Sophia said. She shook her head. "No, you're probably right. About Rizzo, I mean. He was a little lit up, he'd won his softball game, had a home run, maybe he thought he'd impress me with his knowledge of current events, or something. You know his parents are dead."

"What does that have to do with anything?" Martin was clearing the breakfast dishes.

"Nothing, I guess, just that he told me his parents were in a fatal car crash about ten years ago. The officers on the scene thought they were relatives of

Frank Rizzo."

"Now that's something to brag about. I cannot believe this guy." Martin stood ramrod straight at the sink.

"No, it's a good story. There was some media confusion at first until the real Frank cleared it up. He made a statement to the press expressing his condolences to the other Rizzo family. He went on about how even though they weren't blood relatives, all Italian-Americans were joined by their heritage." Sophia wiped the kitchen table with a sponge.

"Well, that's original, a eulogy from Frank Rizzo. What a load. I wonder if that gets him a lot of dates. How did *that* come up?"

"He brought it up, and I asked him if he was related to the former mayor."

"That's direct."

"Come on, you live in Philly, someone's name is Rizzo, you have to ask. Who knows, he could be proud to share Frank's name." Why was she misrepresenting Joe Rizzo to Martin?

"That's *scary.*"

Sophia shrugged and dialed the phone. "Buck Dallas or Jack Webb," she said into the receiver. "Yes, Sophia Gold," she paused, "an interview? Oh, of course, with Ronald and Bill Scott. Well, can you let them both know I called? Yes, thank you."

"What was that about?"

"I ran into Buck Dallas yesterday at Whitemarsh Rock. He told me they were interviewing the Scott's today. Maybe they'll know about Ronald's mental status."

"Do you really think they'll tell you?"

"It's worth a try."

******

Charlotte looked more gaunt and tightly wound than ever. She met Sophia and Martin in the sitting room. Every surface in the room glimmered in the morning light. The yellow roses from the other day were replaced with majestic white calla lilies. The flowers, with their statuesque green stems and creamy white blossoms, were more perfect than anything Sophia had seen in any painting or photograph.

"How are you holding up, Charlotte?" Martin asked.

She ignored him. "I want this person found. I want this person caught."

"We're working on it, Mrs. Keats," Sophia said, "Can you tell us anything else about Campbell?"

"Haven't you talked to those horrible Scott people, the ones who run Whitemarsh Rock & Limestone? Jackson was always nice to that man, Bob, or Bill or whatever his name is. But the nephew, there was something about that boy, something wrong." She stood to pour tea from the service sitting on the table. The china was a delicate but bold pattern of black and gold, twining foliage, exotic unicorns, satyrs and impish monkeys. *Etiquette trumps tragedy*, Sophia thought as Charlotte poured three cups of fragrant tea and gestured to a pitcher of milk, plate of lemon slices and sugar bowl.

"Why is no one investigating that boy?" Charlotte asked, incredulous.

"We are Mrs. Keats. I am and so are the police. Rest assured if he is guilty, we will find out."

Charlotte Keats folded her hands in her lap and sighed imperceptibly. "Good. I know he did it."

"May I ask what is it that makes you so sure?" Sophia said.

"Oh, isn't it obvious? The person, the killer..." she said the last word with a venomous tongue. Sophia wondered just how much anger was simmering beneath the surface, and if it would ever boil over. "...the killer committed the crime at the quarry; they must have some knowledge of our business. And that boy is disturbed. Always has been. Jackson was too nice to that family. He used to row with Bob Scott."

"Bill," Martin said softly.

Charlotte looked over at him in shock, as if she hadn't realized he was in the room. "Pardon?"

"Bill Scott. He's the owner."

"Right. Does it matter who the owner is? It's the boy I'm talking about."

"Ronald."

"Ye-es. That's it." Charlotte sighed, having successfully directed the conversation. Sophia wondered if she'd known the names all along but was merely playing a role, a role that Sophia had yet to figure out.

Sophia had goose flesh although the room was comfortable, artificially temperate. "Mrs. Keats, do you know someone named Joe Rizzo?"

"*Joe* Rizzo?" Charlotte touched a manicured hand to her neck. "Don't you mean Frank Rizzo, dear? What does he have to do with Campbell's death?" Disdain washed over the room like a wave.

Unconsciously, Sophia stood. "Actually, I do mean Joe Rizzo. No relation to Frank. He works at the quarry now. Well, he works for Red, O'Brien Constru—"

"I know who Red is. I'm not a trophy wife."

And no one said you were, thought Sophia. Martin shifted uncomfortably in his chair.

"Okay." Sophia bit back an apology. "Anyway, I was wondering if the name sounded familiar to you. Joe Rizzo."

"Not in the least. Well, besides that it's a Rizzo, which is unfortunate for the young man, being named after such an insufferable city official."

"Yes, well," Sophia, said, attempting to digest the gamut of personality traits Charlotte Keats had revealed since they'd arrived.

"Will that be all?" Charlotte asked. "I do have some things to attend to."

Martin stood obediently. Sophia felt like Lieutenant Columbo without the cigar and bad raincoat. She sat down again, and crossed her legs, feeling at once powerful and awkward.

"How is Zoë, by the way?" she asked casually.

"She's here, upstairs resting. Sumner Howard's daughter is here with her."

"Jane?" Sophia asked. *So, Jane doesn't deserve independent mention anymore, she's someone's daughter. Someone important.*

"Yes, Jane. You'd think that woman still summered here. When she was younger, she spent a lot of time—Jackson doted on that girl—it was really quite, well." Charlotte stood. The meeting was over.

"Why is Zoë here? Is she all right?" Sophia remained seated.

Charlotte nodded. "She's been staying here since the memorial, which I think is best, safest for everyone. But, she insists on going home tomorrow. Jane promised to stay with her in Center City. 'It's the least I can do, Mrs. Keats, after all your family has done for me,' she said to me. I'll say. And, as relieved as I am about Jane's departure, I just don't like the idea of Zoë staying alone in the big house downtown."

"And the dog, Max?" Sophia showed no signs of leaving.

"Oh he's here as well, tearing up my garden like a wild animal." As if on cue Sophia saw a red streak fly past the sitting room window. Max was probably in seventh heaven—the Keats mansion had a huge yard—although Sophia wondered if he missed Campbell. Maybe he was more Zoë's dog.

Then Sophia remembered the makeshift dog bed in the back of Campbell's Jeep. In that moment she felt more compassion for the dog than she did for Charlotte. She stood, thanked the woman for her time and followed Martin out of the house.

28

July 12^{th,} 3:11 a.m.

Zoë went into early labor. She sat bolt upright in bed and began to weep. Perhaps it was fear, physical pain, lack of sleep, stress, loss of her husband—there were many reasons for tears.

Jane heard her from the suite next door. They were in two rooms joined by a large bathroom, a part of the mansion's small guest wing that opened onto the back patio and swimming pool. Reluctantly, Charlotte had had the second guest room made up for Jane. The room had been hers years ago; the décor still reflective of Jane's taste. Jackson had insisted the room be kept as it was, as if his long lost daughter might return to the nest someday.

Zoë lay in the darkness remembering the early days of her life with her husband. The sun shone brightly throughout the summer months and family members literally frolicked in and out of the house. In the winter, the entire estate was decorated with tasteful Christmas lights. Single stem candles lit the windows of every bedroom and the overwhelming scent of pine and cinnamon permeated the senses. She'd considered herself so fortunate then. Fortunate to be married to a man who loved her, and to be a part of such a wealthy and prestigious family with roots and stability.

She'd long ago given up on her own parents, who flitted from one continent to the next, rarely to land in North America, never to stay more than a fortnight before heading off again. She had wanted something more secure, something traditional. Was that too much to ask? And now she was being punished for her superficiality and greed.

She was pregnant against her will; and she was now at the mercy of a cold and difficult woman.

She cried out in pain as another contraction shot through her body.

Jane sat on the edge of the bed. "How far apart are they?" Jane asked, reaching for her sports watch.

"I don't know. It hurts."

"We better tell Charlotte. You should get to the hospital."

"I don't want to. It hurts too much." Zoë's voice had transformed into that of a weak child, frightened and alone.

"You have to, it's time. I'll be there." Jane slid easily into her role as caretaker.

"But—" she cried. "God damn it that hurts." Zoë clutched her belly, willing the pain to subside. It did not obey.

"I know. Try not to think about it. Come on, can you sit up?"

Zoë screamed again. Her agony rang out into the corridor. Charlotte appeared at the door in a perfectly pressed raw silk robe and matching slippers.

"Oh, my, looks like you've beat me to it, haven't you, Jane?" Charlotte's voice was icy but thick with sleep. "I guess you heard our poor girl all the way through the bathroom walls. We'll have to do something about that." Charlotte's slippers clopped across the hardwood floors. She picked up a white phone. Campbell had named it the "Keats Courtesy Phone." Zoë thought of it more as the "Keats Spy Phone" but had never said as much.

"Yes, Mitchell. We'll need the car right away. Zoë's in labor. No ambulance. I said 'No.' Bring the car and come to the guest wing and help me. Now." Charlotte replaced the receiver with a definite click.

Zoë's overnight bag was still packed from her arrival that afternoon. Silently she held her belly waiting for the next wave.

Jane stood. "I'll get dressed."

Charlotte gave her a look. "Oh, here's Mitchell. Mitchell, her bag is there, make sure she gets in the car safely. I will meet you out front." Mitchell, of Charlotte's house staff, took over while Jane slid into the bathroom.

Within minutes they were in the car, Jane having buckled herself in next to Zoë, who was braced for the next contraction, the air laced with tension.

******

Chestnut Hill Hospital does not see much action, especially the emergency room, and rarely prominent families. This was the stuff of newspaper headlines. The staff came alive immediately. Their largest donor stood before the admitting desk, triple-strand pearls around her neck, a list of doctors to summon at the ready. Zoë was whisked away to a private room while the admissions staff got busy on the phone to Zoë's doctor, the Ob/Gyn on call, and probably the hospital administrator for all Zoë knew. The red carpet had come out; she'd ride it as long as she could.

Several hours and an epidural later, Zoë was actually giving birth. She was in a daze but saw Jane hovering over her. Somehow she had the sense that Charlotte was there too, sitting placidly in the far corner of the room. She had some recollection of raised voices as the anesthesiologist worked on her.

"...Not leaving her to... baby alone, Mrs. Keats." Jane's voice had been firm but calm.

" ...Not family, young lady. I'll kindly ask you to... I will stay with her."

"Hah, that's a laugh." Jane's voice raised an octave. "You'll never last in here."

"How dare you, you ingrate. Do you have any idea to whom you are talking? Fine. I'm not going to lower myself to argue with you. We'll both stay." Charlotte had acquiesced and Zoë saw a blurry image of her sitting on a side chair by the window, occasionally rummaging around in her purse. *Probably looking for smelling salts*, she thought, *or a handkerchief to cover her nose. Bitch.*

And then the baby was coming and there was no time for listening to others or focusing on blurry images in the corner of the room. She was numb but aware of her son making his way into the world. The pain was gone and had been replaced by a strange euphoria that only intravenous medication can achieve.

She tried to push when the voices told her to, tried to stop when they told her to do that, but mostly she just felt numb and fabulous and scared and overwhelmed and then she did feel something, something leave her body and then she was holding him, a tiny human being, covered in placenta and whatever else babies are covered in, and then he was snatched away from her and she fell asleep and dreamed of swimming in the ocean with Campbell on their honeymoon on Kauai.

29

Sophia tracked Martin down at his office. "She's had the baby," she said without introduction.

"She's not due for another month."

"I know. She went into early labor this morning."

"How did you—what happened?"

"I called the house this morning looking for Charlotte. The maid told me. She'll probably get fired. She even told me what hospital. Chestnut Hill, can you get here?"

"On my way. Is she alright?"

"She's fine. Resting. The baby was small though, five pounds or something. But the doctors say he'll be fine."

"Charlotte?"

"Pinched."

"So-phia."

"Well, she is pinched. But she's okay, I guess. It's Jane I'm worried about."

"Who?"

"Jane, Zoë's friend. Well, the family friend."

"Hmm, yes, Charlotte has some issues with her."

"That she does. Still, Jane seems to be the only one who is actually concerned about Zoë in all of this," she paused. "But I'm not too sure about her myself."

"Why's that Soph, classism raising its ugly blue-collar head again?"

"That's cute. No, she's hiding something. I think she's in love with Zoë. I

146

mean, you know, *in* love with her."

"Oh for Christ sake. That's ridiculous. Jane Howard is as conservative as they come. Can you keep your crazy theory to yourself for an hour? I'm on my way."

"Sure thing, Kemosabe." Sophia punched the end button on her phone and felt a shadow come over her. A waft of citrus hit her nose and she looked up into the statuesque presence of Jane Howard.

Both women were silent. They stared at each other. The hospital din was the kind of white noise that might have blocked out Sophia's conversation with Martin. Jane broke eye contact and moved to a bank of pay phones.

Sophia made an exaggerated point of walking away. She paced by the window and watched two young candy stripers giggling in the parking lot. They had just piled out of a Mercedes SUV and were galloping up the driveway with long limbed, well-tanned bodies their hair flapping against their backs like manes. *Great genes abound in Chestnut Hill*, Sophia thought.

She turned to watch Jane on the telephone. The woman balanced a date book on one knee, and held the phone receiver in the crook of her neck.

"...Unavoidable family emergency... Don't know when I will be back... Soon as possible of course."

Sophia moved closer to the pay phones, stopping at a strategically placed water fountain for a long drink.

Jane's voice had softened, her tone conciliatory, her hands still. "Yes, Ted, yes. I know. Well, the merger is all set. Leigh can handle the paperwork. She's ready. Yes, I know. Look, it can't be helped. What? Oh, my aunt, she's in the hospital. Right. Thanks. No, look she doesn't like fanfare. I'll tell her though. Thanks, right. Talk to you soon, right. I'll be on email if you need me. Bye. I will, right. Okay. Bye." She hung up.

Sophia stepped forcefully on the fountain foot pedal and got a huge mouthful of tooth-numbingly cold metallic Philadelphia water. She wiped her mouth and felt her cheeks deflate as the drink forced its way down her gullet. Jane was watching her as she moved away from the phone.

Sophia smiled at her with every numb tooth in her mouth. "Sounds like she's going to be okay," she began. "And the baby is doing well too, so I hear." She gave Jane a gentle pat on the arm. "Isn't it wonderful? You know, in the face of this tragedy to find joy."

"Yes. Wonderful." Jane eyed her suspiciously. "You know, you sound a little like a Hallmark card. I wouldn't think that was your style."

"Ah, well, everyone's a sucker for a baby, right?" Sophia looked around, leaned in to Jane. "Zoë is lucky to have a friend like you, someone who could leave her job, come to stay indefinitely, someone who was around on the holiday weekend. Guess you're used to things at the Keats mansion—I hear you've spent a lot of time there." *And,* Sophia thought, *you lied to your boss about why you're still here.*

Jane smiled knowingly. "Charlotte has always resented me, but Jackson was like a father to me, an uncle. Campbell was jealous too, after all, I was the only girl."

Not really, thought Sophia, *since you're not even a blood relative. Really, Charlotte is the only "girl."*

"We're the only family Zoë has. Did she tell you about her parents?"

Sophia nodded, wondering about Jane's word choice—"*we're* the only family."

"All I know," Jane continued, "is I am not leaving Zoë's side until they catch this killer. She could be in danger too. No one—especially Charlotte—seems to care about that."

She had a point there. "Haven't the police been keeping an eye on her, the family?" Sophia gestured to the officer sitting—or rather sleeping—outside Zoë's suite. "Never mind," she said when she saw the man was asleep. "I see your point."

Jane nodded. "I'm sure I'm just being overly protective, but—"

"Hey, at least someone is," Sophia said, still confused about the mix of emotions she felt toward Jane Howard. "I'm sure Zoë really appreciates the emotional support. God knows she's not getting that from Charlotte. In the meantime, I'll try to catch a killer."

Jane's face went dark with fear. A thin smile crossed her lips as she turned towards Zoë's suite. Sophia moved towards the elevators and heard Jane behind her. She was waking up the officer and the tone of her voice was forceful. It was the voice of a woman used to getting her way. It was the same tone Sophia had heard—muffled from the vestibule—in Zoë's home days earlier. And, interestingly, the same tone Charlotte used.

148

30

July 13th, 9:10 a.m.

In the morning cool, Charlotte Keats walked in the garden. She clipped a few roses, some hydrangea, and carried them to the kitchen in a large flat basket. The scent was mesmerizing. Hydrangea had always seemed gaudy to Charlotte—the smell overpowering, the plant too sturdy and strong, full and abundant. But Jackson had loved the pastel flowered bushes and had insisted they maintain them. Charlotte wondered when the gardener would ask her if she wanted them removed. The plants had flourished since her husband's death. And the small Asian man still came twice a week to tend them and the rest of the flora. Kwon had been a member of the family longer than Charlotte herself. He spoke no English but had a gentle, golden touch. The garden was rich and ripe with color, clipped and smooth with design. Charlotte imagined he understood. She would keep the hydrangea.

Today, she cut a few blooms and was assaulted by the smell, the memory of Jackson. She put the flowers in a majestic crystal vase and set it on Jackson's desk in the library, infusing the air with aroma, shocking the room's earth tone colors of rust, green and gold with an explosion of pastel.

She drew the drapes against a sharp and blinding sun casting odd shadows against the wood's grain. When Jackson was alive, he used to sit behind the huge mahogany desk smoking cigars, reading, working, always silent and steady. She closed her eyes to prolong the memory.

Across the room, Charlotte sat back on a plush overstuffed chair that promoted napping and poor posture. She allowed herself to sink into it, surprised as her body relaxed into the down pillows. With the house staff off and Zoë at the hospital, she had the house to herself. She was both relieved for and overwhelmed by the solitude.

The note sat on a silver tray, folded neatly in fours. It was a single sheet of plain white paper, like the typewriter paper she used to get for Campbell and Clayton every September. Her sons called it computer paper; typewriters were relics to them.

They would all go to Chestnut Hill Stationery and spend twice as much for binders, paper, notebooks and pencils than the boys' classmates. Their mothers, or staff, went to Woolworth's or Rite Aid and bought in bulk. Charlotte delegated many tasks to her staff but the purchase of back-to-school supplies wasn't one of them. And, after making their purchases, they would walk a short distance down Germantown Avenue to the ice cream parlor. They'd listen for trolley cars to see who would hear the tram first. Campbell was always more alert than his brother to the familiar wheeze, clank and spark of an oncoming trolley. Charlotte allowed them to eat in the car once a year, on back-to-school shopping day, and they would get chocolate ice cream all over themselves, their clothes and the blanket Charlotte had laid out in the back seat of the car. It was a small ritual, but one which she remembered with fondness. As children, they were so much easier. One year she even got ice cream for herself and the boys had squealed with delight, amazed to see their mother's indulgence.

Charlotte leaned forward in her chair. Next to her sat an antique side table adorned with a brass lamp. And, on a silver tray next to that sat the note, its sharp-cornered edges harsh against the flowery, ornate tray on which it sat. She'd read it several times since this morning and could almost recite the content from memory. She opened it again and her back stiffened against the plush folds of the chair. She mouthed the words silently as she read:

Your family is growing. Now you have two grandchildren. But, you will never know your first. You will not be allowed to ruin another life.

This could not get out. She picked up the phone and dialed. "Can you come to the house? It's urgent. Yes, now." She hung up softly and stood, smoothing her gardening clothes. She would shower and change, that would shorten the wait. She went to leave the room but turned back, knocking the silver tray to the floor with a heavy clang. She left it simmering like a cymbal, snatched up the note and made haste to the wall safe.

The safe was hidden behind another of Jackson's passions, the art of the late nineteenth century. The Jean François Millet painting was worth hundreds of thousands of dollars. Charlotte had often wondered aloud why he'd want a rendering of such crude people—peasants. He'd always answer the same way: "Realism, my dear. And there but for the grace of God go I. Besides," and he'd chuckle, "don't you think it's ironic that I use it to cover the safe? Where's your sense of humor, dear?"

Charlotte preferred the more carefree, delicate, sophisticated works of the Impressionists and had filled the rest of the house with other priceless originals. Her living room boasted the vivacious charm of Renoir's celebrations and the unmistakable atmosphere of Monet's points of light. The wall safe stared at her, it's numbered dial positioned on zero, just as she'd left it. She opened the safe and placed the note inside, along with the others.

******

Martin was used to being summoned by Charlotte Keats. But he wondered about his lover. Charlotte was the client, so he'd go, but he felt the conflict in his gut and wondered when, all of the sudden, he'd gained a partner. In the span of a week, he and Sophia had fallen back into a comfortable but exciting rhythm. The momentum of the case kept them in constant contact, and in work mode. The intellectual stimulation was as intoxicating as the sex. He felt like a whirling dervish though, not stopping to breathe, to watch where he was going, or warn the rest of the world. Like with every physics experiment he'd ever done, there would be a reaction—an equal and opposite reaction.

He parked by the back door and let himself in through the kitchen. He moved to the library, knocked softly and entered without waiting for a reply. Charlotte sat at Jackson's old mahogany desk, her pale skin framed by a bouquet of purple and blue. Martin started seeing her there, a ghost in shimmers of light that forced through the curtains. The room was dark and cool; it felt formal and cavernous compared to the rest of the world. He was grateful he'd dressed business casual—sport jacket, polo shirt, slacks—and not Saturday casual. The day threatened another record—the upper-nineties. Outside, the skies looked like cotton candy, an almost unnatural shade of flawless blue. Martin had passed hundreds of bikers, joggers, and volleyball players on his drive to Charlotte's. He'd taken Kelly Drive, telling himself it would be faster than the expressway. Surely there would be a back up of some kind on I-76, there often was. But as he wove past the Art Museum, the boathouses and sculptures, slowing for the occasional jaywalking Philadelphian taking advantage of the summer weather, he looked to his left and saw traffic moving smoothly along the highway. He would have done anything to be stuck in a ten-car pile up right now, anything to prolong the journey.

He stood over the desk and whispered Charlotte's name. She nodded and rose. She would tell him when she was ready. The scene was set for that. Charlotte Keats' guard was as down as he'd ever seen it. And seeing that, he knew Sophia would not be there, nor would Charlotte allow him to share this with her. He felt his chest constrict.

"I must show you something," she said.

She went to the far wall and stopped in front of a painting. Martin remembered it as one of Jackson's favorites. And, he knew the safe was housed behind the canvas. Charlotte spun the dial with manicured hands and the safe clicked open, softly shedding light into the room. Charlotte handed Martin a gray oversized envelope, unsealed, its flap tacky to the touch.

"What is this? Another one?" he asked.

She nodded. "From that horrible man Ronald Scott. *He* killed my son. When will the police figure that out? When Martin?" She slammed the safe door shut and went back to Jackson's desk.

Martin followed her, sat on a side chair and shook the envelope contents on the desk. A pale blue petal fell from the bouquet and flitted to the floor. He began to read.

"Oh my God. Charlotte. Another grandchild? Have you shown these to the police?" He put down the note.

"No. Why should I? Zander knows."

"How can they be from—?"

"It doesn't matter. That man killed my son. That's all there is to it."

"Then what, Charlotte? What do you want me to do?"

"I don't know Martin. I just couldn't stand it any longer. One came this morning. That one." She gestured to the table.

He picked up the white sheet, waved it at her. "This is a threat Charlotte. You could be in danger. Or Zoë, or Campbell, Jr."

"I know that. That's why the police must arrest that man."

"What if he's not the one? What if this—?"

"He is the one. I want him arrested. I want this to stop."

"I think we should tell the police. We need to show them these notes. We ought to have done it sooner."

"No. Can you imagine the press?" She stood and stiffened. "They just need to put him away. And, you are not to tell your girlfriend, Sophia."

Martin looked shocked.

"Do you think I'm an idiot?" she asked. "I had two sons. I know what is going on between you two. Let me tell you something Martin Duncan, if you want to keep your job, you will remember our attorney-client relationship."

He hated when clients threw that in his face, as if attorneys couldn't possibly remember that the most sacred of oaths on their own. "And what do you want me to do about the note then?" he asked.

"You are going to continue to help me. You and Zander. And that's all there is to it. These notes are private." She looked him square in the eye. "And Ronald Scott will spend the rest of his miserable life in prison. Period."

31

July 13th, 2:15 p.m.

The flowers sat outside her apartment door. One dozen long stemmed red roses in a box with baby's breath and ferns. She started to call Martin to thank him, and then remembered Joe Rizzo had said something about sending her flowers. Might they be from Joe? If so, how had he gotten in her building? Her neighbors were as careful about letting in strangers as she was.

Maybe they were delivered to the front step, a neighbor saw them and put them outside her door. There was no cardboard box around the vase though, no packing material. Just a simple bouquet, her name scrawled on the card in block letters. The handwriting was not Martin's, she realized. And there was no message, just her name. Sophia did not get a lot of flower deliveries, but she had *seen* them before. This looked personal. She trembled.

The phone rang in her hand and she picked up, wary, half expecting it to be Rizzo, asking if she liked the flowers, as if he'd known she just got them.

"Hey, it's me." Martin's voice was cell-phone shaky.

"Hey." She breathed deeply but didn't feel better. "What's up? Where are you?"

"On my way back to the office from a meeting. Just wanted to say 'hi.'"

"Well, hi. What meeting? It's Saturday."

"Oh no big deal, a different client, Whitehouse asked me to handle it," he said. "What about you? How's your day?"

Sophia wondered whether to tell him about the flowers. Part of her wanted to; maybe he'd send her some next time. Another part of her wanted to slap the first part. No self-respecting grown woman *needs* her boyfriend to send her flowers, nor should she feel wanting because he does not. She said nothing.

"Soph? You there?"

"Oh, yeah, sorry. Good, my day's good. Just working."

"Okay, well listen, I'm pulling into the garage now so I'm going to lose you. I'll see you tonight."

"Sure, see you later."

She stared at the card. Martin would have asked if she'd gotten the flowers, asked if she liked them. Besides, he would never have delivered them himself, she realized. He'd have called Willow & Reed and had them do it. A dozen long-stemmed red roses. She knew. Joe Rizzo had written it himself, delivered the flowers himself, been at her doorstep.

She looked through the box for another note, something identifying the sender. She found nothing.

She did have a boyfriend, didn't she? But, that wasn't it. She had been down that road before with Martin and it was paved with Kleenex and Ben & Jerry's New York Superfudge Chunk. The break-up had been tough, a lot of crying, too much ice cream, and then—when she'd come down from the sugar high—introspection, big issues, values, what about children, the importance of money, prestige. Joe Rizzo was different. And attractive. What might be down *that* road?

What about the investigation? He was, technically, in it. Was he a suspect? No. But, she had to figure out why seeing Rizzo had alarmed Zander Jarvis. Martin had given her his take on it. Yes, in fact he had explained it away with a flourish. She put the flowers in the kitchen and sat down at her desk. Her mail was in an angry pile next to the computer and her rent was late. Sophia logged on to the Internet, paid some bills, and tried to clear her head with mundane tasks.

******

Martin looked at the phone after he disconnected. Call time: 00:48. Not even one minute. He'd have to talk to her more tonight, and the longer they talked the more time would pass without his telling her what he knew. About what it might mean for Charlotte, Campbell's death. And, yet he couldn't tell her anything.

Martin descended into the parking lot's depths, finally found a space and slid his car into the tight opening. *Poetic justice*, he thought. Had he really needed the Seven Series BMW? Regan had thought so, surprising him with it when he got the partnership. He had a new Pennsylvania license plate, the "You've Got a Friend" grammar fiasco a thing of the past. For a time the state's motto had been a poorly constructed phrase, today it was utilitarian: "Keystone State." Martin's vanity plate said "PRTNR-3," special order by Regan Whitehouse Duncan. She'd found the double meaning clever. Partner in law, partner in marriage (although their marriage was anything but a partnership) and "3" for number of years they'd been married at the time. It was vain and ostentatious, and Martin had loved it because Regan had. Because he had arrived. Or so he'd thought. Today, he wanted to destroy the car, ding its doors in small parking spaces, mar the wax sheen by parking under trees, near pigeons. He wanted to take paint and write random numbers and letters over the sharp yellow PRTNR-3 that announced itself every time he opened the trunk.

He grabbed his briefcase, activated the alarm and took the elevator to his office, the halls a summer Saturday quiet.

32

"Police have made an arrest in the brutal murder of Campbell Whitmore Keats, son of philanthropist Charlotte Keats and the late quarry owner and industry pioneer Jackson Keats. Ronald Scott of Whitemarsh Township has been charged with the crime. Scott allegedly killed Keats at the Keats Quarry on Thursday July Fourth between nine p.m. and midnight. In 1989, Scott served one year of a three-year sentence on a first-degree misdemeanor and has a history of mental illness including institutionalization to treat paranoid schizophrenia. Police are calling this swift arrest an example of our legal system at...."

Sophia turned off the evening news in shock and went to answer the door. Martin stood, grinning ear-to-ear holding a bouquet of flowers.

"Did you hear?" He pecked her cheek. "It's over, they got Scott! These are for you. Great job." He handed her the flowers.

Yes, she thought, *they got Scott, but did they get the killer?* "I didn't really do anything," she said closing the door, "but thank you."

He followed her into the kitchen. She stopped short when she saw the roses. His flowers were a lovely multi-colored arrangement, a floral celebration, but they were not red roses, the flowers of love, passion, courtship.

Martin came up behind her. "Well, looks like someone beat me to it. Where did those come from?" His voice was unnaturally steady, his mouth clenched.

"Oh, these. I meant to tell you before, I think they're from that guy Rizzo."

"What?" His jaw tap-danced, tooth against tooth.

"Yeah, it's no big deal, he just sent me flowers. I'm not interested in him or anything," she lied. She was actually quite interested in him, in a way she couldn't figure out. On the one hand, he was sexy, family-oriented, even. On the other hand, what was his connection to the Keats case? How did he get her address, get into her building?

"Oh," Martin said drawing thick eyebrows toward his nose.

"Actually it's kind of," she searched for the word, something that wouldn't startle him, "off-putting to tell you the truth." *Why do I care what you think?* she wondered, explaining herself anyway. "They were outside my door. The flowers."

"You mean out front, downstairs, right?" Martin had already made clear his oppressive concern about her building's safety.

Last summer, a woman had been attacked across the street in Fitler Square. The neighborhood went on alert. In the end, the attacker had been the victim's ex-boyfriend. A domestic dispute. It could have happened anywhere, even in the comfort of the victim's own home. Her ex- had simply chosen the park.

"No, actually outside this door." She motioned toward the front door of the apartment.

"Jesus Christ, Sophia! Off-putting? I'd say it's more than that."

And yet another linguistic failure between Mars and Venus, she thought.

"Hey, if you'd done it, we wouldn't be having this conversation right?" She felt defensive of Rizzo, although she didn't know why. Maybe it was just resistance to Martin's concern. "Martin Duncan, respectable lawyer delivers flowers to his girlfriend's doorstep, isn't that romantic?" She stopped, huffy.

He ran his fingers through his hair. "You're right. I'm sorry, it's just, what do you know about this guy?"

"You mean his *ilk,* Martin, is that what you mean?" *Here comes the class issue rearing its ugly head again,* she thought. "He's a fine person," she said. And then, almost an afterthought, "Although, I never did give him my address." She wished she could take the words back.

"What?!" Martin was incredulous.

"Well, I am listed." Again, she was defending a man who had effectively invaded her privacy and made presumptions about their relationship.

"Yeah, and so is the Queen of England, but you don't just pop over. There are ways to do things. Etiquette," he said.

"Aha, so that's what's bothering you. He's rough around the edges. He's not reading Emily Post. He's making up the dating rules as he goes along. Well Martin, we can't all be well-bred." She snapped and left the room. She was angrier than the conversation merited.

Martin followed her into the living room. "What was that about?"

"I don't know. It's just the snobbery. I've had enough." Sophia folded her arms across her chest.

Martin sighed. "Not this again."

"I'm sorry. But, you're, well, you are part of that world." She softened her tone, "I think it's just Charlotte though, this whole thing, the case, the feeling I have that for some reason, Campbell was killed because of his privilege."

"What are you talking about? Ronald Scott killed Campbell. You saw the news. Maybe he did kill him because of that, but I think the guy is just crazy." Martin twirled a finger at his temple. The universal, and oh-so-politically-correct, sign for mental illness. "Maybe he *was* jealous of the Keats' success. Can't you just leave it alone?"

Sophia looked at him. He was breathing hard and sweat glistened on his forehead. Martin still had a thick head of hair, but he'd brushed it back earlier, in frustration, and it clung to his scalp now slicked away from his face.

He looked different, ominous.

"Are you all right? You're all sweaty. What's the matter with you?" she asked.

"Nothing. I just don't want to fight with you, Sophie. I'm worked up that's all. This Rizzo guy, the case. I was so excited to have it be over and I came here to celebrate with you and you're not with me on it." He sat down.

"You're right," she said. He looked hopeful and then not. "I'm not with you on it. I need to think things through a little more. I need to work it through. I'm sorry, Martin," she said, "I need some time alone."

And their dance began again in earnest. She knew he would leave. Reluctantly, but he would go. This time, she didn't know if she wanted him to come back.

He left quietly, angry, after placing the flowers on the kitchen counter next to the roses. The flowers he'd brought, still in their green tissue, were tied with a purple bow. Two packets of Flower-Last, a floral preservative, were attached to the wrapper. She found a vase, dissolved a packet of Flower-Last in water and arranged them, a huge assortment of tulips, irises, snapdragons, and alstroemeria framed with deep green lemon leaves. She looked at the roses: simple, elegant, beautiful. She decided to put the other packet of Flower-Last in that vase and moved it to the sink. She gathered the stems gingerly, avoiding the thorns and lifted them out of the vase. A white card fell from between the stems, and landed on the floor with a soft thud. It was damp, having fallen into the bouquet to rest on a piece of fern. She picked up the card and smiled.

Rizzo probably wrote a private note that only she would see, figuring a nosy neighbor might read a visible card. She opened it and read:

These are for your funeral. You're next.

33

Sophia rose early Sunday morning.

In the middle of the night, unable to sleep, she'd stripped the sheets to purge Martin's smell from her bed. She still slept poorly. Getting flowers for your own funeral will do that to a person. Luigi, on the other hand, had made a meal of the roses' baby's breath, batting the cheap filler around like a dead mouse. Between his antics and her fear, Sophia was wide-awake at six a.m. She didn't want to be.

If you're going to threaten someone with flowers, have the decency to cut the filler. She tossed the whole lot, the roses, the baby's breath and ferns in the garbage chute and went down for the newspaper.

The Philadelphia Inquirer had a front-page story on Ronald Scott's arrest. The story featured a photo of Scott looking terrified—or crazy—depending on your bias, and was positioned next to a professionally done portrait of Campbell Keats, handsome and full of promise. Sophia read the story and then went for a long bike ride. The city had that sleepy Sunday morning feel about it. She rode out to the art museum, where a special Rembrandt exhibit was opening that afternoon. She looped the Drives and by the time she was home again, the day had shaken off its cobwebs.

The apartment was quiet; at least no one had been there since she'd gone. The windows were still locked, tape across the doorjamb intact. She wanted to be home. Wanted to stay home. While riding she'd allowed herself to think about the day and the overwhelming need she felt to confront Charlotte Keats. But, she didn't want to leave the sanctuary of her apartment. She'd been violated last night, threatened. Who was this killer? And was she really next?

Yet, she was pumped for a fight and relieved she'd gotten rid of Martin the night before. She didn't want to think about him, the emotions of it. She needed to be angry, not afraid. She needed to take action. She thought about getting in the car, heading out to Chestnut Hill. But Charlotte was still the client, and it was Sunday morning. The courtesy of a phone call was the least she could do.

The truth was, she just did not want to go out. *How can I be a good PI if I am scared of my own case? Get a grip.* She picked up the phone. "Hello. This is Sophia Gold, is Mrs. Keats in please?" Where would the woman be anyway at this time? Maybe church, but surely she'd not be gone long?

"No, ma'am she's not. This is Ginny. Is there something I can help you with?"

Sophia remembered the woman who had served her lemonade. It seemed like years ago. It had been just over a week.

"Hello Ginny. How are you?"

"Fine ma'am, and you?"

"Ginny. Please, don't ma'am me. It makes me feel a hundred years old. Call me Sophia."

"Yes ma'am. Sophia."

"When will Mrs. Keats be back? I'm on my way to see her."

"Oh, she's gone for the entire day. She's at church, and then going to a benefit at the art museum with Mr. Jarvis."

"With whom?" Sophia asked, surprised.

"Oh, it's a new exhibit, I think, the Keats Foundation is sponsoring it and there's an opening today. She does a lot of work at the museum." Ginny hadn't heard the question.

"I see," Sophia said. "Did you say she was with Zander Jarvis?"

"Yes, ma'am—Sophia. She sent for him early this morning."

Sophia wondered if she'd *sent* for Martin as well. They'd all be together again—The Three Musketeers. She felt a chill. Maybe she should get in the car, go to the museum, and break up their little party. She felt impulsive, out of control. She didn't like it.

"So, Ginny." She sat down; willing herself to relax, think before acting. "I saw the paper this morning. They arrested Ronald Scott. Mrs. Keats must be relieved to have this over with. You all must be."

"Yes, we are. It was frightening. Especially the notes. I imagine there won't be any more of those." Ginny was multi-tasking. Sophia could hear water running and dishes clattering.

"Yes," she said. Then it registered. "Notes? What notes?"

"Oh—I thought you knew. I really shouldn't say." Ginny's regret was tangible. "Oh dear God," she whispered. The water sounds stopped.

"Ginny. You can tell me. I won't say anything," Sophia said quickly. "Listen, I'm on my way to the house. Can I talk to you when I get there?" No response.

"I'll be gone. I have the afternoon off, and tomorrow too," Ginny said and gave a nervous laugh. "Mrs. Keats gave me an extra day off." Silence.

Shit. Sophia would have to keep her on the phone. She could do this. She didn't have to run around like a crazy person. It was about time she learned that. Her knee-jerk reaction to stress and problems, was to act, go, move, do. She wasted a lot of time and energy that way.

"So, you have the day off tomorrow, that's nice," Sophia said wondering if she sounded as stupid as she felt. Who gives a shit about a day off? What about the notes?

"Yes, ma'am." The ma'am was back, but that was the least of Sophia's worries. "I haven't had a Monday off in thirty years," Ginny said.

"Why do you think Mrs. Keats decided to give you the day off?"

"Who knows anymore." She stopped. "Oh dear, there I go again. I'll just say she's been through so much; maybe she wants the house to herself for a change, to be alone. Can't say's I blame her."

"Ginny?" Sophia paused.

"Yes?" Her voice faltered.

"Tell me about the notes. I'm trying to help find Campbell's killer."

"I can't talk to you anymore about that."

"Was Charlotte getting threats?" Sophia pressed.

"I need this job. Mrs. Keats will never forgive me." Ginny sounded close to tears.

"She'll never know. I won't tell her where the information came from, unless I absolutely have to, legally. What if the wrong man is being charged with Campbell's death? The Keats family could still be in danger." And of course there's always justice.

"You mean? I thought Ronald Scott wrote those notes." Ginny sounded shocked.

Sophia had to fight from snapping at her. *What notes!?* "That's just it. I don't know. He may have. Charlotte never told me about any notes. Don't you find that odd, Ginny? She hired me to investigate her son's death. Don't you think she would have told me, given me every clue, every opportunity to find the killer?"

Ginny was silent. She probably cared about Campbell a great deal more than she did Charlotte.

"Ginny," Sophia asked, gripping the receiver like her life depended on it, and it probably did, "how long have you been with the Keats family?"

"Over thirty years," she said. "Clayton was in diapers." Her voice clouded with tears. "Poor boy. He died so young."

Campbell died young too, Sophia thought. *Isn't that who we've been talking about all this time?*

"And Campbell?" Sophia asked.

"I cared for him too," Ginny's voice changed, "He was a hellion, that child."

"Campbell was?"

"Oh well…. " Ginny's conscience was like a living breathing organism. "He was just always into something. Mischief. Even had the police here once or twice. Boys will be boys, I suppose, but his little brother was such an angel. Poor Clayton. He was just—"

"Yes?"

"He just couldn't make it in this family."

"I thought he died in a boating accident."

"Oh, he did. But somehow, I think he just gave up. Charlotte was so hard on them both. Campbell, he was tough. He had lots of friends, other rich boys with time and money to burn. But Clay, he needed love and support, encouragement. He was a gentle child." She blew her nose quietly.

"Ginny, please, tell me about the notes."

The woman sighed. Sophia heard the scraping of a chair against tile. That was a good sign. She was sitting down. "Well, there were several, I think. Only one or two that I saw, but maybe more. One was just the other day. It was in the flower basket. The one Mrs. Keats uses. She's the only one who uses it, but I moved it from the greenhouse to the back porch for her. I've been worried about her and it was my day off the next day so I—"

"Uh huh, so the note?" Sophia interrupted.

"Right, so the note was there. I didn't know what to do. It had to be for her. She's the only one who—well I didn't open it, but it was the same paper. The same as before."

"Before when?" Sophia asked, trying not to scream.

"Oh maybe a month or so. I guess it was May or June, I'm not sure. I know it upset her because she went immediately to the library and locked the door behind her. I could hear her—" Ginny stopped herself, embarrassed. "Well, I couldn't help it, but I could hear her open the safe. She put it in the safe; at least I think she did. Then she made a phone call. But I didn't listen," Ginny protested, "I didn't. I don't know who she called."

"It's okay, Ginny. This is helpful. Don't worry. You're doing the right thing by telling me." Sophia thought for a moment. "When did the last note come? What day was that?"

Ginny paused, "Well, the staff day off is Saturday, so it would have been Friday. It may have been before that, but I doubt it. The gardener comes on Thursdays and he would have seen it. I mean it was right there in plain sight."

So, it was someone who knew the schedule. Or who got very lucky. How difficult would it be to find out when the staff was there? Sophia thought it through. Watch the place for a week or two; homes like the Keatses' tend to be run like businesses. There is nothing random about when the gardener comes, the pool man, the maid. Charlotte would have a fixed schedule, one likely to be rigid, even in the wake of her son's murder.

"I really must be going," Ginny said suddenly. "I'm due at my daughter's this evening and I have the laundry to finish here."

"Ginny, where do you live?" Sophia asked. *Did it matter?*

"Why here, of course…"

Maybe it does, she thought.

"In the carriage house out back, but on my days off, if I have an overnight, I go to my daughter's over in Camden. She has a new baby, just a year old this month." She sounded light again, joyful. Sophia remembered Ginny as a beautiful, older black woman with gleaming white teeth and a clear complexion. She wondered if Ginny would have been hired had she been darker-skinned, or at all today, now that Jackson was gone.

"I really need to speak with Charlotte. When can I do that?" Sophia asked.

"She'll be gone all day," Ginny replied.

Yes, you already told me. "What about tomorrow morning?"

"She's always home on Monday mornings, she does paperwork and such. Never misses." Ginny sounded worried.

"Okay. I need to speak with her about the case but I will not tell her what we talked about. Trust me Ginny." Sophia hoped she wasn't lying. "Whatever happens, we cannot send an innocent man to jail."

34

Why had Charlotte lied to her about the notes? Clients lied all the time, but rarely about something so potentially important. They lied about minor things—lies of omission usually. Threatening notes were not minor. Or, Sophia thought with sudden clarity, clients lied about things they wanted to hide. What was Charlotte hiding?

This was more than control, this was conscious, calculated.

Sophia thought back to her first impressions of the woman. Charlotte Keats' primary concern had been, on the surface, for her son, but something else was at play. She wanted secrecy, she wanted to keep the media out of the investigation, she mistrusted the police.

Charlotte's need for control was one thing, but how much was she guiding the investigation? Had she hired Sophia for her expertise or to manipulate her? And perhaps with that to guide the press, the police, the ultimate "guilty" party for this crime. Jackson Keats had used the media in the past. Maybe the answer was in the press, and in the past. She thought about firing up her computer and searching the Internet but she needed greater access, greater *physical* access. She needed to touch the newspapers and magazines, to smell the telltale odor of history. Sophia was out the door in minutes.

******

The Free Library of Philadelphia main branch sits majestically on Logan Circle, just yards from Sophia's favorite haunt, The Rodin Museum.

Logan Circle is a charming park—smack in the middle of Benjamin Franklin Parkway—a roundabout with benches and trees and an oversized fountain in the center. The Circle marks the spot for many of the city's cultural haunts—like The Franklin Institute, where Sophia learned about electricity and raced through the giant human heart exhibit, and The Academy of Natural Sciences, where she marveled at the life-like stuffed bears, lions and buffalo. Of course, there's also the incongruous Philadelphia Juvenile Courthouse. Yet another anomaly in a city full of them.

Sophia was a frequent library visitor, both for business and pleasure. She knew the guards by name and the various locations of archival information, periodicals, literature, non-fiction, art and an impressive collection of old LPs. Her introduction to jazz—John Coltrane— had come about one rainy Sunday afternoon at the library. She'd closed the place, headphones on, lost in a new sound.

Today she breezed through the security entrance, nodded hello to Sam— the man had been on Sunday patrol since Sophia was a girl—and made her way to the newspaper archives.

Hours later, after a combination of microfiche, paper archives, and reluctantly, Web surfing, Sophia had a clearer picture of Campbell Keats. The Keats family's media savvy dated back decades before the *Fortune* magazine spread, which was by the way, impressive PR. Why hadn't she done this in the first place? She had been as mesmerized by Charlotte Keats as anyone.

Reading between the lines, Sophia deduced that Campbell had been a very bad boy. Several stories, often front page, reported on escapades of Campbell's youth—even borderline criminal activity—only to disappear in subsequent issues of *The Philadelphia Inquirer* or *The Daily News*. One story about Campbell struck a particular chord, if only for its geography. There had been an altercation between Campbell, Zander Jarvis and some local "South Philadelphia residents." Zander wasn't mentioned by name—merely as a prominent justice's grandson— but it had to have been Zander. Sophia knew his history too; his grandfather had been a Philadelphia legend in his own right, and certainly powerful enough to keep his son's name out of the papers. The South Philadelphia residents were unnamed. Had Rizzo been among them? The so-called "altercation" had taken place outside The Saloon restaurant on 7th Street where one of the locals worked. There was no follow-up story. Sophia could have checked with Tariq to see if charges had been filed but she knew the answer would be "No."

She then checked philanthropic activities immediately after each of these events. Invariably, the Keats family—namely Charlotte—followed Campbell's mishaps with unprecedented donations to this foundation or that, a new wing here or there—anything to divert attention and possibly, Sophia thought, to buy good press and bury the bad.

Charlotte Keats had been protecting her son and her husband's family name from day one. Perhaps it hadn't been Jackson behind the *Fortune* story after all. Maybe Charlotte was the engine of this public relations machine. The question was how far would she go to protect the Keats name? If Campbell's past had truly come back to haunt him, them, would she sacrifice her son to save face? Was Charlotte behind Campbell's death? Not having thought that was possible, Sophia choked on her thoughts. Could a mother murder her own child? She certainly hadn't done the deed; she would have hired someone to do it. Zander. Martin. Sophia flashed on the memory of them talking at Campbell's funeral. And what of the threats against her? The break-in. The flowers. The hang-ups. Was she doing her job too well? It couldn't be. And yet....

Suddenly, the library was stifling. Despite high open ceilings, cool marble floors and adequate air-conditioning, Sophia began to sweat. She felt faint. She gathered her papers and printouts, forwarded saved searches to her home email account and left the building. She had walked to the library and was grateful for the vacant time before arriving home. The streets are wide and expansive near Logan Circle; streetlights few and far between. She didn't know what to think; she could only feel. She was sick, angry, confused. She needed time to absorb what she'd seen, to test out her theory in her head, to let the dust settle.

Sophia spent the rest of the day at home resisting the urge to go, move, do, solve. She knew she needed time to process the case, the threats, this new information. Her alarm system in place—tape across the doorjamb—she locked herself in the apartment, pushed a credenza in front of the door for good measure. When she'd returned from the library, there had been two new hang-ups on her machine. She unplugged the phone. She didn't need to hear from anyone else today, especially her anonymous new friend, whoever it may be.

Thoughts of Martin with flowers, Charlotte's poise, Zander, Joe playing softball, Zoë's new baby, Jane at the hospital, Ronald Scott, and the funeral all flitted through her mind. She picked up around the apartment while listening to Billie Holliday and then switched to Lyle Lovett for major cleaning. She scrubbed and mopped and ran the vacuum, cleaned the kitchen and tossed out old condiments, crusty horseradish, moldy Kalamata olives and a jar of salsa, that when she opened it burned the insides of her nostrils.

Later, she opened a bottle of Valpolicella Ripasso she'd been saving to drink with Martin. She drank most of it with Ritz crackers and a hunk of Brie she hadn't the patience to soften. She blasted Emmy Lou Harris's *Wrecking Ball* and cried to Emmy Lou's renditions of Steve Earle's "Goodbye" and Jimi Hendrix's "May This Be Love." Luigi joined her on the couch, bathed, napped and kept her company through the tears. By the time the CD had run through Daniel Lanois' "Blackhawk" she was cried out, a little drunk and sick of sitting around. She got up off her ass and shut herself in the bathroom. An hour later she was scanning negatives of Matteo Rizzo catching pop flies in Wilson Park.

35

Monday morning, Sophia was ready to venture back into the world. She checked the window and door locks, put new tape across the doorjamb and gave Luigi an especially big hug. He was not amused and squirmed away, retreating under the bed.

She finally found her car, parked on Panama Street by Taney Playground. Saturday night isn't the best time to find parking in Center City. She had circled the area for ten minutes before slipping into a spot. She went to the trunk to stow her cameras. Never leave home without them, especially after a break-in and a death threat. With a pang of guilt she thought of Luigi. *No one is going to break in today*, she thought. *If they'd wanted to steal my possessions, they had their chance. Someone is just trying to scare me and it's working.*

She went to close the trunk and slipped on something. She looked down at her shoes, now covered in dark, slippery greasy liquid. She peered under the Saab, following a fresh trail of fluid up the street. She'd parked on an incline and there was no mistake, whatever it was, it was coming from her car. Sophia's stomach dropped. Someone had tampered with her car. *Why didn't I take auto shop in school,* she wondered? *A lot of good an art degree does me now.*

She popped the hood to check the engine. Sweat popped on her upper lip—liquid fear. *I don't even know what to look for. I pissed someone off recently, a former client; that guy I dated six months ago—what was his name—Jerry something?* Or, the more likely scenario, it had been the killer.

She thought of the flowers, the hang-ups, the break-in. *Someone is trying to kill me, just as they did Campbell Keats.*

She locked the Saab—a lot of good that would do—and walked up Pine Street to see her mechanic. Of all the conveniences one could hope for, it was an auto mechanic within walking distance. Vinnie Morano's shop had opened twenty years ago—also the last time the place had been cleaned. She peeked in the garage door through smudged glass and saw Vinnie leaning over the hood of a black Porsche Boxster.

"Yo, Vinnie," she called out. Music blared. He wasn't quite open for business yet, although, he never really was. Vinnie didn't encourage walk-ins.

Rather, he serviced a regular clientele in and around Fitler and Rittenhouse Squares. For many, owning a car was a luxury downtown, parking a fantasy. Sophia figured Vinnie made most of his money renting parking spaces on the side. His shop was full of rarely used expensive foreign-made cars buffed to a perfect shine available for their owners, day or night. Sophia knocked on the glass. Vinnie looked up and smiled, motioned to the side door and met her there, unlocking it from the inside.

"Oh, it's my favorite Italian detective. *Come va?*" he asked arms spread wide in an open hug. He kissed her cheeks, one side then the other.

"*Ciao,* Vinnie." Vinnie was teaching Sophia to speak Italian. Every time they saw each other he'd introduce a new word or phrase. He was a methodical man.

"*Oggi, facciamo le lezioni,*" he said definitively.

"Vinnie, sorry, I can't do lessons today. I've got a problem."

"Eh?" he asked, pretending he couldn't understand her.

"*Ho un problemma,*" she said slowly. He nodded. "*Con la macchina.*"

He smiled. His student was learning well.

"Vinnie, I can't do Italian right now. My car—there's a pool of something under it, grease or something. I think someone fucked with it." Suddenly she sounded stupid. She hadn't even tried to start the thing. Maybe it was fine.

Vinnie raised his eyebrows. "You kiss your momma with a mouth like that?" he asked, grinning. "Okay, I can see you're upset. *O Dio,* Sophia Bella, when are you gonna get a safe job? What about your pictures? Why don't you just take beautiful pictures?" he asked gesticulating as only an Italian can.

"Vinnie, I do photography, I do both," Sophia said, steeling herself. "Listen, I'm working on this case and I've been getting threats lately. I'm sure it's nothing. But you can never be too careful, right? Can you check it out for me? *Per favore?*"

"Threats? *Mamma mia, mi fai impaziere.*" Vinnie was already grabbing his tools.

"I know I drive you crazy Vinnie," she said, translating. "Listen I'm down by Taney Playground so you should lock up here first."

"*Madonna*," he grumbled. "Taney Playground." It was only a four block walk, but Vinnie wasn't nuts about exercise. "We'll take this baby." He patted the hood of the Porsche he'd been working on.

Sophia raised an eyebrow.

"They pay me to keep 'em running, how else am I gonna do that? Hop in."

Traveling at the speed of light, Vinnie pulled the Boxster into an empty driveway in front of the Saab. The driveway's town house looked deserted, its owners off making the all-mighty buck. The garage door had an official looking sign on it that said "DON'T EVEN THINK OF PARKING HERE." Vinnie gestured at the door, flicking his left hand under his chin, the Italian "fuck you."

Sophia laughed, got out of the car and pointed Vinnie to the back of her car. He looked at her hard and slid under the car with a flashlight. When he came out, he was not smiling.

"That's brake fluid," he said. "Somebody cut your brake line." He sat down wearily on the curb. "If I didn't know better, I'd say someone's trying to kill you. Good thing you were parked on this hill here. You'd've never seen the grease otherwise." Vinnie ran his grubby fingers through thick black hair. He looked up at Sophia.

"You're sure it's the brake line?" she asked softly.

Vinnie gave her a who-do-you-think-you're-dealing-with look and nodded. "Ey, I know what I'm talking about here," he said. "By the way, you should bring the car in more often, your brake fluid needed changing. See how dark it is there?" He pointed to the puddle. "That's not good."

Sophia gulped. She looked at the ground. "Yeah, I'll get right on that Vinnie. Change my brake fluid. Good idea." She sat down next to him on the curb.

"Scared now?"

She nodded. "I'm scared. But I'm close too. I'm going to get this asshole."

This time Vinnie didn't comment about her language.

"Listen, I really appreciate this," she said. "*Grazie mille.* You saved my life."

"No," he said, "*You* saved your life. If you hadn't seen that grease, you'd be out there right now, no brakes or nothin'." Vinnie gestured to the Schuylkill Expressway.

Stay-at-home mothers and nannies were flocking to Taney Playground across the street. The park butted up against the roar of the highway; an odd union of progress and pastime. City life.

Sophia felt sick. *Turn it into anger*, she thought. *Turn it into anger and find this asshole.* She had to get to the Keats mansion. She had to confront Charlotte about the notes.

She didn't have a car.

Vinnie read her mind. "Tell you what, take the Boxster. I'll tow the Saab to the shop and fix her up for you. Find this *bastardo*, make him pay."

Sophia was shaking her head. "I can't take this car Vinnie, what if someone sees me?" The Boxster gleamed and had a vanity plate that said "NOTGLTY." She figured it for a criminal defense attorney's. She definitely did not want to be seen driving it around the city.

"Take it already, the guy's in the Bahamas. You're my, eh, niece, for cryin' out loud." Vinnie smiled conspiratorially. "I can't let my niece borrow a car from my shop? Go already. Drop me at the shop. I'll take care of this." He pointed to the brake fluid.

Death grease, Sophia thought. *That stuff'll kill you, if it doesn't harden your arteries, it'll wreak havoc on your car.*

"Thank you." Sophia kissed his cheek. "So, what do I owe you Vinnie?" she asked.

He touched his cheek where she'd kissed him. "*Niente, cara.* Just be careful."

173

36

The Porsche hugged the road quite nicely, thank you very much. And the brakes were stellar. Crisis averted—for now.

Sophia made it to the Keats home by noon. She pulled in to the driveway as the Montgomery County Coroner was zipping up a body bag and heaving it into the back of a van. A single squad car sat idle, its driver hunched over a clipboard. She watched in shock as the black van pulled away without fanfare. The cop didn't even look up. Sophia pounded on his window.

"Ma'am?" he asked through the glass.

"Officer. What the hell happened here?" Sophia waved her arms toward the road.

"Watch your language please ma'am," the officer said getting out of the squad car.

What is wrong with these people? Is it really fucking important that I watch my language when another person is dead here? "Excuse me," Sophia said smiling through clenched teeth. "It looks like the medical examiner was just here, Officer Miller." She looked pointedly at his nametag. "Can you tell me what happened?"

"Who are you ma'am?" he asked, pen poised for report writing.

"I'm working for Mrs. Keats." Sophia showed the officer her PI license. *Just tell me who's dead damn it!* "Is it Mrs. Keats? What happened?"

"Mrs. Keats?" He laughed. "Oh, no, the maid I think. Looks like an OD. Pretty cut and dried."

Well, since it was the maid, who gives a shit, right? The maid. Ginny!

174

Sophia ran to the side of the house and saw yellow crime scene tape floating like Desert Storm ribbons around the carriage house. My God, how far would Charlotte go?

"Cut and dried my ass," Sophia said and stormed toward the house. Officer Miller shrugged, went back to his clipboard.

******

Sophia saw a silhouette in the library window next to the kitchen. Charlotte sat at the desk with perfect posture, a neat pile of papers at her side. Sophia remembered the library as a dark, cool room with large sofas, walls of leather bound books and a huge mahogany desk.

Sophia went to the kitchen door and, finding it unlocked, let herself in. She moved softly to the library. She heard Charlotte get up from the desk, her heels clicking on the hardwoods. Click, click, and then nothing—she must be on the carpet—click, click, and the library door opened.

"Hello Charlotte. I hear there's good and bad news," she said. "What happened to Ginny?"

Charlotte jumped. "What are you doing here? How did you get in the house?"

Sophia pushed her way into the room. "Well, I came to talk to you about the case. Little did I know Ginny would be dead when I got here. What happened? Who killed her? Couldn't have been Ronald Scott. That's the bad news. After all, he's already been arrested." Sophia was fuming. "That's the good news. By the way, I do hope the Rembrandt opening went well yesterday. So nice that you've been able to get on with your life."

Sophia had said a mouthful and was breathing heavily. She couldn't accuse Charlotte yet; she had no evidence and could still be in danger herself. She paced the room. The walls were adorned with paintings all in heavy, solid frames. She noticed a Thomas Eakins—perhaps Philadelphia's most famous 19th century artist—on one wall, a lone scull gliding across the Schuylkill River.

"Not that it's any of your business Miss Gold, but Virginia took her own life last night. She overdosed on sleeping pills. It had nothing to do with Ronald Scott. Perhaps the pressure got to her, perhaps she was unhappy. I don't know why she did it. We'll never know," Charlotte said evenly.

"She's been here thirty years. How can you not know anything about her? Was she suicidal? She didn't seem so to me!" Sophia shouted. She stopped short of explaining that she'd questioned Ginny, knew she'd had plans to see her grandchild, not kill herself.

Charlotte took a deep breath. "I will have that officer remove you from my home, young lady, and we can terminate this relationship right now," she said, gesturing outside. Officer Miller was still filling out reports in his squad car. "Do not speak to me in that manner. Lord knows I have been through enough."

"Yes, Lord knows," Sophia said and plopped down in an overstuffed chair. Despite her height she was suddenly engulfed in pillows.

Fine, she thought. *Don't tell me about Ginny, I'll get what I came for and get out.* She crossed her legs as forcefully as she could from mounds of down.

"I am surprised though, how did they finally get Ronald Scott? I understand he has a record. But for the murder, I mean. Was there some evidence I don't know about?"

Charlotte sharpened her gaze. "I see Martin told you about the notes."

"Martin?" Sophia asked, her stomach rising in her throat.

Charlotte's anger was a controlled heat. "I should have known he would betray me with pillow talk. Well, I suppose it's just as well. I will tell you about the notes. However, and I mean this," Charlotte almost spat the words, "I will have your license revoked if the police ever find out about these notes. Ronald Scott is already in custody. He has no alibi for the night of Campbell's murder and will be sent away for a very long time for what he did to my family. The man is crazy and the police know it."

Martin. Martin had known about these so-called notes all along. That bastard. Sophia hid her surprise well—let Charlotte think Martin had been the one. Fine. He should have been the one. Ginny was dead. She had confided in Sophia and now she was dead, possibly by Charlotte's hand. Poison would be Charlotte's style—no muss no fuss and the next best thing to a suicide overdose. Charlotte certainly had opportunity; the victim lived in her backyard. The matron was still talking and then click, click, clicking to one of the many paintings on the wall. Sophia turned to watch her.

Charlotte stopped at a beautiful stark painting that reminded Sophia of Jean François Millet's *The Peasants*. It probably was a Millet, another original. How sanctimonious. What a way to stick it to the common man—hide your wall safe behind Realism—literally. The painting would be a constant reminder of the toil and physical work most people endure every day. A reminder to you, the elite, that you are above it.

Charlotte clearly considered herself above it, the law, other people. Sophia wondered just how far above, and outside, the law she'd really gone.

Then Sophia thought of the quarry. If hauling huge stones around wasn't toil, she didn't know what was. Perhaps Jackson Keats had, in fact, been a man of integrity. A man with an awareness of his roots. She realized that she had done little to confirm what others had said about him save her brief stint at the library. She had been looking at him through Charlotte, if at all. She put the thought out of her mind. He's gone and Campbell's gone too. This case is about Campbell—and Sophia's opinion of him had disintegrated after yesterday. She felt only contempt for Campbell Keats. Who shared her feeling? Surely Ronald Scott did, but not enough to kill him. She was sure of it.

"Here." Charlotte put a carved cherry box on the side table next to Sophia's chair. She stood in front of her, blocking the light from the windows. The room was dark and cold and, despite the furnishings and the human element, felt empty. Sophia reached across the table and turned on a lamp. She thought she heard Charlotte huff but she didn't care anymore. She'd been lied to, by her client and by her lover, and she was going to find the truth, with or without them.

There were three notes, all on plain white paper, all folded neatly into squares. "Did you handle these?" Sophia asked.

"Did I *handle* them? I *read* them. In order to read them I had to touch them." Charlotte stared at her unblinking.

"I was just thinking about fingerprints," Sophia said.

"My fingerprints are on those notes. Your *lover's* fingerprints are on those notes." Charlotte said the word with a sneer worthy of compliment. "I don't imagine you want your beloved Martin to be a suspect, now do you? Besides, we know who wrote those notes. It was Ronald Scott." Charlotte pulled up a side chair and sat down. She towered above Sophia who fought to sit upright in the over-stuffed chair. The women stared at each other like two cats about to shed blood.

Sophia thought about fingerprints. Was it too late? Should she even think of crossing a woman like Charlotte Keats? If she planned to accuse her of murder then all bets were off. Anger flashed through her. *"A woman like Charlotte Keats?"* she repeated to herself. A woman who puts her pants on one leg at a time, a woman whose shit stinks just like mine, a woman who may have blood on her hands? With a surge of relief, Sophia realized she had a pair of latex gloves in her backpack. If nothing else, the gloves would give Charlotte pause. She put them on with a snap and opened the notes.

Charlotte was struck silent.

Sophia opened each note and laid them on the ottoman across from her. They were all written in the same hand, a neat block lettering that looked oddly familiar, like the lettering on an architect's plans.

"Which one came first?" she asked Charlotte.

"I really do not see why you have to wear gloves, for goodness sake," Charlotte said.

Please direct the witness to answer the question, your honor. "Which note came first?" Sophia asked again.

"That one." Charlotte pointed to the ottoman, almost touched the paper and then pulled her hand back as if from fire.

"Then?"

"That one, then this one." Charlotte indicated the order in which the letters had arrived. Sophia arranged them chronologically.

"When?" she asked. Sophia was fed up and somehow Charlotte knew it. The balance of power had shifted, although for how long was anybody's guess. A woman like Charlotte Keats would not go down easy.

Charlotte pointed to each note. "Late May, early July, Friday."

Sophia looked at the first note. It read:

Your family has ruined mine. You will pay. God will make sure of it.

Sophia looked up at Charlotte who was watching her intently. At first blush, it did sound like Ronald Scott. She remembered Bill Scott's talk of God, affirmations.

She moved to the second note.

How does it feel now? Maybe you should go to confession, like a good Catholic.

"You said this one came in early July?" she asked. Charlotte nodded. She was pale and stiff. "Before or after Campbell's disappearance?"

"The day after."

"Before or after I came over with Martin?" Sophia had to know just how complete the deception had been.

"Before," Charlotte said.

So, Charlotte had hired her under false pretenses and it was likely that Martin had been in on it, from the beginning. She couldn't ask Charlotte, she had to assume he'd known. She thought about Ginny. Sophia moved to the last note.

Your family is growing. Now you have two grandchildren. But, you will never know your first. You will not be allowed to ruin another life.

"When did you get this one?" she asked, although she already knew the answer.

"Saturday."

"Two grandchildren? One presumably illegitimate? That could be bad for the Keats image," Sophia said.

Charlotte's face went pale. "That man is crazy. Ronald Scott is delusional. I have no idea what he's talking about." She touched her neck.

Right, she thought, *and I'm the Tooth Fairy.* "How were the notes delivered?" she asked.

"That one," Charlotte pointed to the most recent, "was in my gardening basket. I use it on Saturdays when the staff is off."

"So someone knew your schedule."

"Perhaps," Charlotte said.

"And the others?"

Charlotte Keats was unyielding, answering Sophia's questions in clipped phrases, her anger palpable. Sophia wondered why she hadn't been thrown out. She imagined Charlotte was still trying to figure out how to handle her, knowing that she might go to the police, or worse, the media.

"I don't remember. In the mail slot or on the porch. I don't remember!"

"Let me ask you something," Sophia said. "Why did you hire me?" Her eyes drilled into Charlotte's.

"Because I wanted to find my son, of course," Charlotte said, composing herself.

"Hmm. It just seems odd that you hired me and then hampered my investigation by withholding evidence. Something doesn't fit here." Sophia crossed her arms against her chest and tapped her foot on the floor.

"I don't care what seems odd to you. I have shown you the notes, now you can see how sick Ronald Scott really is and that is that."

"You know, I think you hired me to frame Ronald Scott. But, I have to say, it looks like whoever killed your son has been—and still is—threatening you. Now that Campbell is dead, why would the notes continue? That is, if the killer is the same person who wrote the notes.... "

And, if so, why hadn't Charlotte turned the notes over to the police? It would simply be more evidence against Scott, and that's what Charlotte wanted. No, Scott had been the scapegoat all along. The note writer was a mystery still. And what of the killer—were they one and the same?

Charlotte flexed her jaw muscles. "Why wouldn't he have written them? Who knows with these crazies? He is sick. We're safe as long as he is locked up." Charlotte stood. The meeting was over. Sophia was dismissed. She stood to go.

Perhaps Charlotte Keats had thought the notes would convince Sophia of Scott's guilt. Instead, they only raised more questions. Why would he continue to threaten the family if Campbell was dead? Who killed Ginny? Ginny had been on her way to see her daughter and her grandchild; she did not commit suicide. And Ronald Scott didn't kill her. He was in custody. Was this mentally ill, weak-willed, highly medicated man, really capable of cold-blooded murder? And who had committed the second murder? More importantly, who was next?

******

"She knows. That horrible PI knows about the notes," Charlotte said into the phone. "I suppose Martin told her. No, I'll phone him next. I need you to take care of it. Don't give me that. You can and you will. I can make your life very difficult. I can take it all away. This must be dealt with. No, I will not have any further questions about my family. There is to be no more press. This case is over."

37

Sophia sped away from the Keats mansion heading for the Plymouth Township police station. She thought about Ginny, her beautiful mocha-colored complexion, her genuine goodness. And Ronald Scott, a decent young man trapped by an unwitting mind. Casualties— literally and figuratively— of a class war. She called information on her cell phone and was connected through to Whitemarsh Rock & Limestone.

"Bill Scott please," she said. "Oh. When do you expect him back? Family emergency. Right, do you know if he is at the courthouse, or the police station? Yes I realize it's personal, I want to help. I'm trying to help Ronald. Yes, right." The line went dead. *Thanks for nothing.* She punched the "end" button and drove like hell, making it to the station in ten minutes.

Her adrenaline pumped when she saw Bill Scott leaving the building, head hung low. "Mr. Scott," she called out to him. He didn't look up. "Mr. Scott." Sophia wondered if the media had already begun hounding him and she felt sorry for the man. She ran after him and touched his arm. "Mr. Scott, do you remember me?"

The man's eyes registered recognition. "From Harrisburg? PACA?" he asked, astonished.

Sophia remembered her lie and blushed. "No, Mr. Scott, I'm not from PACA. Actually, I'm a private investigator. I want to help Ronald."

"You want to help Ronald? Why?" The man's head still hung low, dejected.

It was do or die time. Charlotte Keats was her client and that relationship was supposed to be private, sacred. Fuck that. She may be the killer. And she

181

had lied; she was framing an innocent man. Martin had lied. They had both used her and for reasons she had to yet to understand.

"Well, technically, Mr. Scott, I work for the Keats family. I *worked* for them, that is. Right now, I just want to find the truth about who killed Campbell Keats."

"Look Miss, the Keats family seems to think my nephew killed their boy. Why should I trust you?" Bill Scott quickened his pace and Sophia followed.

"But, I don't think he did it. He couldn't have. He's too sick, isn't he?" Sophia grabbed his elbow. "He's been sick for years now. He's not violent. Even without his medication, he's never been violent, has he?" She'd done enough research on paranoid schizophrenia to know that the illness rarely caused violence, homicidal or otherwise. Someone else was stalking the Keats family with threatening notes and maybe that same someone else had killed Campbell. Neither crime fit Ronald Scott. She remembered him as almost flat, his features dull and blank, his eyes moving quickly from one side of the room to the other. He was weak and scared. He was not a killer.

The man shook his head. "No, the boy is not violent. Some with his condition are, but not Ronnie. He's terrified. And, he takes his meds every day. I know because I monitor him. He lives with us, my wife and me. He no more killed that boy than you or I did, Miss—"

"Gold. Sophia Gold. That is my real name." They stopped walking and stood on the sidewalk outside the police station. The occasional uniform passed, spit-shined shoes squeaking in the mid-day sun. "Mr. Scott," Sophia asked, "when did you first find out about Ronald's condition?"

The man looked down at his feet again, his neck reddened. "Oh, they caught him back when he was a teen. He was arrested then too."

"Caught him at what?"

"He was in the park." Bill Scott shored up his strength. "He was," the man sighed looking suddenly old and very tired, "pleasuring himself in the park, in front of children, in broad daylight."

"Oh," she whispered. What do you say to that? They stood for a moment in silence. That explained the first-degree misdemeanor and the prison time. Pennsylvania doesn't take lightly to indecent exposure, especially with children involved.

"Why would he go to jail though, if he was sick?" she asked.

Bill Scott shook his head, his shoulders slumping. "He'd just turned eighteen, and like I said, there were kids there. They arrested him just like that. A bunch of mothers made a stink 'cause their kids were playing in the park," Scott's voice caught, "he didn't even know enough to be humiliated. His mother, my sister, had run off a few years before that. She never was very good at taking responsibility. Ronald's father disappeared when he was born. The man was a no-good louse." Bill Scott looked to the sky, as if to ask forgiveness for speaking ill of others.

"How did you find out about his illness?"

"Couple of months after he was released from prison, my wife and I heard him in his room. He was talking to someone. Yelling. Only no one else was there. Then he tried to commit suicide. Took a whole bottle of aspirin. Judy, that's my wife, found him passed out in the bathroom. We rushed him to the hospital, had his stomach pumped. They made him see a psychiatrist. They do that for suicide attempts."

Of course. You have to try to kill yourself to get psychiatric attention, otherwise you just get locked up, she thought.

Scott shrugged. He seemed to be thinking the same thing. "He was diagnosed then." Tears welled up in his eyes. "Thing of it is, he's on suicide watch now. I don't know if he'll make it sitting in prison, even if it's only a few days." Bill Scott had become a father to a troubled boy, a boy who might never really function as a man in this world. Sophia felt tired and sad.

Suicide watch. That upped the ante. Although she knew none of this was her fault, Sophia felt she'd then have another death on her conscience. First Ginny, then Ronald. "Mr. Scott, I really do want to help Ronald. Anything else you can tell me would really help. Where was he on July Fourth?"

"He was supposed to go out—he's actually making friends again and living a pretty normal life, but he came down with something that morning and stayed home. Judy and I were away so he was at the house alone."

"I thought he told the police he was with friends."

"He did. He lied. He's so scared of the police now that he just plain lied."

So his alibi hadn't checked out. Convenient for the cops, and Charlotte, disastrous for Ronald. "Do you have any other children, Mr. Scott?" she asked.

"Bill," he said. He saw the confusion on Sophia's face. "Please, call me Bill. And no, we don't. Anymore. We had a girl, Amy, about Ronald's age, but she died of leukemia when she was ten. They were best pals."

My God, Sophia thought. *What family hasn't seen tragedy, death, something horrible? Life is just getting through the bad stuff. If you're lucky, you have a little fun here and there, a few laughs, love.*

"What's happening now? Where is he now?" Sophia asked.

"He's in there." Scott gestured to the station. "They're keeping a close eye on him. Guess they'll evaluate him soon, see if he's fit to stand trial."

"Does he have a lawyer yet?"

"They've appointed someone for him. Hasn't shown up yet. We just flat out don't have the money, Judy and me. We just can't." Scott looked pained.

"Listen, I'm going to check some things out too, today. Here's my card. Will you please call me if you need anything or have any questions?"

The man nodded. "Why are you doing this, Miss Gold? Why would you want to help us, especially if you work for Charlotte Keats?"

"I don't work for her anymore," Sophia said, "I work for myself, and I don't believe Ronald did it. Someone else did and I'm going to find out who it was."

Bill Scott walked away shaking his head and staring down at her business card as if it had a fascinating story to tell.

******

Sophia turned to the station entrance. She wove her way through uniforms, plain-clothes cops and the occasional citizen, catching Webb and Dallas on the front steps. Webb was carrying some files; Dallas held a cell phone.

"Ah, the illustrious *Ms*. Gold." Buck Dallas mocked political correctness. He had an especially cocky air about him.

"Gentlemen," Sophia said, "and I use the term loosely. Where are you off to? Taking a little break after a harrowing experience catching a killer? Where's the silver platter, or did you already return it to Charlotte Keats?"

Jack Webb looked at her dead-on. "What can we do for you, Ms. Gold? As you know, we've made a legitimate arrest. I would think your job is complete, is it not?" He paused. "Although, there is the death of the maid to look into."

"Yes. There is that," Sophia said dread washing over her.

"Oh, so you know about Virginia Amos?" Webb had an odd look on his face.

Sophia nodded. "I ran in to the ME this morning at the Keats home. That place is a hazard. Hope I'm not next." She joked, almost.

"So you knew her?" Dallas was smug.

Sophia felt faint thinking about Ginny again. Maybe it was the heat, probably not. "I'd met her, talked with her." She looked up at Webb. "What happened?"

184

"OD," Dallas said.

Webb reached his arm out to curb his partner.

"B.S.," Sophia replied, "she knew something."

"Well, we just got it this morning. So, we can't comment," Webb said staring at Dallas, "at all." He turned to Sophia. "Are you okay? You look a little pale."

"Who me? I'm peachy. Why wouldn't I be?" She smiled falsely. "Look, about Ronald Scott. I don't think he's your man." She looked pointedly at Webb. "And neither do you, am I right?"

Buck Dallas jumped in. "The arrest's good. His alibi was for shit, the guy has priors, and there were witnesses. What the hell's your problem?"

"Priors?" Sophia asked with a grin. "Are they coming for you next? You want to tell me you've never done it, Dallas? So he whacked off, big fucking deal." Sophia shook her head. "The kid is sick. He didn't know what he did was wrong. I hope you know he was hospitalized; he's a paranoid schizophrenic. You do know that don't you?"

"He 'whacked off,' as you so elegantly put it, Ms. Gold, in a park full of little children," said Webb. "He was diagnosed years later. We don't even know if the two are relate—"

"Not related? What planet are you from? Of course they're related." Sophia crossed her arms across her chest. "I'll give you indecent exposure. Although, I bet a psych eval then would have revealed his problem, saved the kid some prison time. Not to mention the hit to taxpayers. But never mind that, you might have another suspect right here." Sophia gestured toward Dallas.

Webb stifled a grin.

"Hey, what the hell?" Dallas looked confused.

"Look, I know what he did, but don't tell me you don't know what happened to him after that, the illness, the hospitalization. He was sick. That was just a symptom. Once he was diagnosed—" her voice was drowned out by the buzz of officers moving in and out of the building like lemmings. Must have been a shift change.

Webb scanned his colleagues milling about on the sidewalk. "We were just going for a cup of coffee, Ms. Gold. Won't you join us?" He guided her toward a coffee shop on the corner. He held a file folder in his right hand and put his left at the small of her back.

Standing in front of the station to talk about the merits of an arrest was probably not wise. Webb knew that. And, Sophia realized, he was too much of a professional to just let the thing drop. Dallas, on the other hand, was celebratory, definitive. Maybe she'd misjudged him yet again. She was misjudging everyone these days. Especially her own client. Clues in this case were few and far between, and those she did find were misleading, perhaps manufactured. She was following her gut, but almost blindly as if through a maze. People get lost forever in mazes.

The coffee shop was a cacophony of spoons tinkling against coffee cups, thick crepe soles screeching across linoleum, and hot oil sizzling something— potatoes or eggs—to an artery-hardening crisp. The pungent smells of warm toast, egg yolk and bacon filled the air. The din was just enough white noise to both let in and block out every sound.

Webb guided them back to an empty booth. A waitress flew out of the kitchen with a tray of food, the door swinging against their booth, effectively blocking half of their table. Both Webb and Dallas had chosen that side of the table. They could see the entire room, but views of them were obscured by what turned out to be a very busy swinging door. Sophia hunkered down across from them.

Jack Webb tossed his file on the table, the contents sliding out towards Sophia. She glanced quickly at the papers and then away. "So, Ms. Gold, you've got something stuck in your craw. Spit it out." Webb stared at her dead-on.

"Ronald Scott didn't do it," she said, "you know it and I know it."

"We have witnesses," Dallas protested.

"Witnesses who saw what?" she asked. "Some guy in a car? Did they actually see Scott?"

The waitress loomed above them. She was a good-looking bleached blonde with a generous bosom and a nametag stuck to one breast. Donna. "What'll it be boys?" she asked, and then eyed Sophia.

"The usual Don," Webb said.

"Bambi?" Donna asked.

"Hey!" protested Dallas.

Webb cracked up. Sophia looked down, hiding a smile and caught another glimpse of the file Webb had tossed on the table. In small capital letters, typed neatly along the file tab, it said: "CONFIDENTIAL, Thomas Jefferson Medical College—Keats, Campbell W."

A single sheet stuck out and she saw a scrawled signature. Above it was a typed note that said:

Conclusions (Sept.12, 2001): Patient exhibits symptoms of azoospermia.

Physical examination does not confirm diagnosis. Recommended testing: hormonal imbalance, urinalysis, testicular failure and/or duct blockage.

Note (Nov. 23, 2001): Pregnancy achieved. Follow up cancelled by patient. Based on previous symptoms, further testing is still recommended.

Someone had handwritten "Sterile?" next to the passage. The note was marked with a red stamp: "R'cd Plymouth Township Police 7/14/02."

Sophia gaped. Slowly she looked up at Jack Webb who was grinning ear-to-ear.

Jack lightly punched his partner's shoulder. "You're so sensitive. Poor Bambi," he laughed. Then he picked up the folder, straightened the contents and stuck it behind his back. "Let's just get that out of the way so we can eat," he said still laughing at his partner.

"Buck, damn it. It's Buck. Why does everyone do that?"

"Oh sweetie," Donna cooed, "you're just so fun to tease, look at that little pout. I could just eat you up." Donna clearly had a lot of job satisfaction.

Buck tried to look tough. "The usual for me too," he said.

"And you, Miss?" Donna's gum was like a powerful acrobat in her mouth, cracking, popping and flipping to an internal rhythm.

"Coffee," she said numbly. "And water please, Donna."

Donna grunted and shimmied off.

Dallas sat back, extending his legs along the side of the table. Sophia had the odd sensation of being trapped; his legs were so long they reached past her to the other end of the booth.

They busied themselves with coffee, adding sugar here, cream there, passing condiments across the table as if they'd been sharing meals their entire lives.

Webb started in quietly. He wouldn't make eye contact at first. "We do have a case against Ronald Scott, it's weak, but we have one. We can't tell you everything. There's a lot of pressure to close this thing, to make an arrest and have it be Scott—a *lot* of pressure," he paused. "Maybe stronger than…" his voice trailed off. He glanced slowly around the diner.

Stronger than what? The actual case? Sophia wondered. "I see," she said. He had shown her the file on purpose. "I knew it. I mean something isn't right about it."

"Sure, something doesn't feel right about it, he's a nice kid, he's sick. He'll probably get put away somewhere with padded rooms. He's not going to jail, not with his psychiatric history, no matter what Charlotte Keats says or does. What can we do? We've got no one else." Webb nodded at Donna as she approached with their food. Dallas had ordered a cottage cheese plate with fruit, Webb a BLT.

Sophia stifled a laugh. "Dude, no wonder people call you 'Bambi.' You're eating the diet plate?" They all laughed, Donna included. Then she walked away.

Buck sighed. "I care about how I look, is that so wrong?" He grinned, realizing he sounded silly. "I do a lot of training and protein—oh forget it. Leave me alone." But he was smiling too and dug into his melon with fervor.

"Scott can't afford a lawyer," Sophia said and Webb raised his eyebrows. "I ran into his uncle earlier. The boy's on suicide watch. And, the trial is going to put this guy through the wringer, mentally and otherwise. Besides, don't you guys want to catch the real killer?"

"We don't know that it's not him," Dallas said through a mouthful of cottage cheese.

"Well I do," Sophia said. She locked eyes with Webb.

"We're puppets on this case, Ms. Gold. The DA is driving the bus, and Charlotte Keats is giving directions. We've got no choice."

"What if there is evidence to implicate someone else?" Sophia asked frantically.

"We can't look for it though. Don't you see? We've got other cases," Dallas said. "Besides, why look a gift horse in the mouth?"

Sophia rolled her eyes and Webb snickered.

"What? That's an expression. Isn't it?" Dallas furrowed his brow. "'Gift horse in the mouth.' Yeah, that's an expression."

"Don't hurt yourself partner, I need you later," Webb said grinning.

"Aw, screw both of you." Dallas went back to his fruit.

"Okay, I'll ask again. What if I find evidence to implicate someone else?"

"Ms. Gold, correct me if I'm wrong, but your client, Charlotte Keats, has found her killer," Webb said.

"You are wrong," Sophia said, "she's not my client anymore. I fired myself. I'm doing this on my own time."

"Okay, but we never had this conversation. Be careful, and if you find something, I mean *really* something, let us know." Webb reached a hand behind his back to adjust the file he held there. "Otherwise," he said, "*sayonara*. I'm about to retire early. Don't fuck it up for me." Webb took a huge bite of his sandwich and shoved it into his cheek, chewing slowly.

Sophia stood, took a swig of her coffee and saluted them both. "Friday, Bambi. It's been real." She turned and walked out. She could hear them chuckling as she went.

38

The investigation had borne down on Ronald Scott like a speeding train—poor guy never knew what hit him. From day one, Charlotte had implicated Whitemarsh Rock & Limestone guiding the police, and Sophia, from there.

Scott's alibi *was* faulty, his past even more so. Witnesses, a couple, had come forth and placed a tall, darkly clothed man at the scene. But that was half the male population of Philadelphia, and could easily have been a hired hit man. The couple had been making out in the trees along Ridge Pike. Sophia guessed they'd been doing more than that, so just how mentally sharp they were was anybody's guess. The boy had seen a figure running to a car parked by the side of the road. The girl had been fastening her bra. What kind of car did he see? A big car. What color? Dark. Well, that's helpful. Sedan, SUV, American-made? Shiny. Hmm, narrows it down. Ronald Scott drove a late-model dark green Chevy Blazer, like a million other people. He kept it clean, like a million other people. How many cars did Charlotte Keats have? What about rental agencies? SUVs are the hot rental item these days.

The police didn't seem to have anything substantial, although Sophia knew Webb was doing it by the book. Ronald Scott had never seen this so-called book. He had no idea what the rules were. Sophia wasn't sure she did either.

As she got on the expressway, she hit a huge semi pile-up and cursed her choice of routes. With a deep breath she told herself everything happens for a reason, put the Porsche in neutral and sat waiting among tons of steaming, idle steel.

190

She got out her cell phone and checked messages again. Another hang-up. Lovely. And a message from Martin. This one she listened to. *"Soph, it's me. Listen, I need to talk to you. I can explain everything. I know you saw Charlotte. Please call me."* He sounded matter-of-fact, as if the call was on his list of to-dos for the day and he'd just crossed it off and was moving on to the next thing. She'd been wrong about him again. *He used me*, she thought. *Maybe he even loves me, or did, but he needs what Charlotte and his law practice can give him more than he needs me.* She deleted the message.

She felt anxiety start to build in her throat. She was stuck in traffic and the killer was still out there, likely relaxing, since there had already been an arrest. Okay, she'd catch the bastard off guard. Unless the bastard knew she was still looking. Well, nothing was going to happen in the next twenty minutes. She sat behind ambulances, Jaws of Life and state troopers all dealing with the scene before her.

The faces of the players appeared in her mind. Who was doing this? She got out her notebook and her library research spilled onto the passenger seat, headlines from the Keats' past. She started writing, first come first served. She wrote:

Charlotte Keats
Zander Jarvis
Martin Duncan
Zoë Cohen Keats
Jane Howard
Frank Reynolds
Ronald Scott
Bill Scott
Ginny Amos
~~Joe Rizzo~~
Joe Rizzo

She had to add Rizzo back. This was not the list of suspects, she reasoned. This was just a list. Besides, Martin was on it too. Maybe he was the killer. How far would he go for his career? He had betrayed her but she couldn't bear to think the betrayal had been that far-reaching. She looked around her, as if she'd be caught—caught both implicating a man she had loved and made love with, and a man she now wanted, Joe Rizzo.

The answer, she reasoned, had to be in Campbell's past. She thumbed the loose pages, the newspaper reprints. Charlotte's motive seemed more and more clear. Ronald's Scott's arrest deflected attention away from the victim.

Reporters would dig up his medical records, sealed or not. They would find out about the public masturbation, the hospitalization, his mental illness. He and his family would be pulverized by the time the trial was over. Whitemarsh Rock & Limestone would be ruined; Keats Quarry still the only game in town.

For the first time since traffic had slowed, Sophia focused outside herself. The expressway was littered with overturned cars. Scared people clutching each other, car doors swung open, air bags like limp bloody rags draped over steering wheels. She'd been lucky. She'd missed the carnage by minutes.

She flipped on the radio to hear confirmation of what she was seeing, although based on her vantage point she could have done the report herself. And as she listened, she saw something that made her heart stop. A red Saab, identical to her own, crushed almost beyond recognition.

"Apparently, this was a hit and run, David," the reporter was saying. "And one specific car bore the brunt of this horrible accident, the semi overturning has, of course added to the wreckage."

"Susan, can you tell us who was hit?"

"State troopers are not releasing that information at this time until they have notified the next of kin. Our thoughts and prayers are with the families of these victims, David."

"Thank you. Susan Richardson, reporting live at the scene."

Sophia turned down the radio. She had been the target. What were the odds that two red Saab convertibles would be on the expressway within minutes, seconds, of each other? The killer didn't know she'd switched cars with Vinnie. And, with a cut brake line, she'd have been dead after a hit like that, if she hadn't already gone off a cliff. Someone knew where she was, what she was doing, and was still trying to kill her.

The Boxster's new car smell was suddenly overwhelming, she opened the door thinking she had to vomit. She didn't. She turned off the radio and was suddenly bathed in a cold damp sweat.

She looked to her left. A family sat in the lane next to her, two kids buckled up in car seats, Mom and Dad in the front. Mom was crying, probably both fear and relief. They'd missed death by seconds as well. *And it's my fault*, she thought. The kids were well behaved. A girl sat on the far side reading. A little boy sat at the window next to Sophia and had just learned to flirt. She waved to him and he giggled. His dad leaned back from the front to check the car seats and caught a glimpse of Sophia. His son was waving madly at her. The man looked at his son and smiled too.

They had the same smile. The same cleft chin. The same green eyes. Sophia felt faint. She reached for her bag. Photos of Rizzo's nephew Matteo had spilled onto the floor of the Porsche. His blue eyes sparkled on film and his smile chilled her to the bone.

She knew that smile.

A horn blared. It was directed at her, traffic was moving and it was Sophia's turn to maneuver between the state troopers making reports and road flares, angry and hot against the asphalt. She tossed the photos on the passenger seat and slid the car into first gear.

39

Zander Jarvis lived at Pennsylvania Towers in Society Hill. Directory assistance had an Alexander W. Jarvis III—a third generation version of a once great and formidable man, a former Pennsylvania Supreme Court Justice. The name had been familiar but without context when she'd first met the cocky, good-looking, brash Princeton graduate. She was putting together the pieces.

Zander worked at the Philadelphia Stock Exchange, that much she'd gotten from Martin at the funeral. She was tempted to go directly there to confront him at the office. But that environment would be too testosterone-heavy. She couldn't stomach the peacocking. She needed him alone. It was nearly four o'clock; maybe he was home already. She'd wait if she had to.

The Porsche decided for her, bypassing Center City and the Stock Exchange for the Vine Street Expressway through China Town, Independence Mall and finally into Old City and Society Hill.

She pulled into a non-parking spot right in front of the Towers, figuring she wouldn't be long. Besides, she thought, no one will tow a Porsche Boxster S, vanity plate "NOTGLTY," from this swanky spot.

She heard a voice behind her. "Is that Sophia Gold?" Zander called. "I assume you're here to see me." He winked, sprinting to the front entrance to finish his run as she locked the car. He glistened with sweat and had a musky, sexy odor, one that would turn sour as his body cooled. A Tom Cruise smile splashed across his face, his teeth more perfect than real. Sophia focused on his face, a single dimple punctuating the left side, a weaker one on the right.

His eyes were an icy shade of blue. She bristled. A leather leash hung loosely around his waist; against a stomach so flat Sophia wondered how gravity held the lease in place. She imagined it rubbing against his hipbones as he ran. A giant Irish Setter barreled into her legs and began licking her hand.

"Nice ride," he said eyeing the Porsche.

"Yes," Sophia said. "It is isn't it? It's a loaner. I've been having some car trouble lately," she paused. "But you wouldn't know anything about that, now would you?"

Zander looked confused. "What? No, my car's in great shape," he replied. "Oh, you mean about *your* car," he smiled, but whether he was mocking or flirting, Sophia couldn't tell. "Gee, uh, I'm sorry to hear your car's in the shop, what do you want me to say? Looks like you've done okay for yourself just the same." He gestured to the Boxster. "Do you need a chauffeur later? I might be able to squeeze you in—in fact it'd be my pleasure."

Pig, Sophia thought. *Either this guy is a great actor or he didn't cut my brake line. Let's try something else.* "So, I'm kind of surprised to find you home this early, Zander. I heard you worked at the Exchange," Sophia said. "Don't you wheel and deal into the wee hours, you know, Tokyo and all that?"

He stared at her. "Not that it's any of your business, but I took the day off today. I had some things to take care of."

Oh really, like trying to kill me? "I see." She nodded. "So you didn't actually call in sick to go jogging with your pooch?"

"What do you want Sophia?" Zander sneered. The dog panted with excitement and fatigue. "I have to get Minnie in for some water, so if—"

"Right," Sophia said suddenly aware of the heat, the back of her neck sweating against her curls. "So why don't I come on up?"

Zander looked down, then shifted to false enthusiasm. "Well, now why didn't I think of that?"

As they walked into the lobby together, the dog almost leapt out of its skin. His master was having a visitor. Sophia couldn't resist.

"You look like Max." She pulled on the dog's ears.

"She's Max's sister. Campbell and I got them together," Zander said.

"Oh, well, no wonder," Sophia continued, grateful for the dog's presence. Eventually, she would have to look in Zander's cool blue eyes and tell him why she'd come, confront him without including the dog in the conversation.

Sophia was ready for the truth. Somehow she didn't think Zander would be.

"I hope you don't mind if I a grab a quick shower first," he said pulling on the hem of his T-shirt. He held it to his brow, wiping tiny beads of sweat, showing off six-pack abs.

Sophia followed him into the cool corridor and onto the elevator.

Zander lived in a massive penthouse apartment with a spectacular view of the Delaware River, tanker ships docked in the port, a tourist trolley car and Penn's Landing, Philadelphia's answer to the outdoor summer concert. Minnie vanished as soon as they entered and seconds later could be heard gulping water in another room.

"Help yourself to something to drink." He motioned toward the dog's slurping sounds. "I'll be right back. Shower-time." He pirouetted to face her, his expression a mixture of malice and sport. "Unless of course you want to join me?"

"I think I'll pass on that," she said. *I don't usually shower with murderers.* "So, you haven't even asked me why I'm here," she said finally.

"I know. I figured we'd get to that. I'll be right back." He disappeared down the hall removing his clothes as he walked.

The kitchen was as she would have expected. Gleaming appliances—all professional grade. The Viking stove was pristine. Sophia wondered if he ever used it. She moved to the refrigerator. Also stainless steel and spotless. She opened it and saw that he likely did use the stove, or he had a personal chef. The refrigerator shelves were filled with fresh fruits and vegetables; jars of pesto and chutney; fresh cheeses; tahini; tofu or feta or something white and cloudy; fresh pasta and an open bottle of Mount Eden Estate Chardonnay, 2000. She took a Volvic from the shelf—there were maybe fifty of them—all single serving size.

Clearly, Zander did not economize.

When she came back from the kitchen, he was sitting in the living room in shorts and a polo shirt, feet on the coffee table, hair still damp from the shower. His eyes popped against the blue of his shirt and the color in his cheeks.

Sophia sat down across from him on the couch. "You know, Zander," she began, "I've been investigating this murder and I don't think Ronald Scott's the killer. I'm hearing things, things about Campbell growing up. I think any number of people might have wanted to kill him. Sounds like he wasn't terribly well-liked."

"I don't know what you're talking about," Zander dismissed. "Ronald Scott's been arrested. He's a wacko. He did it." Zander tugged on Minnie's ears.

"Yes, well, that *is* the technical term for his condition," she replied.

He looked at her hard. "You are a real pain in the ass, you know that?"

"Yeah, can't seem to shake that," she paused. "So, you and Campbell were best friends." It wasn't a question.

"Yes. We were," he hesitated, "we grew apart after college. I, uh, hadn't seen him in awhile. Besides, high school was the usual, you know, parties, girls, drinking." Pensive, he touched his chin. "You probably *don't* know," he said, "what were you doing in high school, studying?"

Sophia took the offense as a compliment and said, "So, you hadn't seen him, huh?" She let that sit. "And yet you were pretty tight with his mother at the funeral. Something going on the side with Charlotte? You know, cleaning up the Keats family dirty laundry…."

"What the hell are you talking about?"

"By the way," she went on. "How well do you know Zoë? Probably pretty well. Do you know her in the biblical sense? And what about Jane? She grew up with Campbell, bet you've known her awhile too."

"Those dykes? I told him not to marry that chick." He laughed. "And Jane, she's so in the closet who knows if she'll ever get out."

"What makes you say they're gay, Zander? By the way, that is the more appropriate, dare I say politically correct, reference to a person's sexual orientation."

Zander looked impatient. "I don't give a shit what they call themselves. They're both lesbos." Zander ran his hands through thick, wet locks.

Minnie, luckily, wasn't picking up any of this. *No self-respecting female, of any species or sexual orientation, should have to listen to this jackass,* she thought. The dog continued to rub against her owner's legs. Then she moved over to Sophia.

"If you and Campbell had grown apart, just how much contact did you actually have with Zoë?" Sophia asked.

"What do you care?" he asked. "She's a gold-digger." He paused and leaned forward. "Can I get you anything else? Coffee, tea or…?" He winked. That beguiling smile—charming, and scary.

Minnie put both paws on Sophia's lap. Sophia felt sorry for her. "So Zander, where do you run with Minnie?" She asked, not really knowing why. Was this now a civil conversation? There were no rules but there was more to say, she was buying time.

Zander noticed the change in tone but answered anyway. "Sometimes we go through Center City. Or we head south to the Italian Market, if we feel like slumming." He grinned with every tooth in his mouth. Those dimples.

Sophia almost spat.

"I'm kidding," he said, "I love the Italian Market. Great meat."

Sophia stared at him in disbelief. The Italian Market was a wonderful rich aromatic display with windows of sides of beef and chickens dangling against gravity, rainbows of fruit and vegetables carpeting the streets, and the thick scent of spices and tea in the air. A clamoring of sounds and voices, accents, Italian mixed with South Philly-speak, dialect, some Vietnamese, children whining, and men laughing the deep barrel-chested laugh that Alexander Jarvis the first, second or third surely never allowed himself. But Zander meant a different kind of market, and a different kind of meat. And, he wasn't kidding.

"So, Dad, why don't we get right to the point?" she said finally.

"Excuse me, did you just call me Dad?" Zander rubbed his hands together. "Is this some kind of sick fantasy? Do you want your Daddy?" He broke into a twisted smile and the muscles in his legs tensed. "I can definitely go there."

"You know why I'm here, and it's not my sick fantasy, it's yours. Did you think no one would ever find out?" She tossed the pictures of Matteo on the coffee table.

"Cute kid," he said.

"You bastard." Sophia snorted at the pun. "He's *your* kid."

"What the hell have you been smoking? Martin's right, you are really whacked."

Whacked? Now that's mature. "Campbell," she said. "Was sterile."

He blinked. "Bullshit."

"Not bullshit. Check his medical records." Sophia leaned forward. "Did you guys fuck all the same women? The 'great meat.' Is that how it was? You just rotated them around like horses on a carousel, didn't you? Including Zoë. You make me sick."

"You can't prove anything," Zander said, still shocked from the earlier bombshell.

Famous last words, she thought. "Oh yeah, ever heard of DNA, Zander? Besides, look at the likeness." She stood and walked to a picture of Zander in his Princeton cap and gown. He was smiling broadly. It was the same smile Sophia had captured in Matteo. She held the pictures side by side. "This boy is your son."

"So what if he is? Who gives a shit? Campbell's dead, he can take the rap, might as well make himself useful. He fucked her too, that Italian bitch."

"Lovely," Sophia said. "But don't you mean he 'raped' her too?"

Zander waved his hands dismissively and laughed. "Tomato, to-mah-to," he said.

"Did you kill him for Charlotte? You know, to save the family name."

"What the—?"

"Who was threatening Charlotte, Zander? I guess she couldn't risk his past getting out—his so-called illegitimate child—so she had you kill him. How much did she pay you? Framing Ronald Scott was the swan song wasn't it?" Sophia's heart rate quickened. "Should have checked it out—your friend was shooting blanks. And, of course, you're Campbell Junior's father too. But Charlotte doesn't know that. That's why Zoë wanted an abortion. She knew. Did you kill your best friend, Zander? Did you kill him for Charlotte?"

"Charlotte couldn't have—what? I did not kill him. I didn't kill anyone. Ronald Scott killed him. Charlotte didn't—you're out of your fucking mind." Zander jumped up from his chair. "And so, I fucked that chick too, so what? I fucked a lot of girls. *I* never killed anyone. You should ask those dykes about it, or your new Italian boyfriend. Why don't you ask them who killed Campbell? Now get the hell out," he shouted. His face looked like a perfect red bell pepper. The uneven flush of exertion had faded, replaced by the unmistakable pallor of rage.

Sophia stood and hoped she wasn't visibly shaking. "You think I'm just going to sit on this? You have two illegitimate children—that you *know* of? You *asshole*." She glared at him, breathing fire.

They locked eyes. An eerie, knowing smile passed across Zander's lips and his eyes hardened to a cold deep ocean blue. "You don't know when to stop, do you bitch?" In two giant steps, Zander had crossed the room to Sophia. He grabbed her by the hair and knocked her to the floor. She stiffened, fought back, kicked at his legs and landed on the outside of her right ankle. She felt something pop. Shit. *That's going to leave a mark*, she thought. He dragged her into the kitchen.

"You stupid, stupid bitch. You had your fee but you couldn't leave it alone, could you?" He laughed. "You are going to be so sorry you ever met me."

I already am, pal. Believe me, I already am. "Charlotte's behind this, admit it Zander. She had her son killed to protect the family name and you're in on it. She thought she'd be getting a grandson so that made it okay. Little does she know Zoë gave birth to *your* child."

Minnie came bounding into the kitchen. She thought they were playing and yipped at Sophia's heels. Zander ignored her.

Her tongue tickled Sophia's leg. The scene was so bizarre, Sophia almost laughed out loud. She heard a drawer open above her head and heard the sound of metal scraping against metal. Zander had a large knife in his hand. A Henckels. *At least I'll go out in style*, she thought.

Minnie barked sharply. Sophia managed to twist her legs around and kick at Zander as he pulled on her hair. He was going for her neck and held the knife dangerously close to bare skin. His other hand had a firm grip on her curls. She grabbed his wrist, squeezing as tightly as she could. His wrists were broad; he was a big guy. A smaller woman wouldn't stand a chance with this maniac. She dug her nails into his skin drawing blood and in a flash of Bruce Lee brilliance, kicked her left leg into the air, hitting him square in the nuts. Poetic justice. Zander doubled over and dropped the knife, letting go of Sophia as well. She grabbed the weapon and noticed a drop of blood oozing down the blade. Instinctively, she touched her neck—her hand came back bloody. Minnie was barking but had backed away into a corner of the kitchen. Zander came at her again. She looked right at him and then stuck her leg out as he approached. Oldest trick in the book. The kitchen floor had been freshly washed and waxed—Sophia knew this from her earlier floor-time—and there's nothing quite like a Mr. Clean shine. Zander's foot caught the edge of a throw rug. He fell hard; face first onto the shiny tile. The jolt knocked the knife out of Sophia's hands and sent it skittering across the floor. She caught him in the solar plexus with her good foot and somehow hit him just right. He was out.

40

Sophia stomped on Zander's hand for good measure. She heard bone crunching and hoped she'd broken his finger. He'd scared the shit out of her. The look on his face had said he was enjoying himself; the timbre of his voice had said he would have killed her. Minnie came trotting over and, thank God for Irish Setters, gave Sophia a big sloppy kiss. She then proceeded to do the same to her master as he lay in a heap on the kitchen floor. *I wonder if Zander plays like this often*, Sophia thought smugly. The dog thinks life is back to normal. The only thing that had scared Minnie had been the knife.

Sophia kicked Zander's side. He was definitely out, but who knew for how long. She moved quickly through the apartment. The penthouse wasn't as large as it had seemed, most of the square footage was used up in the kitchen and living room. There was a master suite at the back of the apartment with an unbelievable bathroom—Sophia couldn't resist looking—and a smaller, but still generous, office equipped with a powerful PC, enormous flat screen monitor, fax machine, copier, two-line phone and paper shredder.

Zander's desk was neat, his papers stacked in orderly piles. *Always a pleasure spying on the anal types*, Sophia thought. On the left side of the desk were work papers, the telltale logo of the Philadelphia Stock Exchange emblazoned on letterhead and notes. On the right was the mother lode. Zander had copies of every note Charlotte had received. Under the notes were newspaper clippings about Ronald Scott, his misdemeanor arrest and release from prison. *Someone else has been doing research too*, she thought. Zander had scared up clips from *The Times Herald*, Norristown's local paper. To

Sophia's horror, Zander also had a file with copies of Scott's medical records.

Guess nothing's *really* sealed.

Yet, he had seemed genuinely shocked when Sophia suggested he'd killed Campbell for Charlotte. And, he'd denied his guilt, but not Charlotte's. Clearly, he was involved in the framing of Ronald Scott, but murder? Reluctantly Sophia admitted that framing a guy for murder and committing murder are two different things. Zander stood to gain from Campbell's death—he suspected he was Campbell Jr.'s father—but did he kill him? Perhaps he hadn't known how far Charlotte would go either. The incentive for him could have simply been to close the book on Campbell Keats. With Campbell dead, who would question his son's paternity? There'd be no reason for Zoë to; she'd lose her inheritance. Although Zander hadn't known of Campbell's sterility, he had slept with Zoë, whether or not she'd been willing. That he did know.

Had Charlotte used Zander to frame Ronald and someone else to actually kill her son? The only other person who came to mind was Martin. Sophia shivered. He'd been at the beach when Campbell died. Or so he'd said. She couldn't yet wrap her arms around that theory. It was clear, however, that someone was framing Ronald Scott, whether or not it was the real killer. Did she have enough information to at least get Scott released? Would Webb look at Charlotte, Zander, and maybe Martin more closely now?

Sophia grabbed Zander's papers and ran to the elevator and out of the building despite the now swollen sprained ankle. Within minutes she was locked in the Porsche. A quick glance in the rearview mirror confirmed the cut on her neck was minor and didn't need immediate attention. She pulled away from Zander's building and sped several blocks until she came to the Old Original Bookbinder's parking lot, pulled in and turned off the car. She looked over at the lobster tank. Poor bastards—if you're lucky, you'll die today, she thought. She was shaking and sweating and pissed off. She dialed her cell phone.

41

Tariq met her at the entrance to Philly's 6th District. Although one of the smallest patrol districts in the city, it was also one of the most diverse and dealt with all types of crimes. One day Tariq would be investigating the death of a homeless person—was it homicide or had the poor soul frozen to death sleeping on a grate—the next, he was called to one of the wealthiest homes in the city where a domestic dispute had turned deadly. He'd seen it all.

"What's gotten in to you?" he asked as she locked the car. "I thought they got your guy."

"It's not him."

"What are you talking—what the hell happened to your neck?" Tariq grabbed her by both arms. "Are you alright?"

Sophia touched her neck. "Oh, it's nothing—well it's not nothing, but I'm okay. I'm telling you Tar it's not him. He didn't do it," she said, "he's being set up."

"But the cops think he did. We don't just arrest people for the hell of it. Leave it alone," Tariq said. "Especially if that blood on your neck has anything to do with this. Take the money and run girl."

"Listen, can you just look at this stuff for me, tell me what you think?" Sophia asked waving a thick pile of pictures, notes, her research from the library. She needed a professional opinion.

"I'm not going to like this, am I?"

"Probably not," she said, "Scott is being set up. I know all about his mental illness. But he's not violent. The guy's on suicide watch for Christ's sake. I owe it to him to at least try. I can't have one more death—" she was starting to hyperventilate.

"Whoa, okay, take a deep breath. Let's go to Nate's, you can outline it for me."

******

A bell rang over the door as they entered the coffee shop—*the* 6th District hang out. Nate, presumably, was sweeping behind the counter and looked up at the noise.

"Whaddya' need Wash?" he asked. The man was seasoned. Curly salt-and-pepper hair, worn dark leathery skin and the palest hint of a tattoo on his arm—it looked like an eagle. The place was spotless, organized and ready for the next influx of cops needing sustenance, camaraderie. Sophia could hear female voices in the back. Waitresses on break? She and Tariq were the only customers.

"Nothin' Nate, we're good, just a table for a few minutes."

"Do whatcha gotta do to catch the bad guy," Nate said, almost to himself. He went back to sweeping and then moved on to scrubbing the grill.

They sat at a booth in the back.

"It was someone else, maybe the mother—"

"The mother?" Tariq interrupted. "You're talking about Charlotte Keats, *the* Charlotte Keats. You have got to stop watching *Law & Order*, girl."

"Okay, maybe she didn't do it—maybe she hired someone."

Tariq was shaking his head, smiling at her.

"She's taking advantage of the fact that Ronald Scott has a past. She's framing him. I know it. He is a likely suspect, I'll give you that, but he's not a murderer. With him on trial, the attention is off the Keats family, off Campbell. Maybe she set him up, even after the fact, to hide something."

Tariq was silent for a long moment. Her words were sinking in.

"Tar? Hello?"

"Why do you say that?"

"Look at this." She laid out the news clippings on a freshly sponged table. "Campbell Keats was a bad boy. He has something in his past, but I haven't found it yet. The articles hint at it, and then poof, the stories disappear. You know what comes the day after each story? A donation, some charitable act by Charlotte Keats herself with major press coverage."

"That could just be a coinci—"

"Come on, it's too *much* of a coincidence. Plus, Charlotte was getting notes. Threats. These." She laid out the copies she'd taken from Zander's office. "I found out about them by accident from the maid. The next day she O.D.ed."

Tariq raised his eyebrows.

"Except I know she was headed to see her grandchild. I talked to her—she was not suicidal. You don't make plans with a kid and then off yourself." She paused to give Tariq time to read the notes.

He whistled under his breath. "Holy shit," he said. "Another grandchild? Blackmail?"

"Who knows? The thing is, and get this, Campbell Keats was sterile."

"Sterile? How do you—?"

"I saw his medical file. No, check that, Webb, the lead detective, *showed* me his file. He knows something's off but there's too much pressure for an arrest. I'm telling you, Tar—"

Nate had made his way to their booth and with remarkable tact avoided looking at the stack of papers. He must have years of experience working with cops and their secrets, Sophia thought. "Now how can you entertain such a pretty lady and not even offer her nothin' to drink," Nate said smiling at Sophia. "No wonder you're still single, Detective. Ain't nobody ever teach you how to treat a lady?"

Tariq grinned. "Sophia, this is Nate, Nate, Sophia."

Sophia reached out her hand to shake Nate's and found it rough and calloused but surprisingly gentle.

"You know what, Nate," she said. "I'm actually starving. I haven't eaten all day. Is the kitchen open?"

"My kitchen's always open, little lady, what can I get you?"

"How about a BLT?" she asked, for some reason overcome by a craving for salted meat.

"Comin' right up. Somethin' to drink?"

"Lemonade, if you have it."

"Fresh-squeezed," Nate said proudly. He turned to Tariq. "What about you Mr. No-Manners, you want something?"

"Just some coffee, and thanks for the etiquette lesson Nate. You're right, a lady like Sophia should be waited on hand and foot."

"I tell you what," Nate grumbled walking away. "She was my lady…."

They both laughed as Nate fired up the grill.

"He's a character that guy. Been running this place for twenty-five years."

"He's charming," Sophia said. "All of a sudden I just got hungry, guess

205

it's the first time I've stopped moving all day. Kind of morbid to eat at a time like this, but . . ."

"Ever been to an Irish wake?" Tariq asked grinning. "Listen, why don't you run through the whole thing for me while we wait."

The BLT had come and gone when Sophia was finished outlining the entire case. She went detail by detail, including the hang-ups at her house, the break-in, her reunion with Martin, the cut brake line, the accident on the expressway involving a red Saab, her interactions with the local cops, and so on. Tariq had questions throughout and, by the time Nate had refilled her lemonade glass twice, he was on board with her theory, at least *in theory*.

"Take it to Webb," he said finally.

"Is it enough?"

"You've got something alright. Who knows about the murder, they'll need to dig some more, but Charlotte Keats' motive is there. If nothing else, they probably do have an innocent man in jail."

"Okay."

"I'm serious, Sophie, just go to Webb. Don't even think about confronting Charlotte again on your own, or Martin or Zander or anyone else. How's the ankle by the way?"

"Hurts, but I'll live."

"Let's hope you do," he said.

42

Sophia saluted Tariq at the curb and threw her backpack in a heap on the passenger seat, the contents spilling onto the black leather.

She'd hit traffic going to see Webb and Dallas but she didn't care. Her neck was crusty with blood. *Interesting,* she thought. *Nate said I was a lovely lady, but said nothing about the blood on my neck. Maybe he's used to ignoring certain details, probably has to be, feeding cops all day.*

Before starting the car she scrounged around in her backpack for a tissue to clean her neck. Instead she found the emergency contraceptives she'd taken from Zoë's powder room. She examined the prescription label closely. She had seen Zoë's name on it before, although she hadn't noticed that the label said "Zoë Cohen" and not "Zoë Keats" or even "Zoë Cohen Keats." She read the dosage instructions. They were the same as those she'd seen on the Internet days ago: *Take two tablets within 72 hours of unprotected intercourse. Take the remaining tablets within 12 hours.*

In the corner was a phone number and doctor's name. Judith S. Freedman, M.D. Phone: 202-555-3409. She stared at it. 202 was a Washington D.C. area code.

Her gut reeled and then settled in an unusual calm. Again, she reached for her cell phone.

43

When Sophia arrived at Zoë's, the sun had set in a hot pink swath across the sky. The more beautiful the sunset, the more it reflected the smog Philadelphian's had generated that day. Ironic. She was tired and already ached from her battle with Zander but was fortified from her meeting with Tariq. She'd promised not to confront anyone else, but that was before she'd found the pills.

The front steps of Zoë Keats' brownstone were a beautiful whitewashed marble she hadn't noticed before, the door a glossy black. The doorknocker had fingerprint smudges on it and Sophia wondered who typically cleaned it. They'd missed a spot. She knocked softly and waited, greeting Jane Howard as the door opened.

"*You?* What do *you* want?" Jane stood in the open doorway.

"Hello, Jane. I'm glad you're still in town, although I must say I'm not surprised to see you. May I come in? Thanks." She pushed her way into the vestibule.

"My God woman, you are a nightmare. Didn't you hear they arrested the guy who did it? Why don't you leave us alone?"

"Us? You mean why don't I leave *Zoë* alone, don't you? By the way, is she here? Of course she's here. She just had a baby, I bet the baby's here too. Gosh, I'd love to see the baby. I just love babies." She was enjoying herself.

Jane's face turned the color of her hair. She let Sophia into the house with an exaggerated bow. "I'll get Zoë. I guess we're not rid of you yet."

"Love your use of pronouns there, Jane. Us, we—very interesting," Sophia called after her and turned to go into the front room. She heard a loud clap behind her as Jane slammed the front door and threw the dead bolt. She ushered Sophia through the vestibule, turned and locked that door with a key and put the key in her pocket. Sophia felt a tingle on her neck. Nope, not rid of me—yet.

"Wait in there." She pushed Sophia, who was resting most of her weight on her left side. Jane caught her off guard and Sophia tripped on the carpet runner, falling and splitting her lip on the cold Italian tile.

For a *Town & Country* girl, Jane had a nasty side.

"Now was that really necessary, Jane?" Sophia asked, trying to keep her voice steady. She fumbled for her backpack and held it close to her chest in case Jane came at her again.

She hobbled into the sitting room. The door banged shut behind her and she heard it lock.

Within seconds, Zoë blew into the room, baby in tow, Jane on her heels. She was feeding little Campbell, Jr. and made no effort to hide her swollen breasts. Breast-feeding is not offensive. In fact, it is a natural and beautiful act between mother and child. But it was—in this context—disconcerting. Sophia would have rather seen a stranger feeding her child at Horn & Hardart's. She'd smile and maybe coo at the baby. Instead, the brazen image was of Zoë and Jane standing together, with little Campbell Jr. suckling away between them.

At that moment, the custom of passing names along through the generations struck her. A long-standing tradition signaling quiet dignity, respect for history and lineage, was at once helter-skelter, the real message distorted beyond recognition. It seemed odd to name your child after your dead husband if you'd killed him, if his real father was your dead husband's best friend who'd raped you. Names had such power, carried so much of their owners with them—how could Zoë not think of her husband when she looked at her son? If she'd killed him, why would she do that to herself? To deflect suspicion? Still, every day, in body, in spirit and in name, she'd be reminded of what she did.

"Sophia. What are you doing here? I thought this was over?" Zoë's demeanor was like an evolution. Every time Sophia saw her, her spirit was stronger. Today, despite dark circles under her eyes, her energy was solid to the core. She stood strong, as if she'd always had a baby at her breast, and this life. Jane here. Her husband dead.

"Zoë," Sophia returned. "You're looking well. The baby looks well. I, on the other hand, don't look so good." Sophia touched her cut lip. "Jane, you brute," Sophia said as coyly as she could muster.

"What happ—?" Zoë stared at her Jane in shock.

"What do you want now?" Jane interrupted. "They arrested the killer. We'd like to get on with our life."

"You're right, Jane. There is a suspect in Campbell's murder," Sophia said pointedly. "But frankly, I am not convinced he did it. I wanted to talk to you two."

"What the fuck could you want from us?!" Jane raised her voice. *And swearing to boot*, Sophia thought. Zoë gave her friend fierce look. Sophia thought Jane actually cowered but it happened so quickly she might have imagined it.

"Jane, the baby," Zoë said.

Jane reached over and smoothed the baby's peach fuzz head. The only sounds were of him suckling on his mother's teat. The kid could eat anywhere.

"Can we at least sit?" Zoë asked, putting a hand to her lower back.

Yes, by all means, let's be civilized about this, Sophia thought.

Zoë and Jane sat on the opposite couch and Jane propped pillows behind her. The dynamic between them had intensified exponentially.

In another lifetime, Sophia might have thought: What a lovely couple: Two loving mothers and their little bundle of joy. Today she thought: Two heartless killers and their little cash cow.

"So, Ronald Scott is in jail," Sophia began. "And you two think you are off the hook. You think you got away with it, but I'm still hanging around. So here's what I think happened—"

"You bitch—" Jane interrupted through clenched teeth and a forced smile.

"You know Jane, babies pick up on your mood and tone of voice. Little Campbell Jr., is getting all of this," Sophia said. "I mean God knows how much therapy he'll need later in life."

"Fuck you. He's a week old. He'll get over it." Jane glared at Sophia, the whole time rubbing the little cherub's head. Zoë looked terrified but remained silent. She stared at Sophia with big eyes, her eyebrows arched to the North Pole.

"What are you going to do, kill me too?" Sophia asked. She looked at Zoë. "Mom? Not your best idea I wouldn't think." Sophia shifted her backpack again so that it was at her side.

"I don't know what you're talking about. We did not kill Campbell. That's what you're saying, isn't it?" Zoë shifted the baby to the other breast. "So we're lovers. That doesn't make us killers."

"Maybe it doesn't make *you* a killer, Zoë," Sophia said turning to face Jane. Something clicked in her mind and she leaned back on the sofa and took a deep breath, readying herself like any good storyteller. "Okay, so here's the deal. You two are lovers, have been since before Zoë met Campbell."

The women sat in stony silence. The only sound was the slurp-slurp-slurp of bare gums against nipple.

"You planned this from day one didn't you? Ending up together. Zoë meets Campbell and thinks her ship has come in. The guy is loaded, and even though his mom is psycho, she agrees to marry him. She figures they get married, she's established as his wife, beneficiary, yada, yada, yada, and then boom, re-enter Jane, there's a divorce with a hefty settlement and you two live happily ever after.

"Maybe Jane even planned to off him at that point. One little problem, Zoë got pregnant. You must have been really pissed about that," Sophia looked directly at Jane. "I mean the little lady was actually sleeping with her husband! She was cheating on you. How'd that make you feel? Angry enough to kill someone?"

"You're out of your mind," Jane mumbled.

"Bet you didn't know Campbell was sterile did you, Janey?" Sophia asked. She looked at Zoë. "What about you Mom? Did you know?"

Zoë stared straight ahead, her eyes cold and small.

"You figured fucking Zander was a good way to get back at your husband since he treated you like shit, didn't he? Or was it rape? They were both assholes anyway and hey, Zander's a good-looking guy, if you like that sort of thing, you know—men. Anyway, it didn't matter because you were going to abort the baby anyway. Campbell would never have to know you were pregnant, and a divorce would be easier without a kid. Bing, bang, boom." Sophia stood and started pacing.

"Only problem is, Campbell finds out you're pregnant. You told me that yourself, Zoë, don't you remember? At the hospital. You were pretty out of it, but you said something about not wanting the baby at first. You wanted an abortion; Campbell found out, you changed your mind, something like that. Not very convincing. What happened, did he find these?" Sophia had fished the contraceptives out of her backpack.

Jane grabbed the pills. "What the hell?"

"They're emergency contraceptives Jane. You know what they are, your doctor prescribed them. Only thing, is Zoë didn't take them all did she?"

"Where the hell did you get those?" Zoë stood. She turned to Jane. "Go get the bassinet."

"Huh?" Jane asked.

"Go. In. The. Kitchen. And. Get. The. Bassinet."

Jane leapt to her feet. Sophia stifled a grin. It hurt her lip to smile. Jane got the bassinet and was back in a flash. Zoë extracted herself from her son's lip-lock and placed him in the little bed. Then she sat back and put her big toe on the edge rocking it gently.

Jane tossed the pills at her lover. "What happened? I thought we decided you'd take them. All of them."

"We did Jane, but as you can see, I didn't." She sighed. "Look, I got them too late anyway; you're supposed to take them in the first seventy-two hours or something like that. Besides, Campbell figured it out. He fucking knew. I started getting sick in the morning after a few weeks, if you can believe that. I've never thrown up so much in my life." The toe pushed harder, veins popping to the surface along her foot. "He was so excited. He'd figured it out. I didn't know what to do then."

Jane was still.

Zoë reached over and smoothed the baby's head. "But I didn't kill him," she added, "and neither did Jane. Ronald Scott did it, right?" Zoë pleaded.

"Isn't that right, Jane?" Sophia sneered.

"I was planning to tell him everything after the baby was born," Zoë's voice faltered. "About me. About us." She looked at Jane.

"You married the man under false pretenses," Sophia said. "You expect me to believe you might not have taken the next step? You were trapped." *But, somehow, I do believe you*, she thought.

"She never loved him." Jane said definitively, her face a mask.

"Actually," Zoë looked exhausted, turned to her lover. "Oh my God, Jane. What did you do?"

"What do you mean 'actually'?" Jane was incredulous.

"Okay, I *did* love him. I was confused. I thought maybe I *could* love him, be married. Live that life. Then I got pregnant. I thought maybe after the baby; after some time had passed he and I could be together somehow, or even you and me. I didn't know."

"You told me—you—I did this for—" Jane's eyes narrowed. She was like a cornered animal ready to strike.

Zoë looked like she was going to be sick. She picked up Campbell Jr.— his body limp with sleep. Her hands shook and she had fear in her eyes. *She hadn't known*, Sophia thought. *Jane had flown solo on this one.* Sophia felt the pit in her stomach grow. She fumbled for her backpack and held on tight.

"You killed Ginny too, didn't you Jane?" Sophia asked.

"Ginny's dead?" Zoë whispered. "Oh God!" She held the baby tighter.

"That nosy bitch got what she deserved," Jane spat. "She knew too much."

Zoë gasped and ran out of the room, her footsteps echoing on the stairs.

"So what are you going to do now Jane, kill me too?" Sophia taunted.

"You're so god damned smart, you tell me." Jane lunged at her with fire in her eyes. Sophia threw her body sideways and hit Jane in the gut. The woman was pure wiry muscle—hard as a rock. She seemed stronger than Zander Jarvis, or maybe Sophia was just weaker now. She'd been in one too many fights already today. In an instant, Jane had her belt unbuckled and whipped it out of her pant loops.

Death by strangulation—it wouldn't take long. The belt was around Sophia's neck, slicing open the cut from her round with Zander. Her blood made the belt slick and Jane was having trouble holding on. Sophia kicked the air, struggling to get up and caught Jane by the ankle. Jane spit in her face—a refined fighter. Sophia was starting to gag. Jane's grip on the belt waned; she went to tighten her hands around the buckle and Sophia threw her down and sat on her hips, for once grateful for every one of her 140 pounds.

Jane screamed and tried to bite Sophia's arm but she was in a headlock.

A siren blared and stopped outside the front door. Sophia could see the red light reflecting in the windows. Jane's muscles seemed to relax under Sophia. Maybe she was giving up, maybe she was bluffing. Sophia grabbed her by the throat, ripping the collar off her shirt. Sophia's arm burned, her shoulder was scraped raw and she struggled for breath. She held on while the police broke the door down and barreled into the house.

Tariq Washington was the most beautiful sight Sophia had ever seen. She'd hit speed dial on her cell phone as soon as Jane locked her in the sitting room. Tariq had heard the whole thing. And, he knew her well enough to know that confrontation was her middle name. She'd said she was going to the cops, but with Sophia, anything was possible.

He strode over to them, and lifted Sophia to standing, well, partial standing, she was pretty shaky. He put a size thirteen foot on Jane's chest while one of his officers cuffed her. She spat and screamed and bitched like Medusa until she finally gave out and sat in a mound on the Oriental carpet, her red locks an angry swirling mass around her head.

Tariq had sent a second officer around to the back of the house. He found Zoë going out through the yard with a diaper bag full of cash, Campbell Jr. nestled in a Baby Björn against her chest and Max by her side. She ran right into the officer's arms.

Epilogue

August 3rd, 11:45 a.m.

They were sitting in the Azalea Garden near the Art Museum.

Sophia's right foot was propped up on a pillow. Matteo had a new kite. He and Maria were flying it, unsuccessfully, but they were laughing and having a good time.

"Zoë wouldn't have gotten the money anyway, at least not all of it, right?" Rizzo asked. He reached over to touch her hair.

Sophia shook her head. "When she got pregnant, Charlotte put a grandfather clause in the will. She convinced Campbell to make the trust fund the real prize. Zoë would have gotten a monthly stipend, you know, for expenses to raise the baby, pay the mortgage, that sort of thing." Sophia paused, "More money than most people make in a month mind you, but not what Jane killed for." She put her head in Joe's lap and nuzzled against his leg. They both watched Maria and Matteo as a gust of wind took the kite two feet and then brought it crashing to the ground in an angry descent. She could hear Matteo giggle from across the park.

"She'll still have to fight the accessory charges," Sophia added. "Charlotte's lawyer—Martin—is claiming she had to have known; she was Jane's lover after all."

"Unbelievable," he said. "Hey. Let's change the subject." Joe ran his fingers through her hair. "Do you know you have the most amazing hair? These curls."

Sophia smiled into his thigh. "Thank you," she said softly. "You know I hated it when I was a kid, always wanted it straight, like Maria's."

"*Sei bellissima*," Joe said, "you're beautiful."

"Hmm, I love the Italian, tell me more."

"Have you been to Italy?"

"No. I've been learning the language," she said, "and now I guess I have a new tutor."

"You should go," he said, "get in touch with your Italian side." Joe grinned like the devil. "Maybe it'll keep you out of trouble." He shook his head, started to say something and stopped.

"What?"

"I still don't understand how you knew for sure. I mean once you got there and Jane locked you in, pushed you, sure. But to go there like that. Weren't you scared?"

"I was terrified. You should have seen her face, Joe. The rage was like another person in the room. So different from the Jane Howard the rest of the world saw. I figured I'd fight her off as long as I could and then—well I didn't know. At one point, I remember thinking okay this is it, she's going to strangle me. I just have to try to hold on. And then somehow, I flipped her." She laughed. "Thank God for cell phones. I *hoped* Tariq was on the other line. Luckily, he heard the whole thing."

"I'm not sure how much I like this job of yours," he said teasing. "I guess it's not really up to me, is it?"

Sophia gave him a gentle shove and sat up, smiling. "Not really." *This is a good man*, she thought. "When I got there and I saw Jane's face, and she locked the door behind me like she did, I knew my cell phone was my only way out. I figured I'd call Tariq—I'd just been with him, I knew he was there—or maybe I could somehow dial 911. Tariq figured out where I was and came right over."

"You must have nine lives," Joe said. "I hope you have at least eight left."

"Oh, I bet I do," Sophia said. "You know, it was the pills that saved me, really, and that finally clinched it. I was sure it was Charlotte. I was on my way to see Webb and I was rummaging around in my bag. The pills were in my bag and I noticed the doctor's name, not Zoë's regular doctor, and the phone number, a D.C. area code. I called the office and they didn't recognize Zoë's name, even though the prescription was for her. So I said I was Jane

Howard. The nurse put me right through."

"So what did you do?"

"I hung up!" They laughed. "I hung up and raced over to Zoë's. At that point it just clicked. Whatever I'd been feeling about Jane—the uncertainty—just clicked. And, I'd suspected she was in love with Zoë. Believe it or not, Zander helped confirm that."

"You are fearless."

"Not really. I felt fear." She looked into his eyes. "I feel it all the time."

He stared back, smiling, paused. "And Ronald Scott?" he asked.

"Off the hook, according to Webb. I guess he's going to go to counseling though, make sure he gets through this okay."

"That's good."

"You know one thing I still don't get? The notes. Who wrote those notes? It wasn't Jane," she said. "You know, the cops thought it was you at one point."

"Did you?" he asked.

She paused, "Yes, I wondered."

He looked hurt.

"Hey, I was doing my job. I didn't like it, believe me."

"What a mess," Joe said.

"I did it." They both turned to see Maria and Matteo standing by the blanket, kite in hand.

"You flew the kite, that's great, Maria. Mattie, did you have fun?" Joe asked.

"No," she said, "I did it. I wrote the notes." She turned to her son, handed him the car keys, "Mattie, go run and get your baseball stuff from the car." They all watched as he bounded across the field to the car. It was parked on a cul-de-sac, safe from busy traffic. Maria fixed her eyes on him as he ran. "I wrote the notes. I wanted justice. Finally, I wanted something from that bitch."

Joe flinched at his sister's language. "Maria! What were you going to do? That's blackmail." His eyes were huge.

"I don't know, I never thought it through. I didn't really want anything, money or anything. I just wanted them to know about him," Maria said. "I didn't want his father to die."

Sophia looked at Joe and held his gaze. He nodded. "You know Maria," she started. "Campbell Keats was sterile. He couldn't have been Mattie's father."

Maria looked at them with tears in her eyes.

217

Her son had retrieved his baseball glove, a ball, and was struggling with the cooler; clearly having decided it was time for lunch.

"Maria?" Joe looked at her.

"I just assumed Mattie was his, but, well," she took a deep breath. The truth finally out, strength coming with it. "They both raped me. Campbell and that friend of his, that bastard Zander. I guess I just assumed—" she started to cry.

Joe leapt to his feet to hug her.

Sophia leapt to hers—as much as a person can leap with a bum ankle— and went to help Matteo with the cooler. She hobbled across the lush grass.

"Is Mom okay?" Matteo asked glancing over at his mother and uncle.

"Your mom is going to be just fine," she said. "How about I help you with that cooler?"

"Oh, I got it." Matteo said with a false bravado he could only have learned from his uncle. "Besides, you're injured," he said pointing to her ankle. "How'd you do that?"

"Oh, I was running with a dog and I tripped," Sophia said. The boy wasn't listening—he was completely focused on his mother and uncle. They stood at the picnic blanket watching with pride as he ambled along with the cooler. "Can I at least carry the glove and ball?" she asked.

"Sure, you can help with *that*." Matteo handed her the softball and glove and lumbered along with the cooler banging against his legs with every step. It took them forever to get back to the blanket, but when they did, Maria and Joe were smiling again and setting up for lunch.

Matteo smiled and went to his mom, sitting on her lap. "I love you Mommy, let's have lunch," he said.

He'd known. He'd known that his mother had just needed some time.

Printed in the United States
22655LVS00003B/34

9 781413 727593